In Transit

A NOVEL

Mary A. Agria

North Fork Naturals

To John, with all my love, for his selfless and unfailing support in pursuit of the dream. . .for sharing the journey.

Deepest gratitude also goes to Dr. Ron Ronquist MD,
Professor George Monahan and Shelley Paulsen NP
for their generous technical assistance;
to Joyce Giguere, Ellen McGill and Arline Smith
for their invaluable help with focus reading and editing;
to Helice Agria and Kirsten Smelser for
their contributions to specialized research;
to my mother, Lydia Metzig for her wisdom and counsel;
to designer Sheila Kromas for her creative advice
and finally to Bruce Hembd of Horndog Web Design
for his brilliant design and ongoing tech support
for the maryagria.com website and blog.

visit Mary Agria online at www.maryagria.com

What readers say about Mary Agria's novels . . .

TIME in a Garden,
a "must-read for the contemplative gardener. . ."
Suffolk Times, 2006

VOX HUMANA: The Human Voice
Weaving, pipe organs and the power of human community.
5-Star Amazon.com review, 2007

"Richly drawn characters who continue to be haunted by ultimate questions of mortality and spirituality. . . pure wisdom." 5-Stars, Amazon.com

"*Time* [. . .] has become one of my top ten best reads. What a true love story should be. The main players are older, wiser, with a better understanding of life and its good and bad times. The characters are beautiful. I loved this book. It garnered positive reviews from our book club." Barnes & Noble, 5-Star Review

"I just loved it and really hated to see it end," San Francisco, CA

"My reading group . . . felt that we had read something enjoyable and worthwhile. I'll treasure this story." Grand Ledge, MI

"Thank you for writing such a wonderful story. I didn't want it to end. I am looking forward to reading more of your work." Cutchogue, NY

"From the very first paragraph until the very last, I was hooked." 5-star ranking, Amazon.com

"A unique voice; excellent, intelligent, witty writing; simply wonderful . . . engaging, interesting and believable writing; pure magic." Gather.com

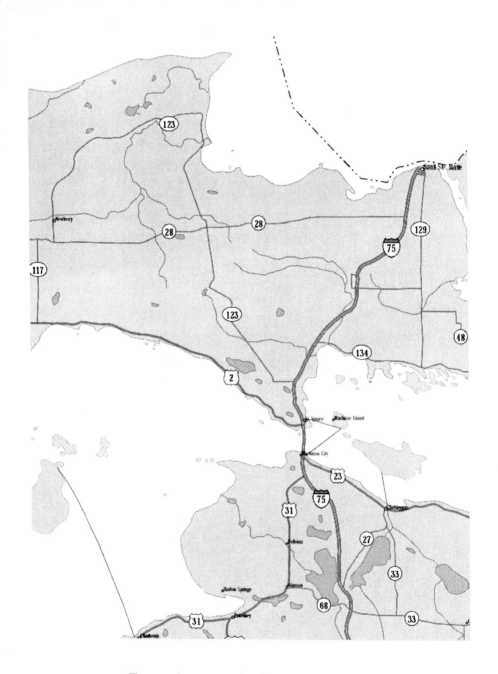

To survive even the hardest journey,
takes only one step at a time,
so long as we never cease our stepping.
Chinese Proverb

One

"You're *leaving*." It was an accusation.

My daughter, Danielle, stood framed in the doorway of her guest bedroom, a hand braced on her pantsuit-clad hip and her brow drawn in a tight squint of a frown. It wasn't like her, but she returned home early from her job as a reference librarian at the University of Wisconsin-Madison and caught me red-handed. I was stuffing a zip-it plastic bag with my toothbrush and cosmetics into the side pocket of the canvas suitcase sitting wide-open on the bed, already full to bulging.

Keep packing. It was that, or confront the hurt and confusion in my daughter's eyes.

My heart ached as I realized it could have been her father standing there in front of me. That tight mop of sandy curls, perpetual Mediterranean tan and intense brown eyes came straight from Dan. But then she was her daddy's girl in so many ways—even that instinct to protect those she loved, as her father had the whole of our life together.

Forty-two years. We would have been married forty-two years last spring, the month Dan died. Yet here I was, walking away from my closest flesh-and-blood ties to those memories, propelling myself into the unknown when everything in me cried out to hold on.

"I'm sixty-three going on sixty-four and your Dad wouldn't have wanted me to live like this," I said, quietly zipping shut the suitcase flap.

"I've decided it's time."

"When did . . . what are you going to do, where are you going to go?" Danielle's frown deepened. "Mom, you don't even have car or a roof over your head to—"

"You forget . . . I *do*. It's sitting, has been for a year now, on that RV pad in northern Michigan."

One small hitch—among other things, the rig was exposed to a brutal upper Midwest winter, without my lifting a finger to protect it. I hadn't allowed myself to dwell on what that could mean. For a split-second, Dan's graphic tales of burst pipes and rodents feasting on electrical wiring surfaced in my memory. The road atlas tallied a hundred-plus miles between Sault St. Marie and that campground, much of it sparsely inhabited wilderness with nary a RV repair facility in sight. I could wind up in the middle of nowhere without heat, water or sanitary facilities and with nowhere to go to remedy the situation.

"The *motor home*?" Alarm resonated in my daughter's voice. "Surely you can't mean that. Daddy was always the one who drove, took care of the repairs. What if you break down on the road somewhere?"

"So, I'll learn," I winced, well aware of how little I knew. "I'm going to fly to the Soo and have arranged for a driver to get me to the campground. If I can't handle the rig, then I'll hire somebody to teach me, if I have to."

Danielle was looking at me with total incomprehension, as if suddenly I had displayed unmistakable signs of dementia. As my eldest, she somehow felt personally responsible to figure out whether to have me committed.

"Mom, it's been so wonderful having you live here. How on earth will we explain this to the kids? It would make the most sense if you would just . . . ," she took a deep breath and came straight out with it, "just *sell* the darn thing."

My mouth felt stiff. "This comes as a shock and I'm sorry for that. I should have told you up front what I was thinking, but I wanted to be sure first, didn't want to seem ungrateful for all you've—"

"You want a place of your own, is that it? Chris and I would be happy to help you find something. Meantime our friend has a great apartment for rent. You can find a car, still travel if that's what you want, but in motels where you're really safe and comfortable, not all alone in that . . .humongous thing—"

It kept coming back to that. "This is my life, honey, and I need to live it. Your dad and I spent some of the happiest days of our lives in that *humongous thing . . .!*"

My voice trailed off on a rising note. The decibel level shocked the both of us into silence.

It wasn't supposed to turn out this way. My husband's dream wasn't a bad one. We would sell our money-pit of a family home, sink a chunk of the profits into a motor home and head wherever the compass or our instincts took us. Together, we had refined this blueprint for a good twenty years before our retirement.

We often laughed at the irony of it, Dan and I. Travel was our business, yet through all those years of marriage, sharing exotic junkets was not an agenda item in either one of our Day Planners.

Eight to five, Dan was racking up frequent flyer miles for an international engineering consulting firm with offices in Lansing and Detroit. I juggled motherhood and a career creating adventures to far away places for my clients as manager of a downstate Michigan travel agency. After hours, I calculated progress by miles on the odometer chauffeuring our children to lessons and soccer practice and play tryouts, usually on my own.

Children grow. Still, even with both Danielle and her brother, David, married and shepherding families of their own, Dan and I slogged away at our respective callings, no end in sight. Fate intervened. My husband turned sixty-two and I was pushing fifty-nine.

"Pack your duds, kiddo!" Dan called out, all nervous energy as he walked into the living room, headed my way.

I looked at my watch—nine PM. My husband had driven crack-of-dawn from our home outside of East Lansing to Detroit for a pow-wow with the powers that be. At something in his voice, I felt a knot tightening in my chest, immediately wary.

"A year's severance, payout for overtime and combat pay," he said. "We're out of here."

You're kidding, the words were on the tip of my tongue, but I drew a long, steadying breath instead. He wasn't kidding. One look at his face made that plain enough.

"Oh, Dan . . ."

He just shrugged. Squaring his shoulders, he tossed the briefcase on the floor inside the doorway and joined me on the loveseat.

"C'est la vie," he said, taking my two hands in his. "Your boss keeps talking about selling the travel agency anyway. I surfed on-line over lunch. Sixteen RVs are listed around here, from camping vans to major bus conversions. What say, Saturday morning we check 'em out?"

It happened just that fast. By close of business Monday we had put our family home on the market, the proud owners of a used thirty-four-foot-long motor home, our very own efficiency apartment on wheels. For two glorious years we lived out our fantasy on the road from one coast to the other and back again.

Ours was relatively modest as motor homes go. No slideouts. No toy haulers, not even a tow-vehicle hitched on behind. Still, whenever it was my turn at the helm, I sat there in white-knuckled terror as if about to move a 747 down the runway. Dan was lovingly amused.

The deal was supposed to be one hour for me at the helm for his every three. More often than not, Dan took pity on me and relieved me at the next rest area.

"Nothing to it, kiddo. Just think of it as a big van. You'll figure it out."

"Yeah sure," I grumbled, "when pigs fly!"

My road *angst* aside, life was good. Dan never tired of puttering and inventing new ways of making our home-on-the-road just that—a home. I nested happily in that cozy space, wrote, sketched, turned ready-to-eat meals into gourmet feasts.

Random geography defined our journey. Greedy for new memories, we clambered through pre-historic mound villages along the Mississippi and trudged along heat-baked pioneer wagon ruts in Wyoming. The rarified heights of Mount Evans in the Rockies beckoned, then the searing flats of Death Valley. Mirror-still glacial lakes in New Hampshire offered a respite after the sun-baked trek east across the farmlands of Canada.

As the months passed, I happily stuck multi-colored peel-and-stick shapes on a large map of the U.S. mounted on the inside of our RV door. Our life journeys, it turns out, are far more elusive to track.

We were bunking temporarily with our daughter and her family in Wisconsin when Dan had his first mini-stroke—within minutes of a major medical center. Their carefully regulated medications gave us another twelve months before the massive clot that ended it all.

The day was balmy, unusually warm for mid-May. We had settled in at a blip-on-the-screen private campground in Michigan's Upper Peninsula, just across the highway from that vast expanse of water we loved so much—Michigan, the "Great Lake", from the Ojibwe *misshikama,* the storied shining waters of Hemingway and Longfellow, the fabled Third Coast.

We had courted, then honeymooned along Michigan's vast beaches and stony shorelines. A lifetime later, from the window in the motor home kitchen where I was making dinner, I watched my husband standing in the deserted picnic area of the campground, enjoying the last of the sunset. I remember thinking how beautiful those dark layers of clouds looked against the pale orange and teal of the sky.

And then I was on the cell phone dialing 911, frantic, stumbling through the wet grass toward where I saw Dan fall. Cradling his head in my lap, halfway from nowhere, I waited what seemed like forever, straining for the sound of sirens.

Mercifully, the EMTs let me ride along in the ambulance on that black and starless spring night—watching my husband's life slip away as the asphalt stretched out ahead of us into the unknown. *Alone.* I had never felt so utterly alone.

"Of course, you've got to stay with family," struggling with her own grief, Danielle took charge, had it all planned. "You can spend summers with me in Wisconsin, then stay with my brother in California when the weather gets snowy and cold."

With no obvious course of action to fall back on, I didn't protest. The months that followed were a blur of tears and deferred decisions. In the back of the ambulance on that rain-slick highway, my heart had ceased to feel and nothing, it seems, could revive it ever again.

We had agreed, Dan and I, when the time came, for our ashes to be scattered over Lake Michigan. A month after he died, with my family around me on an isolated promontory half-way up the Door County Peninsula, I forced myself to honor that part of my bargain.

The sky that day looked surreal, a cloudless, garish acrylic blue. My son and son-in-law read from Tagore and T.S. Eliot, Daniel's favorite authors, heart-searing passages about undying love and the dark night of the soul. Dry-eyed and shivering in my trench coat in the cutting wind, I watched my dreams vanish like trails of smoke over the sun-drenched water.

Our motor home was not on my radar. It stood abandoned where I had left it in that campground on the Upper Peninsula. Instead, as a widow without a permanent mailing address, for the next twelve months I fought my grief and depression shuttling from airport to airport and child to child, from Wisconsin to the California high desert.

This was a journey of another sort—a terrible detour without visible signs of ending. Through those bleak and awful days, my children Danielle and David and their families were kind, patiently indulgent toward that shadow of a woman haunting their guest rooms for weeks and months at a time. Time passed.

And then I awoke one ordinary spring morning shaking and pale, unsteady on my feet, as if having survived a high fever. It would soon be May again. Dan had been dead almost a year.

As I stared into the mirror in my daughter Danielle's guest room, I saw something that had not been there in all those intervening months. It was a desperate resolve to begin anew.

Against all odds, I saw evidence that I could yet reclaim all that vanished muscle tone from a year without regular workouts. My hair, though graying, still retained more than hints of the chestnut brown of younger days. The tracery of lines that bracketed my hazel eyes testified to remembered laughter as well as pain. While my heart felt ancient and scarred, there was a flicker of something akin to hope in that sad twist of a smile, hope I had thought was gone forever.

With my daughter safely off at work, I spent the better part of two weeks on-line googling resources for women RVing alone, then another making follow-up phone calls. I still couldn't bring myself to tell Danielle, quietly grateful she wasn't home to question the priority-mail printed matter arriving on almost a daily basis.

I hooked up with a chat group for single RVers. There seemed no point in postponing things any longer. This time after Danielle left for work, I rummaged through the attic for my suitcases.

And so here we stood, my daughter and I. Her face began to crumple and she looked away.

"Mom . . . I'm sorry, but this is *so wrong*."

I cleared my throat, tried to soften my tone. "Honey, I know you're worried, truly I do. But please try to understand. I would never forgive myself if I just forgot or shelved all those dreams your dad and I had without even trying to . . ."

Words failed. I had no idea what I was trying to do, just knew that I had to do it—something, anything but curl up and die, dependent on others for some sense of purpose and direction.

"I wish you would reconsider, give it time," Danielle said slowly, "make sure this isn't just some—"

"Some crazy Zen throwback thing, reclaiming my lost youth on the back of a Harley," I finished for her.

"More or less, it had occurred to me."

Inwardly I cringed, but managed to keep my tone light. "I came of age in the sixties, remember—have no desire to get back in a pup tent. A motor home isn't exactly roughing it. Plenty of creature comforts, just not an awful lot of room. I lived in the rig for almost three years, after all."

Danielle exhaled sharply. Small victory, I sensed that the steam was going out of her arguments.

"Well, at least let Chris, the kids and me drive you up there," she insisted, "help you get settled. We've got a long weekend coming up and Chris can be pretty handy—not like Daddy, but with the small stuff anyway. You and I and the kids can wash and wax the outside, get the interior shipshape again."

I didn't dare cave in now or she would pounce on it, in a heartbeat. "Thanks," I said. "Really . . . thanks, honey. But, no, this is something I have to do."

Alone. That word kept cropping up again and again in my head. I didn't allow myself to say it.

I had been a travel agent, for crying out loud. If I couldn't even get myself from Point A in Madison to that campground and tackle what may or may not have happened to my home-on-wheels in my absence, how on earth could I ever take that beast out on the road. Besides, if I truly was going to do this, there was no time like the present to start.

My daughter was rigid in my arms as I hugged her. I persisted anyway, wishing so very badly that she could bring herself to understand.

"Honey, honey, I love you so very much," I whispered. "And believe me, I appreciate what you've done, what you're trying to do—"

"*But . . .?*"

I looked at her, managed a weak smile. "*But . . . I'm going.*"

❖

I went. At the moment of truth at the airport, I found myself battling tears as my daughter hugged me, with a silent urgency, as if both our lives depended on it.

On the map the puddle-jumper flights across Lake Michigan seemed like a straight shot. In real time, the trip quickly deteriorated into a maze of hubs and plane changes, threats of flight delays as thunderstorms moved through the region.

When the limo service didn't show up at the airport in Sault St. Marie, against my better judgment, I chose to trust on-the-spot Owen and his older model mini-van. My driver had wanted to see his cash in advance. I quickly discovered why.

Curbside outside the Soo terminal, Owen tossed my three suitcases quickly into the cargo area and shoe-horned himself behind the wheel before I caught the unmistakable whiff of alcohol. Warning lights started to do their little whirling dance in my head.

"Are you sure you're up to this?" I hesitated. "It's not too late to leave me at the nearest bus stop."

Owen just chuckled, turned the key in the ignition. "Could'a used another hour or two of sack time, but ya gotta know, it takes one heck of a lot to stop old Owen. I ain't lost one yet!"

Primitive as sobriety tests go, but at least I didn't see evidence of any open containers. It half-occurred to me to offer to drive myself and let the guy sleep it off in the back. At least whatever Owen's limitations as a chauffeur, speeding wasn't one of them.

He had help there. Something seemed to be wrong with the engine. We rarely hit more than fifty miles an hour unless we were heading downhill, unlikely on Route 2. Except for a few stretches of rolling dunes out of St. Ignace, the terrain flattened out and the chill waters came to what seemed like feet from the road, separated only by narrow strips of sandy beach struggling to survive the gales that battered them on a regular basis.

13

I began to appreciate just how vulnerable and exposed those lonely little beaches felt. Tightening my death-grip on the shoulder belt with one hand, I clutched the wad of bills to pay for the trip with the other, too queasy from the movement of the van to lean down and stash them in my wallet.

"So, whatcha doin' then way out here by yerself anyway, Lady?" Owen shot a gap-toothed grin in my direction.

Good question. "I'm picking up my motor home, at the Northern Lights campground, west of St. Ignace."

At the start of our little junket, I had handed my driver a locator map for Northern Lights that I had pulled off the campground's website. Unfortunately, that useful bit of knowledge disappeared almost immediately into the morass of empty soda bottles and crumpled fast-food wrappers on the floor under and around the front seat.

"Wouldn't have pegged ya as the campin' type," Owen persisted. "Them suitcases of yours look more like a cruise or somethin'."

"Travel agency. I used to work for one. The luggage was a retirement present." It seemed prudent to minimize Owen's distractions. "Is traffic always this heavy?"

"Not to worry. Ya just settle back, Little Lady, and enjoy the ride."

Not likely. Still, I took his advice, closed my eyes and leaned my temple against the cool glass of the car window, a great cure for headaches.

"Wake me, will you," I said, "when we get close."

"Gotcha, Lady."

Maybe my daughter, Danielle, was right—this is nuts. A little late, I admitted, to come to that conclusion. Right now I wasn't in the mood for I-told-you-so's.

Somewhere in my half-sleep and half-waking state as the van lurched its way along the lakeshore, it occurred to me that I had not been this utterly on my own since I headed off to college, my freshman year at MSU. I hadn't thought about it in ages, how utterly forlorn and

14

abandoned I felt sitting on the bunk in that dorm room as I listened to the sound of my parents' footfalls retreating down the cinder block and tile hallway.

I had never been away from home before, but then my four suite-mates and I had bonded quickly, friendships that held for the duration of our college years, even beyond. Within less than a year of graduation, I had married. Through those and all the later changes of my life, other human beings—my family, neighbors, bosses and co-workers—had defined the parameters of my world.

Wherever this Kerouac-ian journey ahead of me was leading, it was turning out to be a leap of faith beyond my wildest imaginings. The terrain was unfamiliar. Words like unsettling, frightening, exhilarating churned in my head—that, and the prospect of change on a scale almost beyond comprehension, not just out there somewhere, but within myself.

For starters, I was older now. I couldn't even fathom how much I needed to learn to survive, much less how I was going to learn it. Exhausted, alternately tearful and resolute, in spite of myself, I must have dozed off.

A crunching of gravel and Owen's hearty, "We made it!" woke me with a start. Disoriented and stiff from bracing myself against the door for much of the trip, I straightened as best I could.

"Northern Lights?"

"A-yup! Shaved a good ten minutes off the trip."

In the back of my mind were wild tales of tourists falling to their knees as they made landfall after a rough cruise. The mini-van had shuddered to a stop in front of a pre-fab double-wide—newly renovated, from the look of it, with cedar shakes and wedgewood blue shutters.

I stumbled out of the back seat and uncurled my crumpled handful of cash, prepared to thrust it in the driver's direction. The bills were sweaty, limp after my multi-hour strangle-hold, but Owen just grinned and pocketed the roll.

Apparently the trip had succeeded in sobering him up. The guy had the look of someone about to hit the head and the nearest watering hole, in roughly that order.

"Good luck to ya, Lady!" he tipped the brim of his wear-stained ball hat.

"You, too."

"If yer ever goin' that way again—back to Soo country—and need a lift, old Owen's your man . . .!"

For the life of me I couldn't think of a response as he slid behind the wheel of his shuttle. Belching fumes from the tailpipe, the mini-van rattled its way back on to the highway from whence we had come.

Alone with my high-end suitcases, I just stood there on that concrete slab outside the campground office. The place seemed way too quiet. I thought I felt a rain drop, but chalked it up to cold sweat thinking about what state my RV might be in.

"Register Here", the sign on the office door said. I cracked the screen and went inside.

The luggage would be safe enough out on the slab for the moment. On solid ground. As for me, I wasn't quite so sure.

Two

"Hello . . .?"

I tried again. Nothing.

The campground office was cluttered in a something-for-everybody sort of way, but well maintained. Directly to the left of the door stood a reception desk that doubled as a sales counter. To the right, a few tightly packed aisles offered a supply of groceries and camper gear. A bookcase crammed with dog-eared paperbacks leaned against a side-wall, apparently some kind of informal lending library.

"Anybody here?"

I wandered down an aisle of shelves chock full of sundry spare RV parts. All the lights in the place were on, but nobody seemed around. When I tapped on a closed door at the back of the large public room there was no response either.

Back at the main desk, a map of the campground and a stack of registration forms lay on the counter next to the cash register. I was about to lean over and snag one of each when I heard the door to the parking lot open behind me.

At the sound I swung around, suddenly feeling very outnumbered. The two guys standing just inside that doorway would have raised eyebrows under the most benign of circumstances.

The one bringing up the rear was clearly a local, late-seventies from the look of it, lean and weathered like an old shoe, with a thinning gray pony-tail that spilled over the collar of his threadbare flannel lumberjack shirt. His companion was taller and a decade-younger, hair close-cropped and a day's stubble shadowing the tight ridge of his jaw. His tailored jeans and crisp button-down shirt smacked of "designer" and the tan windbreaker bore the logo of an upscale sporting goods brand.

The two seemed as taken aback to see me as I was to see them. I noticed the younger man's eyes narrow as he took in my pleated gray dress pants, coral cashmere shell and heavy, oatmeal hand-knit sweater coat. All of it, I suddenly realized, was badly rumpled after nearly twelve hours on the road—yet way too urban-chic for some campground on Route 2.

"Arvo, I'll handle this," the guy said as he ground to a halt a safe distance from where I was standing.

"You betcha, Boss."

Arvo—the name sounded Finnish. Whatever his origins, the older man kept going toward one of the grocery aisles. Wiping his palms on his well-worn work pants, he began noisily to replenish the stock from a huge cardboard box stashed at his feet. That left me alone with the younger of the two, the guy ostensibly responsible for the place.

"You look lost," he said.

Lost. You could call it that. I started to react but the "boss" beat me to it.

"I saw those suitcases sitting out there," he said.

"They're mine."

"I didn't see a rig."

By now the man was staring at me with what I judged to be a mixture of contempt and a no-nonsense resolve to get me out of there as quickly as possible. Thoughts racing a mile a minute, I realized—mortified—what must be going through his head.

Good grief, I thought. This guy manages the place and he thinks you're a hooker or some kind of a druggie, looking for a handout, or all of the above.

"You've been . . . you've got my camper," I stammered. "A thirty-four-footer. My son-in-law says he called about storage back in—"

I found the date, even the month slipping out of my grasp. How excruciatingly fast and slow time moves, and what strange moments in our lives make us aware of its passing.

As introductions go, mine was sounding pitiful, even to myself. A muscle twitched along the stranger's jaw as he weighed what I told him.

"Must be the Class A back there," the man nodded. "The old owner left a note about agreeing to store it. Nobody asked, but we winterized it anyway. I've got the bill here somewhere."

My relief was so sudden and intense, I could taste it. For a split-second, I felt light-headed, almost giddy. Whatever damage the motor home had suffered from its season of not-so-benign neglect, things could have been a great deal worse.

"Of course, I'll be glad to pay it," I said, "whatever it is."

"We've been checking it over about once a month and starting the engine regularly as well as the generator. It's going to need some elbow grease after all that time standing empty, but otherwise it seems okay. I'll walk you back there if you like. We've got a set of keys."

"I'd appreciate that." Mine had gone missing in one of my many moves over the past eight months. "You ought to know, too, that I've got some stuff coming—a couple of cartons—I gave this as the delivery address."

He nodded. "We'll keep an eye out."

Together, though with a conspicuous distance between us, we headed toward the back of the campground along a winding network of narrow gravel lanes. This wasn't a new campground, but apparently under new management.

Around twenty of the shaded lots showed evidence of very recent upgrades in water and electrical hookups. The rest were primitive, obviously set aside for tent camping. Most of those could have stood a good weed-whacking.

"You sure have a lot of equipment and pipe stashed out here," I said.

"I'm sure you couldn't miss that mountain of gravel piled up near the entrance, either. Unfortunately, the driver just dumped it and took off and Arvo and I haven't had the time to get it out of there. Plan is to double the area for RV-camping by the end of season."

"I gather that you . . ."

Whatever pleasantry I intended, out of the corner of my eye I had caught a glimpse of the grassy picnic area with its open-walled, roofed shelter where Dan had collapsed. It was bare of its tables and equipment for the season, but still one place I would never, ever forget. I stumbled and quickly averted my eyes.

"You need help there?" a solicitous voice at my elbow offered. "Those potholes can be tricky."

I shrugged off the hand that shot out prepared to intervene. My sandals were taking one heck of a beating on that uneven surface of the road. Concentrating on every step, I managed to pick my way around the rough spots.

"Face it, I'm not dressed for this."

"I guessed your gear is probably in that rig," the manager chuckled sympathetically. "No problem. We'll have you fixed up soon enough."

Our break-neck tour of the grounds came to a halt in front of the motor home, nose-end in and all but buried in a thicket of low-lying branches and grasses. We were quickly losing the light and this time the raindrops were coming in multiples.

Emblazoned on the side of the vehicle was the motor home's brand name, *Courage*, absolutely light years from what I was feeling right now. For an awful moment, a crying jag seemed a distinct possibility.

Dan would have made light work of this. Sure and unflappable, he would have simply taken hold and backed out that rig until it was free and clear. That was no longer an option.

"I don't . . . I'm really sorry, but I haven't . . . I don't think I can back it out of there." I tried not to sound as panicked and distraught as I felt.

"You're really *alone* out here?"

By now I'd have thought it was fairly obvious. Speechless, I nodded. How on earth was I going to back up, dodge the trees and still swing the back end of that camper enough to connect with the gravel road curving behind the vehicle?

The manager's frown was back. "Listen," he said, suddenly cautious, "if this is some kind of weird *custody* fight we've got going here . . ."

"*Custody?*"

I drew a blank. As in, just *what* was he implying here?

"It's happened before," the guy shrugged. "The divorce isn't final yet and you're getting a jump on the major asset."

Anger flared red-hot blotting out momentarily anything but the total and utter folly of my situation. The survivor in me roused itself with a vengeance.

"My husband is . . . *dead,*" I spat out the ugly truth of it. "He had a stroke and died in this campground. And the only one who owns this rig is *me* . . . !"

Silence. I just stood there my hands balled into fists at my side, daring the guy to say one more word. He blinked, as surprised as I was by the intensity of my reaction, but recovered quickly enough. I wasn't expecting an apology, but got one.

"That was . . . rude, insensitive," he said. "I'm sorry."

In all fairness to the man, I had the feeling that out here, he and his fellow-employee Arvo had pretty much seen it all.

"Yeah, well, I called ahead," I said, "but obviously whoever was on the phone didn't bother to tell anyone I was coming. You help me navigate this thing out of here and I'll get it out of your hair."

Pure bluff, I realized the minute I said it, considering that the rest of my belongings were still en route with the Northern Lights address on the shipping labels. The guy's eyebrows arched and a muscle began to throb along the line of his jaw—visibly uncomfortable with the direction all this was headed.

"Look, we've started off on an unfortunate foot here," he said slowly. "I'm Paul Lauden, the new owner of Northern Lights. And you're—?"

I hesitated, then found myself extending my hand in greeting. Paul Lauden's hand closed around mine, although judging by the haste with which he relinquished it again, he certainly seemed as uncomfortable as I was with the situation.

"Elizabeth. Lib, actually. Lib Aventura."

"Spanish, right," he guessed, "for *adventurer*."

A flicker of a smile played at the corner of his mouth. But then at least he didn't add how wildly inappropriate the name was, given my circumstances.

"Italian." I felt vaguely irritated that I felt obliged to explain. "My husband's family was Italian. Apparently some over-zealous immigration official decided the spelling on their passports was beyond hope and grabbed at the name of a town in Florida instead."

Chuckling softly under his breath, the campground owner had begun sorting the fistful of RV keys that he had retrieved from behind the registration counter, obviously in search of the ignition key. The plastic tag on the ring caught his attention and he held it up for a closer look.

"Senior Travel," he read. "East Lansing."

Now the guy had a problem with *that?* Time was passing here.

"I worked at ST Tours," I said. "Managed the place. Booking cruises, organizing senior tours, packaging family theme-park vacations—"

"Interesting."

"Yes, it was," I said, "and for better or worse, it's my turn for the road trips. That is, if you *skip* the twenty questions and help me get my

22

rig out of this jungle."

Even as I lashed out at him, I knew I was way out of line. Paul Lauden could have let my motor home rot here in the woods and hadn't done so. Mercifully, whatever he thought about my manners or lack of them, he kept it to himself.

"I *could* do that easy enough—get you on your way," he said evenly. "But there's a heck of a storm brewing out there, Ms. Aventura. In your shoes, I'd settle for getting that rig squared away on a pad before it hits. It wouldn't hurt to give the thing a road test either, before planning anything too drastic."

He was right, of course. It would be dark in less than a half hour and as I stood there pondering my options, or better said my lack of them, the first heavy drops of rain had begun to fall.

"All that makes sense," I mumbled, forcing what I hoped was a conciliatory smile, " and I certainly do appreciate your offering to move the rig. Could I help somehow . . . maybe watch out for possible close encounters with those tree trunks as you back out of—?"

"Not necessary. Though if you want, you can walk ahead and pick out a spot that appeals to you."

"Thanks. Yes, I'll do that."

This was no time to get picky. My rain gear was also in the motor home. While he backed the rig out, I set off cross-country and quickly settled on what looked like a wide spot mid-campground, rimmed on both sides by stands of birches. He had just eased the motor home in place on the gravel pad when a clap of thunder told me it was time to duck and cover.

Paul had the only keys. Hunched against the cold drops that were starting to fall faster now, I waited while he sprinted around to unlock the side door of the coach. With some difficulty in those gusts, he held the outer and screen doors for me. I stepped inside.

The wind was howling as I fumbled for the panel of light switches just inside the door. Mercifully, the battery seemed to be holding a charge. One of the inset ceiling fixtures cut through the gloom enough for me to see what I was doing.

"It's going to get nasty out here." Gingerly, Paul shut the screen behind me while he stayed outside on the step. "No sense for both of us to get wet. Just stay there out of the rain, while I hook you up—"

Before I could protest, he had struck off toward the back end of the camper and the huge hinged door panels that concealed storage compartments for electrical cable and the water hose. Propping open one of the panels, he deftly began stretching out the electrical line toward the outlet box to one side of my campsite.

"You don't have to do this," I called out to his retreating back. "Really . . . I can manage!"

Paul stopped, half-turned and looked at me. Droplets of water had begun to cling to his temples and hair—showed signs of soaking through the shoulders of his jacket. His smile was knowing, even a little sad.

"I can think of better times to learn to do all this, can't you?" he said quietly. "Do you know where the internal switch is for the electrical system and the thermostat for the furnace?"

"Yes." I hesitated. "I think . . . I'm pretty sure . . ."

"You're hooked to the campground water supply now, so there's no need for the pump. You have pressure without it."

Pretty much he was describing my state of mind at the moment. "And the refrigerator?"

"If you set it on Auto," he said, displaying far more patience than I had a right to expect under the circumstances, "the electricity will kick in. Some folks get nervous using propane when they're sitting on an enormous fuel tank. And don't worry if you smell what seems like fumes. When the furnace kicks on, it'll probably smell like gas for a while, but that's just dust."

As an afterthought, I managed to choke out yet another "thank you". Paul Lauden just kept going.

Within minutes the lights in the motor home were blazing. I had water and the furnace was running. And none too soon.

The rain was coming hard now on the roof. Anxiously I looked around me at the compact living space, that dinette and its bench seats hard up against the galley kitchen and the living room with its pull-out sofa-bed and tiny end tables, the built-in bed and bathroom at the back. I could live here, I found myself thinking—relieved at how homey the space felt, in a small-scale dollhouse sort of way.

But then, I hadn't been running around out there in that weather either trying to make sense of all those plugs and cords and hoses. When Paul poked his head in the door again, I was dismayed to see he was drenched.

"Come on in . . . please," I said, "It's really awful out there."

Out of breath, he did, clutching awkwardly at the motor home doorframe. His steel-toed work boots left dark puddles on the carpeted stairs.

"You didn't have to . . . it was good of you to handle all that," I told him.

"No problem. Glad to help."

"Do you need . . . I assume you need me to sign something," I offered, "register or something like that."

He shook his head. "Forget it for tonight. We'll get the logistics squared away in the morning, if it ever stops raining. And feel free . . . if you have problems, just put out an SOS. I assume you have a cell phone."

Fishing around in a shirt pocket, he came up with a now crumpled and soggy business card with the name of the campground and a phone number. The card was attractive but homemade, temporary from the look of it, using one of those computer templates.

"Thank you," I started to say, "I really appreciate—"

"Have a good night," he said.

With that he was gone, shutting both inner and outer doors tightly behind him. I shivered, half at the finality of the sound and half at the eerie silence that followed.

The night was turning out as advertised, dark and miserable, but inside the camper it would soon be comfortable enough, except for the occasionally shuddering sound of the wind outside. The air didn't have that cooped up smell, but then I remembered Paul Lauden telling me that he had checked on the vehicle from time to time. More than a just quick look-around, I was beginning to realize.

But then we'd settle up tomorrow, he said. Right now I had a daughter back in Wisconsin who would be thinking I had fallen off the face of the earth.

A tight knot around my heart, I checked the bars on my cell phone. To my relief there was service, barely. Thank goodness I wasn't going to have to stumble across the campground in the dark and bother the guy again to use the phone.

Punching in my daughter's number, I heard her pick up mid-ring. "Mom. . .you're all right! We've been so—"

"I know, honey. Sorry about that. It was getting dark and starting to rain. I had to get settled in."

"The trip . . . it went okay, then?"

I chuckled softly, remembering my wild ride of a day. Point was, even with all that had happened, I was here and in one piece.

"Fine. Just fine. People have been very helpful."

As the campground owner said, some things—like sharing the gory details—would keep until tomorrow. I had to hope it would be funnier in the telling by broad daylight.

"I haven't eaten since breakfast, though," I told her. "I've really got to scrounge something up for dinner and get ready for bed."

I cringed, knew exactly what she would be thinking as soon as the words flew out of my mouth. Here I was, a day on the road and already I was starving myself to death.

Silence. Danielle had picked that up from me, a calculated counting to ten while you weighed your response. It helped me balance my two worlds all those years—Lib the professional go-getter and Lib the wife to a take-charge road warrior who saw it as his role when he was home to walk through hell-fire if need be to take care of his "girls"

26

as he liked to call us.

In the end, tragically, it was a battle he couldn't win. And I was beginning to fear that in some ways Dan's death had upended my daughter's world as much, maybe more, than it had my own. I had struggled with the same grief-stricken awareness when my own parents had died. The passing of the generations is a sobering business.

"For a while anyway, Mom," she said carefully, "do me a favor and check in a lot, will you? Until we're sure you're—"

"No problem."

We said we loved each other and broke the connection. Badly as I knew I had to get away, I had to admit I found myself missing my family around me already, even my Danielle's often maddening mother-hen tendencies. She came by them honestly, watching me struggle to cope with her adolescence. Still, how unsettling it felt at this stage in my life, to find those particular chickens coming home to roost.

A blast of wind caught the motor home and shook it on its newly-graveled pad. Senses heightened, I tried to sort out the unfamiliar creaking sounds as the coach steadied itself. Up front over the bucket seats something was tapping against the roof outside, though not heavy from the sound of it. Closer at hand, I picked up the rhythmic drip of the faucet in the kitchen area.

"Make a note," I told myself, trying to master my rising anxiety level. "Read up on how to replace washers. And figure out what's loose up on that roof."

There was no answer except the muffled roaring of the wind. "Travel light," Dan had always told me, "it saves on gas and broken axles."

Not this light. Not alone, with that darkness closing in around me out here in the middle of nowhere and the temperature dropping by the minute.

"Something warmer," I muttered as I got up from the dinette table and began scrounging in the clothes cubbies. Jammed on top in one was a blue fleece sweatshirt, Dan's X-L acquisition on Mackinac Island

27

from spring—our last spring together—with the location subtly emblazoned in raised embroidery on the front.

Burying my face against the soft knit, I found myself fighting back tears. No time for that now. Made awkward by my haste, I slipped out of my crumpled travel clothes and pulled on the shirt as a makeshift nightgown. It came nearly to my knees.

The tile in the kitchen area and bathroom felt glacial underfoot as I padded about checking for leaks and fooling with dials on the refrigerator, fretting whether its door seal was solid. I kicked off my shoes, snagged a pair of Dan's woolen winter hiking socks from the open bin as improvised bedroom slippers.

"Better," I concluded. Then too, the furnace slowly seemed to be making a dent on the chill.

I wasn't hungry. Still, common sense told me at least I should put together something to tide me over until morning. A half-hearted search through the pantry turned up a dehydrated package of soup that seemed to have survived nearly a year of fluctuations in heat and cold.

In the process, I noticed that someone had taken the precaution of removing the canned goods and the worst of the perishable items I remembered having left behind in the cupboards. The small refrigerator also had been emptied and propped open slightly to keep the insides from molding.

I owed these Northern Lights people a bundle, I decided, if not a major *mea culpa* for being so paranoid. My situation could have been so very much worse, frighteningly so.

It took a dozen frustrating tries to light a burner on the stove but soon the smell of chicken soup was wafting through the motor home. By force of habit, I laid out a place setting complete with napkin and napkin ring, then sat down at the table.

"Lib and her mobile Maison Chick," Dan used to tease, but then I knew he secretly loved those tiny touches of civility that had softened the rougher edges of our life together.

As a couple we had our share of rocky moments and there was

never enough money, never enough time. Still, through it all and especially in those precious final years, we shared a playful intimacy, memories that even now lingered in this space we had treasured together.

The rain had steadied to a persistent drumming on the roof of the motor home. I was having trouble concentrating, but forced myself to finish most of the soup, then cleared the dishes, rinsing them in the cold water of the sink. It would take a while before the water heater had made a dent on the icy well water flowing out of the tap.

The bed was still made up as Dan and I had left it. Not warm enough, I concluded, for that biting spring air out there. After spreading a spare sleeping bag over the blanket and coverlet, I clambered under the covers and reached up to turn out the light overhead.

The motor home was plunged suddenly into virtual darkness. In the distance, I heard the faint rumble of trucks on the highway. The bed felt empty, yet strangely alive with Dan's presence.

With a muffled cry, I buried my face against his pillow. Drawing it tight against me, I gave in to the rising tide of anxiety and grief I had been fighting ever since I got on the plane that morning, fourteen long hours earlier.

Dan. Even thinking his name hurt, like a wound that would not heal, aching and raw at the very depths of my soul. Shoulders shaking with the effort, with no one to hear or care, I wept.

Three

Morning light filtered in through the slat blinds. It had to be at least nine. Confused and disoriented, I squinted at my watch. Closer to ten—but then my inner chronometer kicked in. I had forgotten the hour time difference between Wisconsin and Michigan.

It was eleven o'clock. I had slept nearly twelve hours straight, curled tight to conserve warmth alone in that double bed at the back of the camper.

Groggy and unsteady on my feet, I eased my aching body out of bed and shuffled toward the kitchen area. Sometime during the night the downpour seemed to have stopped. It took a split-second to recognize the new sound I kept hearing for what it was—a faint but persistent tapping on the motor home door.

"Ma'am, are you okay?"

"Fine," I lied, "never better."

The tapping persisted. "It's Arvo, Ma'am. Arvo Lammi. Boss sent me over with a thermos and some fresh biscuits—thought maybe your propane was running low."

I unlatched both screen and outer door, not caring what kind of impression I was making as they swung outward. This was not the time to worry about fashion statements. Dan's oversize fleece sweatshirt and knee-high wool socks served their purpose as the chill breeze hit me.

Arvo flashed a sheepish grin. "Gotcha up, I see. Still a mite nippy for this time of year, Ma'am. Boss thought some coffee here might be good."

Thrusting a multi-cup thermos and a foil-covered recycled pie plate in my direction, Arvo fidgeted waiting for me to take it, a booted foot propped on the motor home step. The smells, I had to admit, were heavenly.

"My stove seems to be working, but thanks."

I reached out and relieved him of the goodies. Arvo looked down at his boots.

"Nothing fancy, Boss says. Though I'll tell ya, he's sure a great cook, that guy."

"Tell your . . . tell Mr. Lauden, 'Thank you'. Oh. . .and would you remind him, too, that I'll stop by around one so I can settle up."

"I'll do that, though ya don't need to be in any hurry to pull up stakes right off," he said. "Good place this, for sure. Good people."

"I'll keep that in mind."

Arvo nodded. "Welcome to Northern Lights, Ma'am."

Dodging the puddles, he disappeared around the back of the motor home. From the high ground of the coach door, I saw that intuitively I seemed to have picked one of the higher RV pads in the immediate area. Even if the rain once again materialized, my home on wheels would be left an island, high and dry, in that little birch grove around me.

Be thankful for small favors and kind neighbors when we least expect it and need it most. I deposited the thermos and pan of biscuits on the gleaming faux-marble counter of the kitchen area and went back to shut the coach door. In passing, I caught a fleeting glimpse of myself in the floor-to-ceiling mirror Dan had installed on the wardrobe door. It was enough to stop me dead in my tracks.

Despite the bizarre wardrobe, this woman staring back at me was anything but the bedraggled waif I had expected to encounter there.

31

Cheeks flushed and salt-and-pepper hair spiked from sleeping on all those unruly cowlicks, I looked like I could have just finished a brisk jog. My hazel eyes had regained some of their sparkle. Despite the fact I was feeling a little worse for the wear in the stamina department, it didn't show.

I was famished. From the smells wafting out from under that foil covering, I decided Arvo and his boss's housewarming gift had all the promise of a gourmet feast. Intrigued, I lifted the foil on the plate and uncovered a neatly arranged cluster of fluffy scratch-made drop biscuits. No packaged stuff here, the slab of butter was fresh cut and a small lidded container held what had to be homemade preserves.

"Wild blueberry?"

I used the old finger-in-the-bowl technique to confirm my diagnosis—Dan and I had picked our share, an exercise in patience. Anyone who ever tasted those tiny nuggets of fruit, growing in such abundance on the sandy hillocks along the marshlands of the Upper Peninsula, knew that all that foraging was well worth the effort.

Dispensing with the niceties of the night before, I used the cover from the thermos as a mug and quickly settled in at the table. Premium blend and fresh ground, I concluded. Arvo was right. His boss didn't cut corners when it came to cuisine.

I attacked the biscuits and trimmings straight out of the pie tin, greedy for every last bite and crumb. For good measure, I ran a fingertip around the bottom of the container of jam. The verdict was messy, but good. I felt like a kid who just raided the cookie jar when no one was watching.

Creature comforts were a good thing right now. The water temperature in the bathroom faucet wasn't hot by any means, but warm enough. Humming under my breath, I showered—if you can call it that, given the water pressure—and washed my hair before the hot water supply gave out. Brief as that was, it was enough to revive even the dampest of spirits.

I pulled on a pair of jeans, sage green tank top and snuggly black fleece jacket, then made up the bed. Although I had to heat water on the stove to do it, I rinsed out the thermos Arvo had brought and redid last night's dishes along with the empty pie tin.

Noon came and went, time to get organized. I fished around in one of the drawers in the end table, scrounged up a notepad and pencil. Comfortably ensconced on the sofa, I started a list, prioritizing what I would need to function again. Groceries, cleaning supplies—by the time I was finished, my jottings had covered a side-and-a-half of the small yellow tablet. Just how and where I was going to find all this without packing up the camper and driving forty-plus miles to the nearest town of any size, I had no idea.

Dan had always managed the logistics. It had never occurred to me how fraught it was to take care of even the simplest domestic chores like grocery runs in that 34-foot beast of a vehicle without towing a car.

Wincing, I stood up and stretched the kinks out of my back. Later, I would worry about all that later.

At the moment, I had some groveling to do. In the clear light of day it was pretty obvious how bizarre my behavior must have seemed to an outsider when I showed up yesterday. By now it also was pretty clear, in my defense, that Arvo was the culprit who had taken my phone call and had neglected to warn the owner I was coming.

After running a brush through my hair and dashing on a reassuring hint of makeup, I grabbed my duffel of a purse from between the front bucket seats and set off for the registration building on foot. The trek was a lot easier in my lace-up hiking boots than in those dressy sandals yesterday as I picked my way around potholes and muddy spots. Unless I was very mistaken, we would see the sun after all.

A flash of movement caught my eye. Head thrust forward in that lurching gate of his, Arvo was just rounding the corner of a gleaming silver Airstream parked in a spot near the highway. It was a vintage beauty, bound to catch the attention of motorists passing on the road.

Arvo looked up, waved and grinned. Then stooping to pick up a tool of some sort he apparently had left lying under the trailer hitch, he loped casually off toward the opposite end of the campground.

A piece of clever marketing, I realized with a smile. Parking that Airstream up front like that as staff housing would make the place look occupied, even upscale in a quirky way. And it provided a measure of built-in security.

No dummie, this Paul Lauden, when it came to running this place. That touch had to be purposeful, the mark of someone who knew the value of details and planned accordingly.

As I opened the office door, I saw he was perched on a stool at the registration counter, apparently entering data into the laptop in front of him. He heard the door, and over his wire-rimmed reading glasses, made eye contact—an intense flash of gray that I found vaguely unsettling.

His smile seemed guarded, preoccupied, as he tucked the glasses in his shirt pocket and stood to greet me. "You survived. Arvo and I began to have our doubts."

I hoped I didn't look as sheepish as I felt. "That obvious, huh. I was shell-shocked, exhausted—could have been in big trouble out there last night if you hadn't offered to help."

"Comes with the territory."

"Maybe. But combined with all the work you've been doing to maintain that motor home, I'd say well beyond the call of duty." I hesitated, as visions of dollar signs flashed through my head. "I shudder to think how much time you put in to—"

"A flat fee for winterizing, seventy-five bucks. Although . . . ," from the look of it he was turning something over in his head, "if you can get around your suspicions that you might have wandered into a hotbed of serial killers or drug dealers out here, I might have a *better* proposal."

For a split-second, I just stared at the guy. As is, that fee for motor home maintenance was nothing out of the ordinary, if anything even low. Better just ignore him, I thought.

"Thanks, but the seventy-five is just fine," I said brusquely. "Do you take checks? Credit cards?

The subtle twitching along his jaw was a dead-giveaway. He wasn't about to be put off so easily.

"For one thing," he said pointedly, "I see your vehicle license is expired. I suppose you could slap an *In Transit* sign on the back and hope the sheriff doesn't pull you over. Though, sooner or later you've got to stay put long enough to deal with it."

"Thanks, but if you just put together my bill . . . "

"You haven't even heard what I—"

"I'm not sure I *want* to!"

I cocked an eyebrow that pretty much summed up my skepticism. So help me, the guy flushed.

"Under the circumstances, I can understand your being . . . skittish," he said slowly. "But if you think this is some kind of a come-on, what can I say—? That's not my style. Sorry if you got the wrong idea. Truth is, I've been thinking of taking on more staff."

Something in my face momentarily stopped him cold. What had any of this to do with me?

"And it occurred to me," he persisted, "your background seems to fit. Senior Tours. Not many of the locals would know how to get a handle on that kind of thing. I hired old Arvo to keep an eye on the desk and help me upgrade the sites. The guy's great with a backhoe, but in the people skills department . . ."

I managed a weak smile. Right now, I wasn't all that sure my own 'people skills' would stand muster either.

"That breakfast he brought over certainly made my day," I said. "Thank you. That was thoughtful."

"Bottom line, Ms. Aventura, if you're not in any hurry to get that rig on the road and could live with a free campground spot, plus expenses, I was considering the possibility of hiring you for the season as a campground host . . . "

"A . . . *what?* You've got to be joking!"

That shoot-from-the-lip response was becoming a very bad habit, totally out of character. In my defense, the guy must be delusional considering he could sense I barely knew the difference between one hookup and another.

"Flattering," I said quickly, when I found my voice again, "really. But a single woman with that job description emblazoned on her motor home door? I don't think so."

Even the attempt to soften my refusal came out far harsher than I intended. What on earth was wrong with me? I had come to the office in the first place fully intending to thank the guy, not insult him.

It could be argued, it wasn't smart for me to dismiss out of hand any proposal that kept me off the highway for the foreseeable future. But then this lunatic Paul Lauden wasn't exactly playing with a full deck either if he thought for a single moment I was up to a job like that. Visibly exasperated, the guy raked his hand over his close-cropped salt-and-pepper hair.

"Lady, you've got one heck of an imagination," he muttered. "I don't know what you think goes on in these places, but I am not running some kind of a . . . back-to-nature Club Med out here. I was thinking of interesting family stuff, one step up from the usual hayrides, rummy tournaments and video nights. Maybe a kiddie parade or something on the Fourth. Period."

It was my turn to look flustered. "I just meant . . . don't couples usually do this sort of thing?"

"True. Except there are more women RVing alone now than ever and both Arvo and I can handle the heavy stuff. Appearances to the contrary, neither one of us has been arrested for anything—correct that, I collected a stack of speeding tickets until I figured out where the local gendarmes hung out, if that's what's worrying you."

"I was thinking, it wasn't such a good idea to be all alone out here, just in case . . . "

"In case, what?" he prompted gently.

Highwaymen, brigands, Barbary pirates. At least the guy didn't dignify my rampaging paranoia by putting a label on it.

"Rowdy guests, maybe."

He laughed, out loud now, shook his head. "Unlikely, when the average age of our clientele so far has been seventy, but yeah—I'm bunked in the back of the office. Arvo is camped out in the vintage Airstream parked near the road. Nothing gets past him, believe me."

I half-smiled, pleased with myself for getting at least that much right. "And the Minnie-Winnie?"

That classic vehicle was parked between the office and my own site, I couldn't help but notice it. Although well maintained, at the moment the rig looked deserted.

"Belongs to an older couple from Green Bay who come over here every couple of weeks on a season pass."

Harmless enough, I thought. "You must get a fair number of transients then, one-nighters passing through?"

Dan and I had camped in places like that. The constant turn-over put a real strain on the facilities and could contribute to a high noise level, generally unpleasant.

"During the week mainly we bring in retirees looking for a base for day-trips in the area," Paul said. "On weekends we get families wanting affordable fun and sun. I also own beach access to a tiny strip of waterfront across the highway. Undeveloped. But then those sandbars out there in Lake Michigan make it fairly safe for small kids to spend the day in the water without lifeguards and minimal adult supervision."

"Sounds nice," I had to admit, "quiet."

"I like to think so. If anything, too quiet."

"And so you're hoping that some events could help, maybe draw more seniors during the week and keep families coming back on weekends."

"Great in theory," Paul said, "but tough to do when Arvo and I are up to our elbows in expanding the water and electrical systems, upgrading the RV pads. It's slow work."

"Backbreaking, from the look of it."

Paul shrugged. "Sure don't need a health club membership.

Bottom line, your coming on board would really help. Spend a season here, give it a shot—get used to living in the motor home. In your spare time, I'll teach you how to handle the rig."

The man pretty much had my situation pegged. Although I had driven the motor home occasionally, my knowledge of handling the sometimes quirky stove, the sewer system and hookups was painfully limited. As for backing up, it was nowhere on the horizon.

True, Dan had kept everything—receipts, warranties, instruction manuals—in an enormous three-ring binder stashed in one of the overhead bins. But then reading technical manuals and handling leaky faucets were two very different things entirely.

"You stay open until, when?"

"We close late-October, although by then we've got to have the publicity out there for the following season. When we shut the place down, you could just get behind the wheel and truck down to Florida or wherever you want to go."

Paul hesitated. "And if it works out and you want another summer . . . well, when the time comes, we can both consider it."

Much as I hated to admit it, the offer made a great deal of sense. Which brought us right back where we started.

"You don't know a thing about me," I said.

My raised eyebrows prompted a quick footnote from my would-be employer. "I know enough. You aren't going to take any guff—from *anybody*. And I suspect those original commercial travel posters I saw on the walls of your motor home are your doing . . . "

I felt a smile tug at the corner of my mouth, pleased that someone had noticed. "Thank goodness for computers."

He shrugged. "Case in point."

"I'm obviously . . . clueless around all that camping gear—"

"You more than make up for it on the business end of a mouse. I'll settle for that."

I didn't have the nerve to hit him with the rest of the equation, that I didn't know my prospective boss either—though by now I had figured out this much. The guy had his hands full running this campground and was dead serious about offering me a job.

He had been more than generous in caring for my motor home. Then, too, there were those biscuits this morning. Maybe, just maybe, it was time to cut him a little slack.

I took a deep breath and shot back. "You've . . . I assume you have an internet hookup?"

He nodded, "WIFI and a computer. You're welcome to use it—that, and software for whipping up brochures and ads. We've got a website of sorts . . . but then you know that, and an adequate digital camera. Certainly some upgrading of PR stuff would help, across the board. I just haven't had the time."

"A land line?"

Cell phone service was marginal. If I didn't make good on my promise to check in with my daughter on a regular basis, Danielle would be sending out the state troopers, maybe even the FBI.

"Unlimited calling plan. Feel free to use the office phone any time you'd like."

"I assume weekends are out, but I'd need time off during the week to stock up on groceries, run errands. I don't have a car."

"Fair enough. Mondays are usually fairly slow. We've got a junker of an SUV for runs to Centerline so you wouldn't have to move your rig. Then, too, I'd let you shop the camp store at cost, though what we stock is limited."

Chewing on the inside of my lip, I weighed the pros of the offer. I couldn't think of a heck of a lot of cons, unless I factored in the prospect of working for this guy.

"Is that it?" he said.

Tentatively, I nodded. "For now, anyway."

At that my companion chuckled and straightened on that stool, as if confident of my answer, arrived at under duress, but an answer nevertheless. "We've got a deal, then?" he said.

I started to bristle. What was it with this guy and his suckerpunch approach to human relations?

Cornered as I was, I couldn't mistake the hint of genuine respect and compassion in that smile of his. Intelligent, a straight shooter—I could think of worse people to sign my paycheck. Apparently from that breakfast he whipped up, at least he wouldn't be asking me to make the coffee.

I forced a smile. "Forget the host idea. I'll try Program Director for a month—long enough to see whether I can get anything going. But in the meantime you've got to teach me to handle that rig."

His hand shot out to shake on the deal. Tentatively, I took it.

"Good for you . . . and me," he added quickly. "Welcome to the staff!"

Good, bad or indifferent, it certainly was not how I imagined my arrival in Northern Lights would turn out, not at all. "Let's just say, Mr. Lauden, for now I'm willing to suspend judgment."

Four

My daughter wasn't nearly as charitable about reserving judgment when I told her what I had done. For what seemed like a full minute, I heard nothing but silence from her end of the phone.

"Are you still there, honey?"

"Mom, you're joking, right? I thought you retired!"

"So did I."

"A campground host?"

"That's what the guy said. More like a program director, though. I'll be handling the registration desk, public relations, arranging weekend events."

"Guy . . .?"

"Paul Lauden. He owns the place."

"Age?"

"Dunno. I'd guess mid-to-late-sixties."

"Married, single?"

"What ever, honey, I have no idea. This isn't matchmate.com. The man apparently drives too fast but he says he isn't an axe murderer or dealing coke. He has some interesting ideas—"

"That's what I'm afraid of . . ."

It was my conversation with myself all over again. Only I was having it long distance this time.

"Honey, I have got to face facts that I'm not ready to take this rig out on the road myself. With free rent, I can buy myself time to get up my nerve. My boss has promised to teach me how to drive and hook up the rig. In the meantime, it sounds like fun. This is something I know, something I can do."

"What happened to all those dreams about the open road and Daddy and—?"

"So that's it," I said slowly. "You think this guy Lauden is some . . . backwoods Casanova and that I'm looking around for an emotional life raft, anything to keep myself afloat."

"I didn't say that."

"But you thought it."

The dead air on the other end of the line pretty much confirmed I was right. I didn't think it would reassure her to mention that when I arrived, my boss-to-be suspected I was looking to start my own little red light district along Route 2.

"Honey, there are worse things than living alone," I said. "I loved your Dad. He's gone. But I'm still here, even underneath all this uncertainty and confusion—not the woman I was, but maybe somewhere in there's the woman I want to become. Someone you, someone your Dad—*someone I*—would be proud of."

There wasn't much she could say to that. Bless her heart, for once Danielle realized she had finally gone too far. "Mom, I'm sorry if—"

"No. There's nothing to be sorry about. You loved your Dad. Believe me, I understand. I had a wonderful marriage, more than a lot of people can say these days. And trust me, I am not looking for another one."

I gave Danielle a second to process my take on things. Every word of it was wrung from the heart, painful but honest.

"So, when is all this supposed to start?"

"I downloaded some of the campground owner's computer files

on my laptop this afternoon. After dinner I was planning to start browsing around in—"

"You must be worn out."

"No." Surprisingly, I wasn't. "Excited, nervous maybe."

"Mom, I don't understand how you can just walk around there as if nothing happened. You were there, in that campground, when Daddy—"

"I have a friend, about my age," my voice was low. "Her husband died in their summer home and she never set foot there again. That's sad, honey. Anyway you cut it, it's sad. We were happy here. Right now I need to hang on to that. It's that simple."

"All this impulsive stuff—it just isn't like you," my daughter said slowly.

"I know."

If anything, the anxious knot in my insides had tightened a notch at that revelation. I was thinking of the past twelve months, lost to me and gone beyond recall, with a mixture of regret and anger. What had happened to the Lib Aventura who had given up her family home and a lifetime of roots, content to follow the road wherever the journey took her?

Problem was, there didn't seem to be a road map for a woman in my situation. I had been thrust into as unfamiliar a territory as it got—without the love of my life as a compass.

"Honey, I've gotta go, but I'll call again. Soon. Really, I will."

If my daughter noticed my voice was shaking as I said it, I had to hope she would think it was just the marginal phone reception. Gently, I closed the cell and laid it down alongside me on the bench seat of the dinette.

On the table in front of me, the ready-to-heat carton from my faux-Chinese dinner was still sitting where I had left it. Shoving it to the side, I slid my laptop into the middle of the clutter and booted it up, then popped the disk my boss had given me into the drive.

Go get 'em, I told myself. This stuff is your stock-in-trade.

Randomly clicking on a file, I skimmed a spec sheet on Northern Lights that pretty much fit with my impressions on that walk-through with Paul Lauden yesterday. A total of 35 acres and 60 sites, mostly unimproved. He had researched statistics for the past five years that showed high occupancy rates for improved sites and marginal ones for tenters.

It was all there. Purchase price. Previous owners. Dates when the campground changed hands, including a brief local press clipping from several months ago:

> Northern Lights, that little gem of a campground on Route 2 west of Bentley is under new ownership and management. Paul Lauden, former CEO of a talk radio station in suburban Detroit, has big plans for the site.
>
> "The name of the game is steady," Lauden says. "By upgrading our sites and facilities, we hope to encourage repeat guests who will come to love this pristine stretch of Northern Michigan shoreline."
>
> No stranger to our neck of the woods, Lauden spent summers with his family in the area for decades. His radio station regularly aired Up-North-Now, a phone-link interview program that highlighted the lifestyle and tourism events year-round in the Upper Peninsula for the down-state market.

The man had long ties to the area. *Married,* my daughter had wondered. From that business in the article about family, it seemed to be the case though I hadn't remembered him wearing a wedding ring.

Certainly sharing this particular little bit of information should reassure Danielle considerably. Clicking shut the file with the press release, I moved on. A flyer swam into focus—two-sided and lined up three to a page.

"Good," I nodded. "Efficient."

Paul's background at that radio station obviously demanded a working grasp of affordable publicity. The design was simple, stark—black and white to save printing costs. What drew my eyes, though, was a stunning photograph of birches and a sandy beach featured on the cover, with a veil of mist rising over the vast Michigan waters behind them. There weren't any credits for what was clearly a professional shot.

Classy, I concluded, really classy. Though maybe it was just a little too much so—a talking point anyway, I decided. If Northern Lights was aiming at repeat business and families, then I would suggest a bit sportier image.

Jotting a few notes on my yellow tablet, I quickly clicked through a series of lesser pieces. I thought I saw Paul's design sense at work in a diner place mat with shared mini-ads from area businesses including one for Northern Lights.

Visit that diner, I scrawled on my tablet. Apparently, Annie's Place was some kind of hub of local social and commercial life. At the very least, it would be politic to check out the place.

By the time I came up for air, it was nearly midnight. Shocked at how the time had flown, I double-checked my watch with the built-in clock on my laptop, then made the adjustment to Eastern Standard Time. I had been working for nearly four hours without a break.

Stifling a yawn, I dealt with the by-now-disgusting leftovers from dinner. My nightshirt was still lying on the bed where I had left it. The familiar ache in my heart at that reminder of Dan was eclipsed momentarily by the throbbing at the base of my skull. Serves me right, I thought, for staring at that computer screen half the night.

I didn't bother to check the expiration dates on the pain killers in the camper medicine chest. Washing the tablets down with the dregs of the coffee sitting around from lunch, I finished my nightly ablutions and crawled into bed.

The silence was so profound, I could even hear the faint clicking sounds of the hands advancing on my backup bedside alarm—not that

45

I had any intention of setting the blasted thing, job or no job. For what seemed like a long time, I just stared up into the blackness, until too tired to keep my eyes open any longer, I finally fell into a troubled sleep.

The dreams that came were a jumble of anxiety-ridden fragments, half-remembered deadlines from my travel agent days, muddy potholes and a bleak, unending highway speeding past before my eyes. *I thought you were retired.* My daughter's words kept flashing through my head.

Retired—from work, from motherhood, from life? If there is a pension out there for grief and loss, from the uncertain human business of living, I had not found one.

The new day woke me. I forced myself to meet it head on, in spite of the emptiness that dogged me as I went through the motions of making breakfast.

Borrow the SUV, I had underlined that item twice on my omnipresent yellow tablet. There was only one more packet of instant oatmeal left in the box and I was getting very tired of chicken soup.

The kitchen area was a mess so I took the time to rehabilitate the place before I did the same for myself. I was on a payroll again, and campground or not, I was going to dress accordingly. Slipping into a pair of my dressier gray slacks, a black cowl-neck sweater and lime green fleece, I topped off the look with my hiking boots. It was chilly in that office.

Good enough for folk music, I told myself. I gave my wayward hair a final fluffing.

It seems I wasn't the only one glued to a laptop. I found my new boss in jeans and what seemed like an endless supply of recycled button-down dress shirts, ensconced where I had left him yesterday on that stool behind the registration desk, attention riveted on the screen.

"Problems, Mr. Lauden?"

His smile didn't seem to make a dent in those stress lines

between his brows. But nice, anyway, I decided, in a low-key sort of greet-the-troops fashion.

"Paul," he said, "please. Unless, of course, you're dead set on Ms. Aventura."

"Lib is just fine."

"To answer your question, Lib, nothing's wrong that about ten more rigs in those sites out there on a regular basis wouldn't fix. You look rested and raring to go."

"Makeup," I chuckled. "After all that commotion with kids and grandkids for the past year, it's way too quiet out here in the bushes. Tough to get to sleep."

At that he momentarily took his hands off the computer keyboard. "I gather you were staying with family, then. . .after—?"

"I really had no place to go," I dodged the fact that I certainly wasn't ready to come back here. "So I wound up riding the red-eye back and forth from my daughter in Madison to my son's house in the California high desert. Both of them, by the way, were clamoring for me to sell the motor home and settle down with one or the other of them."

"But you couldn't. I understand."

Something in the way Paul said it, told me he did. Unless I was very mistaken, under that hit-me-with-your-best-shot composure of his, I sensed the faint aura of deja vu.

"You have a family, too?"

"A son, downstate. Josh."

It wasn't much of a pause, but one that spoke volumes. If I hadn't been tuned in, I would have missed it.

"My wife, Ginny, died," he said, "two years ago."

"I'm sorry."

"It happens," he said softly. "And we just keep going, right?"

"Try to anyway . . . "

My voice quavered, broke. For a split-second, a shadow clouded his expressive gray eyes. I remembered that look, captured in the head-shot of him with the newspaper clipping about the new campground

47

management.

A good looking guy, that's for sure, with strong and determined features—a no-nonsense way of confronting you straight-on, as if you were the only person in the room. And yet, something told me, this man was far, far more complex, tougher to figure out than I had assumed.

"You . . . I don't suppose you had a chance to look at those files I gave you?" he said, suddenly all business.

I knew that reaction, the mark of a consummate survivor. When all else fails, throw yourself head-long into your work.

Goodness knows I had plenty of practice over the years turning to my job to ground myself when Dan was on the road. I was doing it again. Only this time, he was never coming back.

Here's to the survivors, the walking wounded of this world—my new boss, it seems, among them. There certainly seemed to be an awful lot more of us running around than I would have suspected a year ago.

"As a matter of fact, I did check things out," I said brusquely, "selectively, of course. Not all the files you downloaded, by any means, though quite a bit of it."

"And?"

"I jotted down a few ideas. Probably nothing that you didn't think of yourself."

"Fire away!"

My laugh sounded nervous, even to myself. "Well, for starters, that brochure has a very narrow niche appeal. Great for the older crowd, but if you're looking for a more active retired clientele or younger families, it may be a little too—"

"Dull."

"Not exactly." I shook my head. "That photograph on the front of the brochure is breath-taking, intriguing as far as it goes . . ."

"But where are the white-water rapids?"

"Not that extreme. But yes."

He made a show of wincing, although from the smile that followed, he didn't seemed at all surprised—or displeased—with my reaction. "Fair enough. So, what do you suggest?"

"Not one of those ho-ho-hokey campground theme park places, that's for sure. I walked that shoreline across the highway for a while before it got dark yesterday. Gorgeous. And that little stream flowing into Lake Michigan . . .?"

"Ours. The access anyway."

"Fly fishing—that cuts across the generations," I said, "strictly catch and release to appeal to the environmentally minded. We get some local to offer lessons in that clearing behind the office."

"Equipment?"

A problem, I suddenly realized. "We'd have to scrounge up some low-end, tough-as-nails fly casting gear. Set up a bunch of truck-tire targets and try to keep people from maiming each other while they learn the basics."

"Easier said than done," Paul laughed. "Do I detect a note of been-there-done-that?"

"Phys Ed my sophomore year at Michigan State. I wasn't much for running or the wilder team sports. Fly fishing seemed as good an alternative to nail at least a B as any."

"Not out of the question for us if we find the equipment," he said. "But what else?"

"That diner in Bentley . . . east of here on Route 2. I've never eaten there but—"

"Annie's. Great food, popular with the locals and tourists." Paul's forehead scrunched as he thought about it. "Annie's a friend of mine—was a big help when I was considering buying this place . . . "

Something clicked in my head. *Annie.* Mortified, I found myself conjuring up an image of my boss, a widower by his own admission, squiring some tall, leggy bottle blond with a generous smile, younger but not too young.

Ridiculous, I chided myself, even going there. But then my daughter had let that particular genie out of the bottle—hell-bent on questioning my motives for going to work for this guy. I seemed to be having a heck of a time putting it back.

"Problems?" Paul said.

"Potential maybe," I told him, scrambling to get back on track. "Annie's could be a good partner if we're thinking about sponsoring events like fish boils, barbecues."

"So, check it out—this afternoon, if you like. I can switch on the answering machine if you want to borrow the SUV and head into town. Annie's is in the opposite direction, though not that far."

"Thanks, I'd like that. My cupboards are getting pretty bare. While I'm in town, I thought I could make a grocery run."

We had barely scratched the surface of my suggestions for the place. I was almost disappointed when Paul suggested we take a break while he showed me around the double-wide, including nitty-gritty stuff like where he kept the keys to the public washrooms, the SUV and the various equipment storage sheds.

"You keep the SUV parked—?"

"Out front," my boss said, "supposedly, anyway. At the moment it's stuck in a mudhole out at the back of the acreage where Arvo had been felling some dead trees to carve out a nature trail. That was before our thunderstorm rolled through the other night. We'll have it out of there in time for you to use it."

"Nature trail . . .?"

My ears perked up at that one. If mini-golf wasn't on the agenda, we would need something that families could do together in less than perfect beach weather or when they get tired of all that sun and surf.

"We lucked out with a little bog back there on the property," Paul said. "It occurred to me to turn it into some kind of nature center."

"Bog—as in cranberries."

He chuckled. "Bog as in that floating, spongy plant-cover that bounces back trampoline-style when you try to walk on it. Ours even has a few pitcher plants and some other interesting fauna I'm still trying to identify. Plus the setting is spectacular, with a clear-as-glass pond and a stand of maples and pine behind it. In late Fall the colors are

50

amazing."

"Sounds promising."

"But environmentally protected. We've gotten a green light from the DNR to build a raised log boardwalk over one end of it. Problem is, it'll probably take until next season to get it up and running. "

My mind was racing a mile a minute. There were a be-jillion ways we could promote the trail as part of a "back-to-nature" package. *Visit nature's sponge-green moonwalk.*

"It's promotable," I muttered. "Have you got photos?"

"Four seasons including shots in the middle of winter. Trust me, it's interesting to fight your way back there on cross-country skis."

Something in the way he said it, got my antennas up. "You're a photographer?"

"Strictly amateur. But yeah, I enjoy putting a lens between me and all that beauty. Catching the moment."

"I'd like to see your work," I said.

He blinked, hesitated. A muscle began to work along the edge of his jaw. "When the dust settles . . . "

His tone told me loud and clear that I had struck a nerve, leaving me no notion whatsoever why or how. It was a brush off—polite, but a brush-off nevertheless.

"Organizing volunteers for events and whipping up promotional pieces are things I could do while I hang out at the registration desk so you and Arvo can play lumberjacks or upgrade sites. Other ideas might turn up, too, if I keep plowing through those files you gave me."

Paul nodded. "Good. In any case, we should make time on a regular basis to noodle around together about the possibilities, you and I."

"I'm looking forward to it."

Five

 As I climbed behind the wheel of the mud-caked SUV late that morning, it finally hit me just how radically my prospects had changed in the last twenty-four hours. Somewhere in the course of that unlikely journey, I had begun to look ahead, not back.

 Truth was, I found myself looking forward not just to breathing life into this little "gem" of a campground, but to a lot of things. First on the list was the prospect of using skills I had pretty much shelved when I retired. I hadn't realized it until that all-too-brief brainstorming session with my new boss, how much I enjoyed—and missed—the challenge.

 The other mile markers were proving to be such simple things, as mundane as crawling out of bed and making the coffee or striking out late afternoon for a solitary walk along the Michigan lakeshore. The prospect of heading into town for groceries with a stopover at Annie's was assuming the significance of a Himalayan expedition.

 My footing in this brave new world could only be described as tentative. All it took was the occasional wail of emergency vehicles on Route 2 to stop me dead in my tracks. Fists clenched and eyes averted, I continued to skirt the spot near the public picnic grounds where Dan had collapsed.

But for all the obstacles and detours, I had a job and a reason to get out of bed in the morning. I had a place to hang my hat. Right now that seemed like a lot.

Gunning the SUV out onto Route 2 headed east, I felt the spring air against my face through the half-open window. The sunlight dancing on the cobalt and turquoise waters of Lake Michigan flickered against the glass of the windshield. A beautiful day.

"Annie's," I read out loud as I passed a fresh-painted wooden sign along the road, "eight miles."

The signboard had great colors, a Grecian blue background and white with golden yellow lettering. Swirling through the blank spaces were stylized green pine trees, like a pennant unfurling in the wind.

As I clocked off the distance, it occurred to me how isolated we truly were in this corner of the state. Although scattered houses stood back from the road in tiny clearings along the highway, much of the landscape consisted of stands of evergreens, greening marshlands and open meadows with standing water or creeks meandering through them.

Four miles and another sign read, Annie's Diner. Northwoods Home Cooking and Greek Specialties. I smiled, had been right about the colors.

Clicking on the turn signal, I started to slow down. Ahead in the tiny parking lot, I could see a dozen cars packed in like sardines in a tin.

I wound up parking along the shoulder and had barely clicked off my seat belt, was working at coaxing the key from the unfamiliar ignition, when yet another vehicle slipped behind me. Quite a crowd for a random weekday.

Snatching my duffel purse from the passenger seat, I got out, shut and locked the door. Even that distance from the diner, I caught the unmistakable aroma of lamb and exotic seasonings wafting through the parking lot. Somebody at Annie's certainly knew how to cook.

The hostess was mid-forties, a brunette with a contralto come-hither edge to her invitation. It was the woman's smile that shattered the stereotype—friendly, yes, but underneath it all, shy and reserved.

"Seating for one?"

"Yes—no . . . I'm not sure." Her question had taken me off guard. "I was hoping to talk to the owner."

"I'm Annie Stavros."

"Lib," I told her, "Lib Aventura. The new program director at Northern Lights."

Shifting the menus she was holding, Annie grinned and extended her hand. "Paul has been talking about hiring someone for a while now," she said. "Good for him! When did you start?"

"Yesterday. . .well, today really."

"Local?"

I hesitated. "Not exactly. I've been storing my motor home at Northern Lights for a season now. I used to manage a travel agency downstate."

Annie nodded. "We can use every bit of help up here that we can get. It's five-hundred-plus miles from just about everywhere, which means in the tourist department it's either feast or famine depending on gas prices—yet we've got some of the most beautiful countryside anywhere. Tragic, really."

"So, you've been here a long time, then?"

"Twelve years, six running this place . . . an eternity for a business in this neck of the woods. The diner itself has been around for decades—a regular revolving door of owners though."

"Your parking lot is full—you must be doing something right," I volunteered. "The smells coming out of that kitchen are incredible."

Annie looked pleased. "How about you join me, for lunch. My regular waitress should show up any minute and for once the customers can do without my schmoozing. You've got to eat, don't you? I'll fix us up with some coffee to start and a table over by the wood stove."

"Great. I'd like that. Mr. Lauden . . . Paul thought it might be good for us to do some brainstorming about stuff we could engineer together as a tourist draw." I paused. "Though the noon rush might not be the best time for us to . . . sorry, I didn't think of that."

"Really, it's fine. I just saw my right-hand gal Rhonda's Jeep pull into the parking lot. Actually now is as good a time as any to get the flavor of the local trade."

She was right. Looking around me, the clientele seemed to have a live-here air about them. Over at the lunch counter, two elderly men—eighties, if I had to guess—were embroiled in a heated discussion.

"Arnie Klonz," Annie whispered as she followed my gaze. "He owns a white-water tubing business though he's been trying to sell the thing for ages. That cronie of his is Emil Dufries, a retired hunting and fishing guide."

"And the guys sitting near the big windows?"

"That's Earl Forester. A fellow 'troll' like your boss and me, but he and his wife fit in quick enough—"

"*Troll . . .?*"

Annie laughed. "The U.P. term of choice for down-staters," she said, "the Michiganders who live down there *under da Bridge . . .!*"

"On the other side of the Straits, I've always heard outsiders pegged as *Fudgies* for all that gooey, sweet stuff tourists take home every summer," I said. "Sounds like I'm going to need a crash course in local-ese to handle it all."

"If you remember that *pasties* are edible, not items from an x-rated bar, and *Yoopers* are just folks from the U.P., you'll make out okay most of the time," Annie shrugged. "Earl's wife, Sonja, by the way, is Swedish. With the biggest ethnic group up here Finnish, the Foresters made their mark right off by cooking up interesting 'generic' Nordic activities at the local historical society that gets everybody involved. Earl runs the nearest service station, ten miles north of here on the county road, in Centerline."

"And that buddy of his over there at the table with the NYFD tee shirt?"

"Pastor Bob, former fire department chaplain from out East somewhere. Bob heads up the volunteer rescue squad. Thanks to his sermonizing at that lovely little community church folks are restoring along the lakeshore west of here, the guy's quite the pundit-in-residence. Funny as all get out."

I hadn't noticed any chapel, lovely or otherwise, on the way over. But then I hadn't darkened the door of a church either since Dan died. I took a deep breath and changed the subject.

"Based on the license plates I saw on the cars in your parking lot, I would guess you get a lot of regulars here," I said. "Good for you."

"Actually, I don't see much of the locals starting in July when the tourist season peaks. Though rain or shine, a group of old dirt farmers regularly still open the place at eight for coffee and the lumberjack platter. In the high season we mainly draw passing tourists at lunch, sick of driving that never-ending stretch from Mackinaw to Marinette-Menomine. Before we close at six, we tend to get the eight-to-five business folk trying to network a little. If you live around here, you had better like to drive!"

"How did . . . .I can't help wonder what made you decide to start up a business in a place like this," I said.

"Am I one of the natives? Not hardly," Annie chuckled. "Actually, I'm Chicago born and bred, but I married a Yooper, John Stavros. Oddly enough, his dad Nikos used to be the school superintendent in Centerline—bought this place as a retirement investment but never ran it."

"John . . . your husband teaches, too?"

It was just a guess. For a split-second, Annie's face took on a distant look.

"Did," she said softly, "Phys Ed and high school science, until the accident two years ago."

"I'm sorry. Tactless of me . . . I wasn't intending to pry. I lost my husband a year ago myself."

"My husband isn't . . . John shattered his spine when his pickup hit a deer. He's in a wheelchair, paralyzed from the neck down."

"Annie, I'm so sorry. I can't even imagine how hard that must be."

I couldn't. For the both of them.

Devastating as it was to see Dan's life ebbing away in that ambulance, I was thinking what it would have been like to watch that proud and active, take-charge man I loved become dependent on me for even the simplest, everyday things. The stroke would have done that. Be careful what you wish for. Annie Stavros stood before me, living proof.

"I'm glad Paul Lauden sent me your way," I told her. Annie smiled. "So am I."

Rhonda the waitress chose that moment to show up at our table. She was toting the most amazing platter of Greek delicacies, fit for an Athenian feast—stuffed grape leaves, spanakopita, and a luscious looking bowl of humus ringed with wedges of pita bread.

"Wow!" I breathed as I bit into the flaky pasty filled with cheese and spices. "I've experimented with Greek cooking myself back in the day, but this is amazing."

"Wait 'til you taste the avenganola," Annie beamed. "It's my father-in-law's recipe for Greek Easter soup. It's to die for."

"Unfortunately, not exactly the fish boils I was coming here to propose."

"We can do that, too. Fish boils, pig roasts, whatever you think might fly—no pun intended."

I left that diner with a doggie bag that would carry me through at least dinner and another lunch. More important, I left having felt I had made a friend.

By comparison the grocery run was a pretty mundane business. As communities went, Centerline was a notch below a "village" and several above a whistle-stop.

The basics were there—grocery, hardware, a small chain economy store, a struggling consolidated K-12 school system and a modest medical center serving an area of seventy miles in either direction. The Chamber of Commerce was an unstaffed storefront with a well-stocked rack of brochures and flyers from the area. Beyond that the amenities were few and far between.

In all those years living downstate while Dan and I raised our
family, I had enjoyed the classic Michigander census humor as much as
anyone. If someone draws a line just above the half-way point on a map
of lower Michigan, the territory from there on up has more deer than
people. It was one thing to travel through a region, I was beginning to
realize, quite another to adjust to living there.

When I got back to Northern Lights, Arvo and my boss were
working near my motor home tackling that latest row of site upgrades.
Arvo was perched precariously on a tractor equipped with a back-hoe
behind and a large scoop loader in front, in the process of flattening a
freshly graded RV pad. Every time the flat bottom of the scoop slammed
against the ground, I felt my teeth rattle.

Athletic looking in a lean, track-and-field sort of way, this time
my boss had topped off his usual uniform of faded jeans and dress shirt
rolled up at the sleeves with a Detroit Lions ball cap. He was using a
chainsaw to attack a low-lying tree branch.

"Enjoy the grand tour?" Paul called out as he spotted me coming.

"Quite a metropolis over there in Centerline," I laughed. "I've got
a cargo area full of groceries to prove it."

"Well, you can see what we've been up against here."

The two men looked sweaty and exhausted, but then two more
RV pads were also finished, their surfaces broader and level, covered
with a fresh layer of gravel. Another half dozen were less bumpy but still
minus that hard-pack surface that would keep heavy rigs from sinking in
the sandy muck whenever it rained.

"Lookin' good," I told them. "How on earth can you manage all
that with one rusty old tractor?"

Arvo beamed. "Ya gotta try it, Ma'am . . . a real hoot. A bit like
building mud pies with a coal shovel."

"Right now I'd settle for not having a heart attack learning to
drive that gigantic rig of mine."

"That's right," Paul grimaced, "I-O-U some road time, though
not on the calendar until after the weekend, sorry about that. We actually

have a half dozen campers pre-registered. The season is heating up—a regular stampede."

"You'll have these new sites done."

"Just barely. But it's probably unrealistic to organize the bread and circuses we've been discussing by then."

"Not three rings, maybe," I said, "though I'll bet we could conjure up one or two."

Paul's eyebrows lifted quizzically in response. I didn't keep him waiting.

"Arnie Klonz was having lunch over at Annie's," I told him, "lamenting that he hadn't sold that river tubing business of his."

"I understand his operation is pretty out of date—truck tire inner tubes instead of those new inflatable rings and just a junker of an old school bus to ferry passengers upstream."

"I gathered as much," I said, "but I talked to him. He would be thrilled to death to rent us the whole operation for a weekend. Dirt cheap. Maybe even for the season. We can advertise funky old-fashioned river float outings."

"You *have* been busy."

"Not as busy as I will be if I whip up a monthly calendar by tomorrow—with your okay, of course . . . "

I plunged ahead, reeled off the list of events I had come up with. Right now that included everything from a fish boil and Nordic weekend, to an Up-North Fourth and a Yooper polka fest starring a local teen-band known for their send-ups of weird Al. Midstream it occurred to me, I had caught my boss off guard, saw the subtle knot of tension building between his brows.

"You managed all *that* in two hours," he said slowly.

"Thank Annie and that clientele of hers down at the diner. She'll handle the food events. The Foresters are committed to organizing the Nordic weekend. Sonja Forester gave me a phone number for the polka band."

"Budget. We hadn't discussed it, but it goes without saying we can't afford much."

"Volunteers so far," I told him, "but guests probably wouldn't balk at modest activity fees."

"There isn't much lead time. It could be tough to get the word out—"

"For the tubing weekend, I agree. We're talking days here. On such short notice I'd stick to plastering up some posters locally. But if we take a chance and promote a month ahead with what I've got so far, we can advertise two-weekend reservation packages on-line or print out coupons for discounts on future stays, salt them around the area—"

"Insurance," he persisted. "At the risk of sounding like a curmudgeon here, we need a rider on our policy for the river tubing."

Lord, the man didn't miss a thing. My heart sank. Insurance doesn't come cheap. Maybe this was more complicated than I thought.

I squared my shoulders, steeling myself to go back to the drawing boards. Paul couldn't possibly miss the disappointment in my voice.

"I hadn't thought of that," I said.

He chuckled softly, shook his head. "About the only thing, apparently. You've certainly hit the ground running, Lib. Relax . . . don't sweat it. I'll call our agent about the rider. As for the rest of it—you've come this far, I'm sure you'll figure it out."

I ventured a tentative smile. "So, you don't think it's totally nuts, then?"

He laughed, clapped me lightly on the shoulder as he started to rejoin Arvo at the tractor. "Crazy all right—like a fox. Go for it!"

That was all the push I needed. Flushed with the heady possibilities, I stayed up to all hours, cranking out drafts of publicity pieces on my laptop. A family-oriented photo of river tubing I found on-line provided the graphics, all sun-drenched smiles and not even a hint what the temperature might prove to be. I had stuck a toe in the water to check before I committed to the event—positively glacial.

Crack of dawn I was back in the SUV and by noon Tuesday there wasn't a single convenience store, gas station or other tourist stop within a 30-mile radius that wasn't plastered with one of our posters:

ROLLIN' ON THE RIVER WEEKEND
at Northern Lights Campgrounds on Route 2
Saturday - noon to 3 • Sunday - noon to 2
Ride Pipe Creek - Huck Finn style
in our vintage inner tubes from summers past.
Shuttle provided.
YOOPERS, TROLLS & CHEESEHEADS WELCOME!

I threw in that final teaser on impulse. Par for the course, Paul picked up on it immediately.

"That should raise a few eyebrows," he said.

I winced. "Thought it couldn't hurt to try to pull an 'Annie's' and go for locals as well as the tourists, down-state and the Wisconsin side. But if you think it's too—"

"Over the top? Quirky? Guess we'll find out soon enough. Personally, I think it's funnier than heck."

We had done all we could. By the weekend, Paul finagled the insurance rider for peanuts after he promised to recruit a student with life-saving training to chaperone the rafters. Tickled to be back in business, Arnie offered to drive the shuttle for gas money and a tip bucket on the dashboard.

Miracle of miracles, we got a few new guests right off the bat, tourists in the area who spotted the posters. Even in my wildest imaginings, I wasn't prepared for what happened next. Complaining about a bad case of cabin fever, locals started calling for reservations, any excuse to get out of the house after a long Northern Michigan winter.

"Fifty percent occupancy and that doesn't even include weekend impulse-stops," Paul said, shaking his head, when he saw the stats. "Who'da thunk it!"

That was the trouble with rising expectations. By Friday I was a quiet basket case worrying about everything that could possibly go wrong.

Just to make sure there were no glitches with the river trips, around noon I donned shorts, T-shirt, ball hat, sun-block and one of Arnie's bulky life jackets. Then I rode a tube myself down the quiet little creek under the anxious eye of our young guide. Arnie followed along on the road in the bus.

I hadn't told the boss my plan. Still, Paul got wind of it somehow and was waiting on the bank as I drifted toward the sandy landing spot, just before the creek crossed under Route 2 and emptied into Lake Michigan.

"How'd it go?" he said.

"Fun. A bit hard on the derriere in a couple of spots, but f-f-fun."

My teeth were chattering. Chuckling, Paul shed his jacket and quickly wrapped it around my shaking shoulders.

"Next thing you know, you're going to file a Comp claim or start asking for combat pay."

I laughed. "I don't remember hypothermia as a line item on that insurance rider . . . good grief, that water is cold. If we set up a coffee and hot cider stand at the end of the run, we'd make a small fortune."

"Not to worry," Paul grinned. "It's going to hit the high-eighties tomorrow, a regular June heat-wave. The creek may be cold but we're sure lucking out with the weatherman."

"Tell that to my feet."

The feeling was returning although they didn't seem to want to make a move to get me back to the motor home to change. My bottom still felt as if it were encased in block-ice.

"I see you decided to lash the tubes together like a flotilla," Paul wondered, "isn't the creek a bit narrow for that in spots?"

"Easier to supervise and more user friendly given the shape those tubes are in. If one deflates, there's always a spare."

"Good thinking," he nodded, "you seem to have it covered, Lib." An unfortunate choice of words, considering my wardrobe at the moment. Embarrassed that I was soaking through his jacket, I shrugged out of it and handed it back.

"Sorry about that."

Gingerly he held the dripping garment in one hand. "Nothing to be sorry about. I wouldn't have blamed you for bagging it after the first ten feet."

Truth was, I had surprised myself by sticking out the run. I hadn't felt that young, that energized in years—except, of course, for the cellulite and age spots. All of which, I suddenly realized, were only heightened by those baggy old running shorts I was wearing.

Feeling very exposed and vulnerable, in more ways than one, I unhooked the closures on the life jacket, thrust it as well in Paul's direction. Time, I decided, to get moving.

"I must look like the Wrath of God," I mumbled under my breath, prepared to make a dash for the motor home

Something in his voice stopped me. "Happy," he said. "You look happy and ought to be. You understand this place, your job, and you're making it work for us. I'm a bit surprised how fast . . . but grateful."

Suddenly self-conscious, I stared down at the puddles oozing out of my soggy water shoes. "Just doin' my job, boss!"

Not waiting for a response, I clutched my bare arms to hold in the warmth and struck off briskly cross-country through the campground toward my motor home. Last time I looked, Paul was still standing there, looking out at the gently moving water of the creek.

Six

What on earth brought that on? Muttering to myself, I fumbled awkwardly at getting the camper door open. Once inside, post-haste I shoved a half-empty cup of coffee left over from breakfast into the microwave.

It was a logistical nightmare getting out of those wet clothes. Wrapped up like a mummy in a fluffy, oversized beach towel, I sat shivering on the sofa while I sipped at the scalding liquid. Eventually I made myself lunch.

The intention was to boot up the computer and put the finishing touches on our June-July activity calendar. But before I could get at it, Paul called on my cell and told me he was heading in to town to the hardware to pick up some fittings and Arvo was back at the bog—which left it to me to man the registration desk.

En route, I saw a car had turned in to the Northern Lights drive and parked outside the office. An older man was standing on the concrete pad, obviously looking around for signs of life. It turned out to be that elderly couple from Green Bay with the Mini Winnie parked on site for the season.

"Got that e-mail of yours about all the doings this weekend," the husband, Gunnar, informed me after I introduced myself and snagged him a registration form. "Inga and I decided we gotta check it out. Inner tubes, huh? You wouldn't catch me dead in that creek, but gotta see who's crazy enough to try it."

"Me," I laughed. "It just took me an hour to thaw out enough to make a fist again."

"We don't want to miss the Nordic fest either . . . for sure. Inga and I are Norwegian, you know. You should taste her krumkake!"

My antenna shot up at that one. "Krumkake?"

By conversation end, Gunnar promised to enlist his wife as a cooking instructor for the Nordic arts and crafts workshop. "Shoot," Gunnar said, "give that woman a camp stove and she would whip you up enough to feed an army."

The sun felt warm, nice after all that time in the creek. I stood for a while on the concrete slab in front of the office, watching the elderly couple get settled on their site. Inga turned out to be this tiny slip of a woman who seemed frail enough that if a strong wind kicked up, she would be gone. But then it was Inga, I also noticed, who clambered precariously on a step-stool to unfurl the rig's awning while Gunnar hovered solicitously on solid ground.

Work intervened in the form of a relentless chirping from my cell phone. I retrieved it from my jeans pocket and groped for the Send button. The caller ID was familiar.

"Paul—"

"Are you in the office?"

"Close enough."

"Senility strikes," he grumbled. "I left the to-do list on my desk in the apartment. It would be stupid for me to guess, forget something and then have to make a second run over here. My digs should be unlocked, usually are."

As advertised, the door yielded to my touch. I blinked, struggling in the subdued light to get my bearings. My stifled gasp as I stumbled over a bright-cushioned wicker basket chair must have registered even over the tenuous connection.

"Problems?" he said.

"I'm good," I managed after a conspicuous pause. "Fine. Working on it."

"The desk or the list?"

"Both."

It wasn't quite the truth. Stunned and disoriented, I threaded my way through the wide-open loft of a room toward what had to be an authentic Stickley-period desk standing off to one side at the edge of the huge oriental carpet that defined the living area. It was impossible not to be distracted, when every square inch of the dark cedar-clad walls around me were hung with magnificent oversized black-and-white photographic prints.

This was a feast for the eyes as resplendent as some high-end Mackinac Island art gallery. On one wall, fiddlehead ferns thrust their delicate fronds upward in a shower of light. In what had to be the apartment's efficiency kitchen, a horizontal image of the creek at dawn was bathed in a ghostly curtain of mist rising above the dark water. Over a throw-draped futon that apparently doubled as Paul's bed and sofa, the vast Michigan sea glistened as serene as a sheet of glass under an ominous November sky. On yet another wall hung the graying clapboard image of a chapel set into the side of a sand dune, its squat steeple thrust almost defiantly above the precarious slope of the hillside. Something, I had to guess a door latch, had caught the light, a riveting starburst of white against the etched and peeling wood of the chapel door.

Museum quality, all of them. The images were emotionally compelling and original, revealing as much about their creator as the landscapes they were capturing. Most unsettling, they had a spiritual intensity that all but leapt off the canvas, like the earth shimmering at the dawn of Creation.

"Any luck?" my boss said. "It's a folded gray sheet of cardstock—right on top of the heap somewhere . . ."

The list. Paul was waiting.

While I rummaged awkwardly on the desk, my gaze kept straying

66

upward, drawn by a small, deceptively understated portrait on the wall above the cluttered desktop. It was a woman in her early-fifties with elfin features and tight-cropped salt-and-pepper hair. A knowing smile tugged at her generous mouth, a disturbing contrast to her wistful, introspective gaze.

I didn't need a signature to tell me this too was Paul Lauden's work, any more than I needed to check out the pencilled title on the mat of the portrait to confirm the woman's identity. *Ginny*—Paul's wife, it had to be. The love transmitted from lens to matte photographic paper projected itself without a word even to an outsider standing in its presence.

I had been loved like that once. The pain of that awareness and the loss that had come after tightened its iron grip around my heart.

"G-got it . . ."

Paul chuckled softly. "You sound out of breath. Take your time. I'm told my handwriting is atrocious, sorry about that."

"Do you . . . I suppose you'd like me to read you the whole list?"

I began with the plumbing fittings, losing my place now and again as I struggled to focus on his barely legible scrawl. If Paul sensed how distracted and on edge I was, he didn't call me on it, though he took the precaution of reading back some of the trickier specs.

"Good," he said, "thanks for saving me a trip. I'll relieve you on the desk when I get back."

He broke the connection. The silence was unbearable. I didn't belong here.

With the feeling that I was intruding on something deeply private, I carefully pulled the apartment door shut behind me. My boot soles echoed on the hard tile.

The office was deserted as I had left it. A fitful breeze had begun tugging noisily at the screen door. I clutched at my bare arms, waiting for the computer to run its boot sequence.

An hour passed, then two. I couldn't seem to focus. Exasperated, I discarded draft after draft of several new posters, then accidentally deleted the best of the bunch, complete with a tricky-to-execute calendar for July and early August.

I was back where I started. After a few choice expletives, I thought about redoing my work, but my heart wasn't in it.

Eventually the crunch of tires on gravel sent me wandering to the porch to investigate. My boss was exiting the SUV, balancing a fist-full of bags bearing the logo, Centerline Hardware.

"We've got company I see," he smiled.

"Gunnar and Inga. They got our e-mail flyer with the upcoming schedule. I recruited Inga to help us with the Scandinavian heritage weekend—"

Paul reacted with a low whistle. "Quick thinking. That means they'll be back. With friends, we can hope."

"Not if I don't get the darn posters done. It took a dozen drafts, trying to get the calendar to line up. Then I hit something, Lord knows what, and accidentally deep-sixed the . . .blasted thing!"

That caveat came out in a fitful rush—petulant, totally out of character. Embarrassed, I ducked my head, intending to go back in the office and give it another try.

Paul's shoulder, abruptly thrust between me and the door, stopped me. "Is there something I ought to know here, Lib?" he said evenly.

The bags of hardware he was carrying were a buffer of sorts between us. Still, as we made eye contact, my chest felt tight and my breath caught in my throat.

"Tired," I said. "I'm just . . . really tired."

My voice shook. For an awful moment I thought I felt tears building hot and salty behind my eyes.

"So, finish the flyer tomorrow," he insisted quietly. "You're wearing yourself to a frazzle and no one expects that—nobody but you, that is. Trust your instincts, Lib. You're building it and they're coming, starting with good old Gunnar and Inga over there."

"Repeaters. Not exactly a fair test."

Eyes narrowed, with what I recognized now as the practiced gesture of someone used to the business end of a viewfinder, Paul processed what he was seeing. His mouth clamped in a taut line.

"That's it . . . enough is enough. You're off for the rest of the day. And Monday, your *official* day off, you're going to collect on some of that road time I owe you."

"Can't on Monday. I have plans."

Exactly what, I couldn't remember, but I knew there was something. Even if there wasn't, I felt cornered and I, for one, didn't like it.

"And just for the record," my mouth felt stiff, "I am perfectly capable of taking care of myself."

His expression unreadable, Paul slowly straightened enough to let me pass if I chose. I didn't.

"I never thought that you weren't," he said.

Awkwardly shifting the stash of stuff he was carrying, he singled out a plain white plastic grocery bag and extended it in my direction. It looked heavy, filled to bursting with what appeared to be rectangular boxes.

"Donut holes," he said, "for those river rats of yours tomorrow. Plus some tea bags and cocoa packets. And just so you don't feel immediately obliged to haul out the office coffee pot, I'll do it—also tomorrow."

I hesitated, took the parcel, all too aware of how very up tight and defensive I must have sounded. "That was . . . thank you for thinking of it," I muttered.

"No problem. Just do us both a favor and cut yourself some slack, Lib—filch a donut, read a book, hang out on the beach. Not an order, by the way . . . just a suggestion . . . "

I went, my thoughts a dark and swirling jumble. I didn't look back.

The motor home was airless, smelled stale and vaguely of breakfast. I cracked the windows, let myself down on the bed, and then without willing it, fell into a heavy and dreamless sleep.

When I woke, it was after six. A quick glance outside told me the storm that had been forecast seemed to have missed us. The breeze barely stirred the low-hanging branch that was wont to scrape against the motor home roof and the air was warm and heavy.

My words to Paul kept sticking in my head. *I can take care of myself.* Somehow if proving it was behind my frenzied workaholism of late, it seemed to be having anything but the desired impact.

Arvo was right that first morning at Northern Lights when he told me this was a good place, good people. Maybe, just maybe it was time I cut not just myself, but them some slack.

As I headed down to the lake with a towel to cool off before dark, I was relieved to notice that despite all my fretting, the results of my hard work turned out to be campers—a half-dozen more of them, their rigs scattered around the campground. *O ye, of little faith,* I thought.

In the distance as I trudged back to the motor home from the beach, I noticed Paul in animated conversation with one of the newcomers outside the office. He spotted me, waved. I broke stride, called out a Hi and returned the gesture before I kept on going.

Saturday dawned and the influx of campers continued. From my informal straw poll as I handled the registrations, they seemed happy and excited ones at that. One of the rigs had decals of a Norwegian flag in the window and the driver asked about the Nordic fest planned for next weekend. Our strategy was working.

"Sorry I was such a . . . grouch all week," I finally offered by way of apology when Paul stopped in the office to check on how I was doing.

A smile twitched at the corner of his mouth but it didn't seem to reach his eyes. "We all have our days."

Whatever he was thinking, at least he spared me the I-told-you-so's. By nightfall, occupancy hit sixty percent, not bad at all for a pre-season June weekend. Four parties had even booked ahead for July and asked to be put on our e-mail Activity Alert list. We couldn't have expected more.

River rafting proved an absolute hit, despite the bracing water. At the end of the run, I improvised a funky Polar Bear Run first-aid station with the munchies my boss had bought and plenty of hot water for instant coffee, tea and cocoa. The modest charge for the treats, shuttle and tube rental more than covered expenses.

It was a jovial case of who's-on-first for our little Northern Lights team while I supervised the goings-on. Paul manned the desk and Arvo, looking like a fish out of water in crisp blue work pants and gray polo shirt, policed the grounds. Arnie's hearty laugh boomed out over the bus speaker system as the shuttle prepared for run after run.

"When your guide yells *butts up*," he roared, "ya better do what the kid says. And fast!"

By nightfall Sunday I was running on empty again, but this time pleasantly so—even with an afternoon camped out in the office fielding requests for firewood, bandaids and bug spray. Around five, with the bulk of our campers headed back downstate, Paul dropped by to lock up for the night.

"I don't know about you," he grinned, "but I'm ready to drop right where I stand."

"That makes three of us. Arvo cruised through here earlier looking pretty frazzled, a first for him."

"Speaking of Arvo," Paul began, hesitated, "I've got this enormous homemade pizza in my freezer and Arvo and I were going to warm it up. It's kind of a Sunday night ritual around here when we can swing it. You're welcome to join us."

I found myself choosing my words. "Thanks, really. . . but no. Right now I'm headed for a lukewarm fetal-position soak in the tub—if you can call it that, a glass of merlot and some down-time with a good book."

"Can't argue with that," he shrugged. "If you change your mind, you know where we'll be—in Arvo's Airstream."

If he was disappointed at my refusal, he didn't show it. So then why did I feel so guilty about my turning him down? It had been a tough

71

week and the thought of making dinner alone right now was not exactly appetizing.

"I'll see you guys in the morning!"

Paul nodded. "Have a good night."

Alone in the motor home, I slipped a CD into the player, cranked up my favorite Celtic rock band, the Drovers, and poured myself a glass of red wine. In the pantry above the refrigerator, I found a low-cal heat-and-eat casserole and stuck it in the microwave.

Keep it simple, I told myself, comfort food. Waiting for the timer to ding, I sat munching on the last of Annie's humus and sipping at the merlot. From outside I heard the faint sound of laughter as a couple from Minnesota camped next to me took their nightly constitutional.

For a split-second my throat felt tight, my eyes scratchy. That could have been me a year ago, settling in for the night with Dan, walking the neighborhood, checking out the other rigs. But then the impassioned sound of the Celtic fiddler carried me away from those dangerous memories.

Hold on, the lyrics kept telling me. Hold on.

I found myself raising my glass to an empty room. To love and loss and the thousand little deaths that we experience every day that shape who we are and who we become.

Doors close. Others open.

I took comfort in knowing I had choices—which ones to traverse and which ones to leave unexplored. But unlike that trip down Pipe Stem Creek I had so carefully orchestrated for the tubers, my journey had no easy points of entry or sandy shores upon which to land. No shuttle followed me as a fail-safe when the waters around me became too cold or treacherous.

"To survival," I said quietly. How I yearned to hear a reassuring Shalom in response.

Instead, the microwave timer sounded, telling me that dinner was ready. I set the container of steaming casserole on the dinette table and waited for it to cool a while before I let myself attempt it.

Seven

I woke Monday morning stiff and aching as if I had been handling that backhoe of Arvo's. Chalking it up to the stress, I took Paul's advice—indulged myself with a leisurely breakfast and a couple of chapters in a dog-eared novel I had found in the office library. Ostensibly Mondays were my day off, after all.

A quick glance at my calendar told me I hadn't been bluffing when I begged off on my first lesson driving the rig. Penned in was a ten o'clock meeting with Sonja Forester to discuss her plans for the upcoming Nordic weekend. Right now I didn't have a clue what, if anything, we would be offering by way of activities, except for Inga and her krumkake demonstrations.

Sonja showed up in a black mini-van with flame detailing on the side that looked all the world like something out of one of the grimmer Norse myths. We had only spoken on the phone and based on that vehicle, I half expected her to climb out from behind the wheel wearing a horned helmet like a Valkyrie in some over-the-top Wagnerian opera.

In fact, she turned out to be a tall and elegant gray-haired woman wearing a silver-blue tank top, jeans and carrying a sewing bag made from a recycled boiled wool sweater knit in a delicate white on pewter blue floral pattern. So much for first impressions.

"Quite a car," I said.

Sonja sighed, shook her head. "Blame it on my husband, good old Earl. He spotted it at a used car auction and just had to have it. I keep hoping our grandson will steal it, but then he's only twelve so we've still got a way to go before he gets his license and can take it off our hands."

I chuckled. "I'm a fine one to talk. My wheels are out there on an RV pad. That thirty-four-foot *Courage*."

"Great name," she said, "if you're planning on driving the thing. You don't tow a get-around car, then?"

"Hardly. I can't maneuver the rig as it is. And if I added another . . . how many feet? Don't even suggest it."

Sonja nodded sympathetically. "Earl talks about buying one, but so far I've been able to distract him. Retiring into that gas station pretty much keeps him out of trouble and his feet nailed to one spot."

"My husband, Dan, and I always fantasized about chucking it all and spending our retirement on the road in a honker of an RV. It was wonderful while it lasted—"

"Annie told me," Sonja said. "I can't imagine having the courage to do what you're doing. Coming back out here all alone . . . "

It was a familiar response, that mix of admiration and thinly veiled relief. There but for the grace of God. Before Dan died, I remembered reacting just like it whenever I heard of someone losing their spouse. Yet, here I was.

"I wouldn't wish it on anyone," I said softly. "But, mercifully, we are never as . . . alone as we think."

My boss, Paul Lauden. Good old Arvo. Annie Stavrous. Arnie Klonz and his vintage inner tubes. Now Sonja, I ticked off the names in my head. Against all odds, this growing little circle was becoming a part of my story.

"Well, you're sure going to have help with that Nordic weekend of yours, kiddo," Sonja smiled. "We've got a wild mix of ethnic folks up here, most of them really proud of their heritage. I made a half-dozen calls and here's what we've got so far . . . "

As I stood there open-mouthed, she trotted out a list of volunteers prepared to teach Scandinavian crafts, Finnish ladies to run a bake sale including items ominously called *niso* and *korppu,* and to top it off, a Viking horde of teenagers that would land on the beach across from the campground.

"You're kidding," I said. "A long ship . . . ?"

"Okay, more like a row boat," Sonja shrugged, "until Earl fitted it out with a huge, detachable dragon head for the prow. Still, you are *not* going to believe it."

"But how on earth will we get all those volunteers together by Saturday?"

"Piece of cake," Sonja grinned, handing me a computer generated roster of names and program times. "It's a done deal. Everybody's coming. With a football team that calls itself the Vikings, the high school kids around here really get off on that stuff every homecoming. They're just looking for an excuse to maraud and plunder. The Home Ec classes made enough costumes over the years to outfit half the county!"

"Sounds absolutely perfect, all of it. Though I'm not sure where to stage the more artsy-craftsy events, especially if it rains."

"That roofed shelter over in the picnic area would work," Sonja said. "If it rains, we'll just scrunch the tables in toward the middle of the concrete pad, hang up a tarp to cut the wind if we have to. Perfect."

I stiffened, repelled by memories of Dan lying pale and still on that hard ground, the EMTs clustered around him. Inhaling sharply, I faced the brutal truth. I had to get beyond this. *Had to.*

"Fine," I forced a smile. "We can find a way to make that work."

"Oh m'gosh . . . almost forgot and Earl would kill me. After dark we'll burn a straw man for the solstice. He loves concocting those hideous things. It's a downright pleasure to see them go up in smoke—you have no idea."

I laughed. "How on *earth* do you come up with all this stuff?"

"Snowed in a lot of the time up here," Sonja shrugged. "You

better have a pretty active fantasy life, love life—or both! You just mention 'party' in Centerline and before you're home with the groceries or a keg, everybody's sitting on your doorstep . . . rarin' to go."

Still laughing, we drew up a modest shopping list for the crafts tables. That accomplished, Sonja got back in her war chariot and headed west.

When I presented Paul with the weekend agenda later in the office, he looked dazed, as if I had suddenly found life on the moon. "And Sonja just up and organized all that?"

"Yup," I grinned, "with a lot of help from the local historical society and the Centerline football team. Why do I get the feeling that folks around here have way too much time on their hands?"

"One way of looking at it, I suppose," Paul said slowly. "But then you're obviously both creative and passionate about what you do. And that, Ms. Aventura can be contagious."

As we made eye contact, my face felt hot. "You give me too much credit—"

"And you never give yourself *enough*. Just say thank you and take the compliment, Lib . . . just take it for what it is. You earned it." There wasn't any arguing with that smile.

"Thank you," I said.

"Better. Now what can Arvo and I do to help?"

I hesitated. "It occurred to me, we could maybe rig up the tractor—front bucket up—like a dragon and use it to pull kids on a hay wagon through the campground on Sunday. But then I'd worry about accidents, kids running to get aboard."

"Reluctantly, I agree . . . too much of an attractive nuisance, plus that thing can be darn unstable with its bucket up. Maybe plan a hayride some other weekend. With that ship-landing business and the bonfire, we already have a full schedule as it is."

"Oh, Lord, I knew it had to be too simple," I groaned. "Burn permits for the bonfire. There's always something."

Paul's eyebrow arched. "I'm still thinking more along the lines

76

of *burn-out,* if you don't learn to delegate, Lib. I'll be on the desk all afternoon, am perfectly capable of dialing a phone."

"And it's Monday. I know, I know, I get the message. Next week I'll even make sure I get my driving lesson. It's just . . . you have no idea how much this job means to me."

"Trust me," he said, "I'm beginning to figure it out."

So was I. For once I didn't wait for my boss to shoo me out of the office. All that chivalry still felt a little too much like my Danielle in action, but then knowing that my co-workers cared enough to watch out for me in return wasn't the worst arrangement in the world either. Not by a long shot.

Solstice Saturday and summer officially arrived. With it came the first team of Sonja's volunteers for the Nordic crafts demonstrations. She and I were just getting the craft work stations set up in the picnic area when I noticed a pop-up camper pulled by a strangely familiar-looking mini van heading for the registration office.

Wisconsin plates. I watched the driver get out—did a double-take. It was my son-in-law, Chris.

Chagrined, it was only then I realized I had missed going on a week in my regimen of check-in phone calls with my daughter. Danielle obviously had decided to take matters into her own hands.

Heart thudding wildly, I forced myself to concentrate on the task at hand helping Sonja lay out the last of the workshop materials. My daughter was already heading our way, her face a thundercloud. A half-block behind her, I saw my son-in-law Chris and my grandkids were still huddled around the trailer, apparently charged with figuring out how to get the thing to pop up as advertised.

"Danielle," I said, "what a surprise!"

There was no avoiding what I knew was coming next. My daughter let me sweep her into an awkward hug.

"So much for calling, *Mom*—I've been worried sick, haven't

77

been able to raise you on the cell phone for days! The office line is always busy. David and I have been on the phone wondering what the heck to do. You're lucky he didn't just get on the red-eye to Chicago, rent a car and—"

"Wait a minute," I let my breath out slowly, "you actually called your brother. You're kidding."

Apparently she wasn't. Danielle just glared at me.

I chuckled, shook my head. "Always my little control freak."

"Mom, this isn't funny!"

On *that* we agreed, it wasn't. Now the two of them were conspiring to have me declared incompetent.

I shuddered to think what spin my daughter must have put on my unintentional disappearance from her radar, albeit for only a couple of days. A genial public school shop teacher with a pert, outgoing slip of wife who ran a craft shop, two sons and a dog, it took a heck of a lot to get David riled up.

"I didn't mean to worry you. Sorry about that," I winced. "Cell phone service here can be dicey and we've been tied up on the office phone planning this Scandinavian arts and crafts weekend. I just lost track of the time. I'll call David tonight and get this all straightened out."

"Yeah, well, you scared the heck out of all of us, big time. The tabloids are full of people who vanish every day under saner circumstances . . . !"

At something in my face, Danielle shifted uncomfortably, softened her tone. "Anyway, the kids were getting stir crazy, so Chris and I decided to run 'em around in the great outdoors for a day or two."

I fought a smile, imaging how poor husband Chris—as unflappable as our daughter was excitable—took to the notion of charging up here, in a camper no less. Dan and I had decided early-on in their marriage that our teddy-bear of a son-in-law was the best thing that ever happened to our one and only daughter, whether she fully appreciated that fact or not.

"You rented that pop-up?"

"Borrowed, from the neighbors. Hope we can get the thing back intact. I'm starting to have my doubts."

"I'm sure my boss or Arvo over in that silver Airstream by the road would be happy to—"

"So, you really did it, then? You're really *working* here?"

I rummaged in the tote I was carrying for one of the monthly program calendars I had been handing out. "Good stuff, I think. Fish boils, a polka weekend with lots of Weird-Al humor. It's been a lot of fun putting it together."

Danielle quickly scanned the schedule, frowned. "You did all this, in what . . . just a couple of weeks."

"Time flies when you're having fun," I told her. "I always loved my work, honey. Only this time I don't have to punch a clock. I like that."

Something like a smile began to twitch at the corners of my daughter's mouth. "I'll admit, you look—"

"Bleary-eyed. Senile?"

"For the record, Mom," Danielle bristled, "I was going to say, you look great, and I'm . . . happy for you. Relieved maybe, but glad."

It was what my boss had said, too. *Happy.* Only I wouldn't have expected to hear that assessment coming from my daughter.

Danielle's righteous indignation appeared to be losing some of its momentum. And unless I was seeing things, my son-in-law already had commandeered Paul Lauden and Arvo into trouble-shooting what was ailing the pop-up mechanism on the camper. Things were looking up.

"By the way," I suggested, "would you like to meet my boss?"

My daughter blinked, but covered with a cautious smile. "Sure. Yeah, I'd like that."

"Hold that thought," I said.

Around us, a growing knot of curious bystanders had wandered over to see what was going on at the craft workshops. My volunteers seemed to have things well in hand.

One little girl, four or five from the look of it, had been recruited to model one of Sonja's paper flower garlands. You could hear her high-pitched squeals of laughter all over the campground, as the girl began to swoop swallow-fashion, her arms spread wide, back and forth across the picnic grounds. The paper ribbons on the circlet of flowers streamed out like a rainbow behind her.

"If you don't need me," I said to my volunteers, "I'd like to play hooky a minute and say hello to my family."

Sonja looked up from her flower-making and flashed a no-problem grin. "Your people came—great! We'll manage just fine. Go, enjoy!"

"You've got an extra garland?" I said.

"Not quite done, but here."

While Sonja quickly fastened the last of the roses on the wire wreath, I took the opportunity to introduce her to my daughter. Then together, Danielle and I headed back to their campsite.

The sun was already burning away the morning dew. Normally by now it would have soaked through my canvas deck shoes. I decided whatever worries I had about rain dampening our festivities were totally unfounded.

"Chris," I called out as we wandered into the campsite. I gave my son-in-law a quick hug. "How fun to have the bunch of you up here!"

Wide-eyed, my two grandchildren Peter and Louisa, were staring at me as if I had just arrived from outer space. It was Louisa who reacted first, launching herself at me like a pig-tailed missile. Her brother piled on in a group hug that took my breath away.

Disentangling myself, I solemnly planted the flower wreath on my granddaughter's chestnut brown curls. She beamed as if I had just handed her a diamond tiara.

"AWESOME!! Thanks, Grama!"

"This man is helping Daddy," Peter said. "Our poppa camper

doesn't wanna pop."

He was trying hard to play the serious eight-year-old trying to pass for ten, but I could tell that subtly my grandson really was eye-balling his sister's present. Time to nip that in the bud.

"They're going to make broad-swords and dragon shields in a little while, too," I told him, in an undertone. "I'll make sure you get the first sample off the assembly line."

"Neat-o," Peter crowed, did a little victory dance.

Head still bent over the camper hinge, Paul looked up at the sound. "Got a little problem here," he grinned, "but as Arvo always says, we're gainin' on it."

"Grama, this man says *you* work here, too," Louisa stammered. "Cool."

I smiled. "I think so, too."

My daughter was conspicuously silent, but I couldn't miss the quizzical look that flashed between her and her husband. By now Paul had straightened and was wiping his hands on a hunk of paper towel my son-in-law gave him, prepared to join us.

"That should do it, Chris," he said. "I've got some silicon spray over in the office that would make the take-down easier, too. When I get a chance I'll bring it over, if you like."

Hastily I ran through the official introductions. With a tight little smile, my daughter extended her hand in Paul's direction.

"Good to meet you Mr. Lauden. Mom says you run a great ship up here."

"Paul, please," my boss laughed. "As for how ship-shape we are, I've started to think that to run a campground it helps to be borderline certifiable."

"I was thinking more along the lines of Donald Trump," my son-in-law smiled. "You've got one heck of a piece of real estate here."

"A bit off the beaten track. But yeah—thanks. The previous owner was dumping it at just the right time. I lucked out. Are you in the real estate business?"

81

Chris laughed. "Not unless somebody is fighting a zoning restriction—I'm in property law."

"Close enough. Where were you when I was negotiating the terms for this place . . . ?"

"Not up here," Chris shook his head, "unfortunately, when I think about what could have happened to Lib's motor home. I did want to thank you for the amazing job you did keeping it in shape the past year. We all owe you—"

"Nothing," Paul said quickly. "You owe me nothing. Lib has more than evened the score with this programming she has been putting together. She made more inroads with the locals than I have at this point."

It felt uncomfortable being talked about, as if I weren't even there. I felt a little like my grandson Peter, digging with the toe of his sneakers to dislodge a particularly large beach stone from the hardened gravel underfoot. A pinched little scowl had set in between his brows.

"I didn't know you were a camper, Grama," he said slowly. "I always thought Gramps—"

"Neither did I, honey. Neither did I."

I forced a smile as I said it, knowing full well Peter couldn't have picked that up on his own. Apparently little pitchers have very big ears. To her credit, my daughter caught it, too—looked uncomfortable.

She wasn't the only one. My boss suddenly had that time-to-bail look about him, as if he sensed exactly what was going on here. It was pretty apparent, my son-in-law and Danielle were not exactly on the same page when it came to my tenure up here in the north woods.

"Lib, you seem to have the Nordic crafts crew in hand," Paul said, "so why don't you hang around with your family for a while. How much trouble can the volunteers get into while you—"

I shook my head, waved him off. "Thanks, but my family will understand . . . somebody has got to keep the day on schedule. Arvo is at the desk alone and you were planning to trouble-shoot the new sites. The ladies should be showing up with their Finnish bake sale any minute."

Out of the corner of my eye, I caught the disappointment in Peter and Louisa's upturned faces. "But if you don't mind," I said, "I'll let my grandkids hold down the fort with me at the crafts tables. Louisa can help Sonja make garlands and Peter can field-test all those cardboard broad-swords."

A chorus of whoops pretty much summed up my grandkids' take on things. Danielle's frown was back.

"Mom, I don't think . . . aren't they a little young to—?"

"Eight and six, practically grown up. And you and Chris could use the time to get settled on the site," I told her. "I'd love having them hang out with me. It'll be fun."

"If they're a problem—"

"There's plenty to keep us busy."

My grandkids were already inching their way in the direction of the picnic area, more or less commandeering my boss as a co-conspirator. As the four of us reached the roofed pavilion, I looked back one last time, winced. Chris and my daughter were still standing there next to the camper, watching us. Their body language pretty much said it all—while my son-in-law seemed supportive enough, Danielle still had her doubts about what I was doing, to put it mildly.

"Seriously, Lib," Paul said, following my gaze, "it's obvious that . . . I'd be willing to bet your daughter probably could use a little quality time with you right now. You've done your homework. Just enjoy the weekend, go with the flow."

Great in theory. Louisa was tugging at my sleeve, the spitting image of her mom in more ways than one. "Grama, you promised to keep us com-paly," she said. "We're going to miss all the fun."

Always the more timid of the two, even Peter was longingly eyeing the craft table where a group of kids were clustered around Sonja. Laughing and jostling, they were using marker pens, glue and shiny faux-jewels to create cardboard replicas of Viking weapons.

"It does look like fun, doesn't it?" Paul said.

He didn't wait for a response to start moving that way, his smile daring Peter to follow. After a split-second hesitation, my grandson did just that, close at Paul's heels.

"Grama said it was okay . . . that I could make one of these swords 'n stuff, too. . .!'"

I heard the excitement in my grandson's voice, sensed he was just waiting for that little push to get him going. Paul thoughtfully hefted one of the finished model battle axes lying on the picnic table.

"En garde," he winked.

Peter's eyes were as big as pie plates. Playfully, my boss coaxed my grandson into a little impromptu duel. The volunteers were in stitches as the two of them awkwardly thrust and parried with the cardboard replicas—especially since patches of paint was still wet and left interesting battle scars on whatever the weapons touched.

"Mom's gonna have a hissy fit," Peter said glumly as he stopped long enough to inspect a splotch of blue on the shoulder of his polo shirt.

"No problem," Sonja said, "water-soluble, it'll wipe right off."

She already had grabbed a handy stain-remover wipe and quickly went to work on the damage. Chuckling quietly to himself, my boss had snagged a wipe of his own and was attacking the blobs of color left behind on his hands.

"Unfortunately, duty calls," he said as he finished. But then he made no move to go.

I had a tight, scratchy feeling in my throat as I saw him chatting with Sonja all the while gently prodding my grandson to pick out a project of his own and join the other kids. This is something my Dan would have done . . . plunged into the moment without a qualm. By the time my boss rejoined me, Peter was happily sorting glittery shapes to decorate the cardboard shield that Sonja was slicing out for him.

"Thanks for getting Peter settled over there," I told him. "He's a great kid but on the shy side sometimes."

"Strange place. Strange people. It's understandable."

"By the way, as you're making your rounds," I said, "I'm sure my

84

family would enjoy it if . . . feel free to pop over to their site if you have the time . . . "

All that came tumbling out before I had a chance to second-guess myself. I could tell by his split-second hesitation, that I had taken him by surprise.

"Thanks, I'd like that," Paul nodded. "Just our dumb luck, though, those water and power lines on the new sites could be wreaking havoc out there . . . "

Our—his choice of words was casual, inclusive pep-talk stuff, something a sensitive boss cultivates as a matter of course. Still, it felt good to be part of this adventure, to know that whatever my daughter was thinking about my role here, even my grandkids seemed impressed.

"Anyway . . . don't work too hard," I told him.

My boss flashed a knowing wink in Peter and Louisa's direction. "I was about to say the same to you."

Eight

Though I wasn't expecting it, Paul relieved me at the picnic area so I could join my family for lunch. Camera in hand, he just showed up and started grabbing shots of the crowds milling around the various craft stations.

"Don't worry about us," he said, "I've got it 'til you get back."

The menu at my family's campsite appeared to be hot dogs and three-bean-salad straight out of a can. I arrived just in time for the propane in their camp stove to punk out mid-dogs. Red-faced, my son-in-law Chris was making noises about building a campfire and roasting them on sticks—not the most viable alternative with Peter and Louisa already announcing loudly how hungry they were.

"It happens to the best of 'em," I said. "What say we just pick up the fixings and finish the job in my motor home."

Looking sheepish, my son-in-law started loading us down with the makings of the feast and our ragged procession set off across the campground. Once at the motor home, I held the door and waited while Chris, Peter and Louisa awkwardly navigated the steps without dropping buns or beans or dogs.

Only Danielle hesitated about coming in. One look at her face was enough to guess the source.

I had shared this space with her father. Whatever the past weeks here alone had done to help me make my peace with that, however tentative, for my daughter those emotions were still raw and unresolved.

"The kids can sit at the dinette," I said softly. "How about we wait on the couch while Chris does his thing with the hotdogs at the stove."

Danielle made eye contact, nodded. "Fine."

I could tell as she clambered into the motor home, her mind was definitely not on the picnic to come. Visibly distracted, she looked around her at her surroundings.

Silent, I gave her the space to shift gears. There was her Dad's favorite flannel shirt hanging on the hook just inside the door. I had left his camper magazines stashed in the wooden book rack, a year out of date. Hard to miss, any of it.

"It must be difficult . . . with all of Daddy's things here," Danielle said.

"Yes . . . and no. He loved living here. I try to remember that and not the rest of it, or how much I miss all of the—"

"Do the others, your boss and that Arvo, know he . . . . know what happened here?"

"Roughly, yes," I told her, "although neither of them were there at the time. Paul only took over the management of Northern Lights months later. They've all been really very good to me."

My daughter's audible intake of breath pretty much summed up her frustration. "I'm sorry, but Chris and I still wish you would move to Madison, Mom. You shouldn't have to work this hard any more and—"

"I'm sorry, too—sorry to disappoint you. But I think hard work is the best thing in the world for me right now."

My heart bled for her. Still, we had to get beyond this, for both our sakes.

"You really can't spend the rest of your life up here," she said, "in the middle of nowhere. Alone."

"I'm not alone. And I'm not stuck up here, either. My boss has offered to teach me to drive this rig."

I hesitated, surprised myself at what came next. "I only promised them a month working here—although if things continue to go this well, I just might consider staying until the end of the summer . . . "

That was more than my boss had been able to pry out of me. If Danielle sensed I was just making it up as I went along, she didn't call me on it.

"And *afterward*?"

I shrugged. "Florida, maybe. By then I should be a pro at handling the rig."

"It's fifteen-hundred miles at least."

"If I take the drive in small chunks, it wouldn't be so bad. Your Dad and I drove that route several times."

Danielle started to say something, stopped. My son-in-law had shut off the stove, and forehead knotted in concentration, was loading the hotdogs and trimmings into the buns. At the dinette, Peter and Louisa were arm-wrestling over one of Dan's brain-teaser puzzles they had found stowed in a cubby alongside the table.

"Peter . . . Louisa, stop that!" my daughter said. "Take your plates over to your Dad and get your lunch."

The edge to her tone was more than called for, enough so that Peter and Louisa looked over at their mother in astonishment. "We weren't being bad," Peter pouted.

"Just do it!"

At that, even Chris weighed in. "They're hungry. This stuff is getting cold, Dani," he said quietly.

Danielle looked down at her hands, tight-curled in her lap. "All right, then, we're coming."

"Honey," I said evenly, "you have got to let this go, let me make my own mistakes and find my own way through this. It really is time."

Eyes swimming with tears, Danielle just looked at me. I had to bite my lip not to lose it myself.

"After lunch, the kids can try their hand at the Scandinavian crafts again. They're loving it. Sonja used to be a teacher and is really very good. Tonight we can all go to the Dragon boat landing and bonfire."

At that, Peter and Louisa perked up. "Dragons?"

"The local high school students are going to come sailing up in horned helmets and fur pelts."

"With broad-swords—?"

"And dragons in the lake?"

I smiled, as I fielded their chorus of questions. "You bet. Right out of Lake Michigan, like Nessie in Scotland!"

"With smoke coming out of the dragon's nose, too?"

"So I'm told."

In fact, at dress rehearsals last night, the director decided not to waste the fire extinguisher practicing that part of the saga. Tough for a control freak like me, but the guy assured me it was going to work, never fear.

"Wow, Grama!" Peter grinned.

"That's what I thought, too."

Her eyes still dark with emotion, my daughter got to her feet and without a word, headed over to the kitchen area to claim her lunch. At the stiff set of her shoulders, I wanted to hug her and tell her that everything was going to be all right. But then, she was going to have to find that out for herself.

The afternoon went off without a hitch, except for one enthusiastic workshop participant who ignored the instructors and hot-glued two fingers together. Paul showed up once in a while with a digital point-and-shoot and grabbed shots of the goings-on.

"Good for PR down the road," he said as I caught him focusing his lens on my attempts to help a young camper unsnarl the ribbons on her May wreath. She had caught it on her brother's Viking broad-sword, and lip quivering, was getting ready to deck him in protest.

"Great shot . . . harried program director saves Northern Lights from mega-lawsuit," I muttered, as I aimed what I hoped was a withering glance in Paul's direction. "At least you'll make the insurance company happy."

Paul just chuckled. Moved on.

I passed on dinner with my kids, deciding it was time to give them all some space. Instead, I invited the craft volunteers to an improvised cookout at the motor home. Paul and Arvo even wandered over long enough to snag dessert—leftovers from the Finnish bake sale.

As the sun began to set, I led a contingent of campers across the highway, including my daughter, Chris and the grandkids, to take in the Viking ship landing. Though I had witnessed the dress rehearsal and knew more or less what was coming, I had to admit even I was surprised at the flair with which the students carried off their part of the day's festivities. As advertised, thick clouds of smoke truly roiled out of the enormous dragon's nose clamped to the prow of the row boat.

A safe distance down the beach, Paul stood with yet another fire extinguisher and buckets at the ready as garage-owner Earl Forester, decked out in a horned helmet and what looked like chain mail biker vest, used a grill lighter to ignite his straw man. It was woefully scaled down for the occasion, he privately complained, because of the fire danger, but when to boot he set off several strings of firecrackers to punctuate the effect, the gasp from the crowd was spontaneous and unrehearsed.

A camper had brought a guitar and we all settled in for a sing-a-long around the campfire as the sun went down. There wasn't a dry eye as our elderly Minnie-Winnie campers quavered their way together through an impromptu solstice folk tune in their native tongue.

All in all, it was one impressive evening. While Chris and my daughter headed back to the campground with the kids, I stayed behind watching the dying fire and making sure the last of our guests got safely back across the road. In the shadowy light, I looked up to see Paul easing down alongside me on the sand.

"Beautiful," he said, "an amazing day."

"Yes."

"Your doing, all of it."

"With an awful lot of help from our friends."

It didn't seem a bit like hyperbole now to describe them that way—Sonja and her crafty history buffs, Earl grinning ear to ear as he waded out to help guide the dragon boat to shore or Annie quietly cooking up goodies, literally, for upcoming weekends. There was a whole world up here, a culture all its own, that I hadn't even dreamt of encountering when I boarded Owen's Shuttle. If I had my way, had pulled up stakes and run the minute my cartons showed up, I would never had experienced any of it.

My life's work had been meticulous planning on behalf of my clients and I had been good at it. How unsettling it was at this late date to learn to live for the moment, to take a day at a time and enjoy each one for what it was and what it was teaching me.

A burnt-through log shifted in the fire, throwing up a trail of sparks, startling as a shooting star against the dark night sky. I steadied myself with the quiet sound of waves lapping at the shoreline, burnished pale silver by the moonlight.

"I like your family," Paul said after a while.

"Danielle is the oldest. Her brother, David, lives outside of L.A. Unfortunately, my daughter seems to be a bit . . . zealous about my welfare at the moment. Sorry about that. I know the timing for her visit was lousy, with so much riding on the weekend."

My laughter was edgy, nervous, and Paul picked up on it immediately. He had shifted slightly so that I could just make out his face in the glow from the fire.

"No apologies necessary," he said. "You're lucky. They care—and you can talk to them. I'd give anything to be in that position."

"Your son?" I said quietly.

"Josh. Thirty going on fifty and he hates my guts."

91

The silence that stretched out between us was strained, awkward. It was Paul who broke it.

"I'm sorry. That wasn't fair. You've got enough to handle yourself without—"

"You don't have to tell me, Paul," I said slowly, "but I'd be glad to listen . . ."

His lack of a response was an answer of sorts. From out on the lake, the muffled sound of a boat motor reminded us we weren't alone. Running lights stood out low against the horizon, gradually moved beyond our sight.

"It's getting late," Paul said finally. "When is your family heading back to Madison?"

"Sunday afternoon."

He shifted alongside me, turning in my direction. "I owe you some road time," he said. "Monday, when the dust settles, I'll teach you how to disconnect the motor home. Then I thought we could drive the rig up to Tahquamenon Falls—correct that, *you* can drive. I'll come along for the ride. Might as well enjoy the scenery and when we get back, you can practice the hookups again."

"I'd like that."

"A deal then."

I shivered, suddenly aware that the embers were no longer making a dent as the temperatures began to plummet. It was still June, after all, and we were one heck of a way north when it came to climate zones.

"I'd better go," I said. "Morning is going to come plenty early."

Clambering to his feet, Paul extended a hand in my direction, inviting me to do the same. I took it, using his strength and balance to regain my footing. For a split-second, my head swam, but he reacted instantly to steady us both. I chalked it up to sitting so long and the uncertain light.

"Are you okay?" Paul said.

I nodded. "Quick reflexes there—thanks . . . !"

"Any time. Do you have a flashlight?"

"Yes. But the fire still needs—"

"I'll handle it."

I hesitated. "Goodnight, then."

Back-lit by the faint glow from the campfire, I sensed him watching as I picked my way through the beach grass. "See you in the morning," he said.

Overtired, I spent a restless night, but took extra time with my makeup to disguise the fact for Danielle's sake. As I wandered over to my family's campsite, I noticed that my son-in-law had started the day off by cranking out pancakes at the picnic table outside the camper. From the look of it they were undercooked in the middle but edible. The label on the maple syrup was from a small cottage industry about five miles west of the campground.

I begged off on the pancakes but shared a quick coffee. A night in the north woods seemed to have done my daughter a world of good. Though she was unusually quiet, she also steered clear of topics that would have put a strain on the apparent truce that had been declared between us.

"I hope you don't feel I'm neglecting you," I said. "This is the first really big weekend we've had and my boss and Arvo shouldn't have to handle everything I've set up all by themselves."

"No problem," Chris said quickly. "After all, we just barged in on you like this. Go ahead and do what you have to do. In fact, Danielle and I thought we would drive east and give the kids a quick peek at the Mackinac Bridge. Maybe cough up the toll and drive across and back."

"I'm sure the kids'll like it."

Danielle didn't look convinced. "I hope so. In a pinch I've got those Game Boys of theirs in the back seat. When we get back, we'll pack up—then if you have time, we would love to take you out to dinner at that place we saw advertised down the road."

"Annie's," I smiled. "I'd like that. But won't it get awfully late for you driving home?"

"The kids can sleep in the back seat. We don't have to get the camper back to the neighbors until tomorrow."

I felt the familiar lump tighten in my throat. "It's been great having you here," I said. "I'm going to miss you."

Danielle just looked at me, her face an open book. I knew what she was thinking. This was my doing, all of it—the miles between us, my decision to go back to work and my commitments at Northern Lights.

"Maybe we can get up here again," she said, "next month sometime."

It was tentative as olive branches go, but I took it. "You know I'd love that, Danielle."

I flashed a high-five in Peter and Louisa's direction and headed off toward the office. As I hit the porch, I noticed Paul had already opened for the day. Ensconced at the computer, he was entering the weekend's stats into the database he had established.

Still half-thinking about my family, I got his attention with a tentative, "Good morning."

"Looking good, all right!" he said. "We picked up another reservation last night at the bonfire for that madcap Yooper weekend of yours coming up in July. Apparently the dragon boat was a huge hit—nothing like our quirky northwoods humor to get the downstaters going."

I laughed. "You know, we really ought to stock some of the regional goodies at the counter—pasties, maple syrup, wild rice, thimbleberry jam. . ."

Paul smiled. "I had thought about letting some local craft folk display and sell their work on consignment in the camp store, but never got around to it."

"Pen," I said. "Quick, before I forget!"

Eyebrow cocked, Paul rummaged on the shelf under the

reservation counter and came up with a sticky-note and a permanent felt-tip marker. "You're feeling okay?"

I laughed. "Art fair, the third weekend in August."

Paul just shook his head. "You're crazy . . . really crazy, you know. A good crazy, more like hyper. Whatever it is, I like it."

In spite of myself, I felt that familiar flush of embarrassment whenever the man shot a compliment in my direction. "You've really got to stop this or I'm going to ask for a raise."

"I gather, since we are now officially thinking ahead, you aren't planning to bail on me any time soon?"

I hesitated. "August. I told you I'd commit to August."

It wasn't quite true. I had told him a month and that would be up after next weekend, the Fourth of July.

A hint of a smile softened the hard planes of his face. Still, he was smart enough not to point out I was already waffling on my self-imposed timetable.

"Just checking," he said.

"I'm not going to let you off the hook, though—about that road trip tomorrow . . . "

He nodded. "Nine AM?"

"Nine-thirty. I'm sleeping in."

"Good for you!"

Abandoning the stool on which he had been perched and maneuvering his way out from behind the counter, Paul gestured in the direction of the now-vacant computer. "It's all yours, Ms. Aventura—ready for you to work your magic."

Grinning, I took my place at the keyboard and began to crank out yet another e-mail program alert to our growing client list. "GET READY, SET, GAS UP THE RIG AND BREAK OUT THE TENT STAKES FOR OUR OLD FASHIONED NORTHWOODS 4th." Way too cutesy maybe, but then I still had the whole day ahead of me to fix it.

Nine

"Anybody home?"

It was Monday, my day off, and I had lied about sleeping in—not likely under the best of circumstances. In fact, I had been back on my laptop for a good hour when I heard Paul's voice outside the motor home.

The weather was getting warm enough that I could leave the door open during the day, with the screen in place as a first line of defense against the assorted flying beasties that were an unfortunate downside of the summer season. Even with that screening between us, a quick glance in my boss' direction told me I had miscalculated my wardrobe for our little junket.

For once he had abandoned his uniform of choice, jeans and a recycled dress shirt, for chinos and a burgundy polo that I couldn't help but notice looked awesome with his tan. He even substituted dockers for those scuffed work boots of his. North-woods chic.

I, on the other hand, had dressed down in jeans, a tank top layered with one of Dan's old tropical-print camp shirts, and sporting a hand-woven headband a friend had brought me back from Guatemala. My athletic sandals were comfortable, which was about all you could say for them.

The two of us seemed out of synch and our outing hadn't even gotten started yet. To add insult to injury, my boss had brought what looked like an even more professional digital camera than the one he was usually toting—judging by the brand name woven into the strap. I hoped it wasn't to immortalize what could easily enough turn out to be my total humiliation.

"I assume you're thinking ahead?" I muttered. "Just in case I *total* the rig—at least, for insurance purposes, you'll be all set to document the fiasco."

Paul winced. "I was thinking it's a nice day," he said. "Great light. If we were wandering around up at Tahquamenon, I might get off some interesting shots."

"Just give me a minute," I said. "I want to run the latest draft of the calendar for August. But come on in."

He did, eyes narrowed at the sudden transition from sunlight to the subdued artificial light in the motor home. Looking both very tall and vaguely uncomfortable in the relatively confined space of my rig, he settled down tentatively on the sofa opposite the dinette to wait, that imposing camera of his lying alongside him.

Truth was, the thought of maneuvering my rig terrified me witless. I took my time keystroking the last few lines into the computer, ignoring how my housekeeping must look with those previous drafts crumpled and strewn all over the floor around the table.

"Good God, you're at it again," he said, looking around at the mess.

"Sorry. I forgot to tell you that once I get going, I'm compulsive. Copywriting, crossword puzzles, any old kind of brain teaser with words in it—once I start, I'm hooked. At least the e-mail alert finally went out an hour ago."

Paul laughed. "Don't get me wrong. Any boss in the world would be crazy to object to any of this."

"But—?"

"It isn't going to get you out of taking this rig of yours on the road."

It was my turn to look uncomfortable. "Avoidance. That's what you think is going on here?"

"It had crossed my mind."

Awkwardly clambering up from the bench seat, I fished the draft of the flyer out of the printer tray and thrust it in his direction. The heaps of rejects crackled underfoot as he made a move to take it.

"Here," I said. "July-August."

"Later."

Folding the page, he stuffed it awkwardly into the pocket of his slacks without looking at it. "You've got the tech manuals for the motor home?"

"Give me a second," I nodded.

The huge ring-binder was heavy, awkward—stashed in a high overhead cubby. Without comment, Paul didn't hover, just let me horse it down myself. It was no easy business and my anxiety level didn't help.

"Good," he said as I finally laid the enormous thing down on the dinette. "A good place to get your bearings, before we start dragging around hoses and shutting off valves. That way when you're on your own, you can always lay this encyclopedia out there on the step, in case you get confused—easy enough for anybody to do when you first start to handle these rigs."

I managed a tight little laugh. "A safe bet, I'd say."

Paul just looked at me. "You can do this," he said.

Thumbing through the manual, he quickly came to a page with the floor plan and schematics of the motor home. My heart slowed as he passed the margin notes here and there that Dan had penned in early-on after we had purchased the rig.

"Water lines," Paul said, "so that you have an idea where to keep an eye out for possible leaks."

With a forefinger he traced the plumbing for the bathroom and kitchen, and in the process, laid out the best sequence for unhooking the system.

"Sounds like Greek to me," I shook my head. "You lost me back there at not activating the pump when hooked to the campground water line!"

"Not needed for pressure—"

"I'd agree with you on that one!"

"I meant in the line," he chuckled, shook his head. "Anyway always hook up the faucet end first not the motor home, run some water through or you'll get air in the line. Instant geyser."

"*Please,* my eyes are glazing over!"

He laughed. "We'll take it slower, if that would help."

The third time was the charm. We moved on to closing the valves, disconnecting and stowing the hose for the waste water. That left only the electrical system, then on to the nuts and bolts of getting the interior road-ready.

"Simple as one-two-three," I said, "on paper anyway."

"Okay," he said, "now we walk it through."

Hunched over the table like that, I had to stretch the kinks out of my back before we got down to the hands-on phase of his little mini-course. Paul just stood there watching me, his expression unreadable.

"Nervous," he smiled. It wasn't a question.

"*Petrified.* But thanks for asking."

"I'll fish the master diagram out of the binder for the time being," he offered, "so we can carry it with us."

"I'd tattoo it on my hand if I thought it would help," I told him.

Step by step, I walked through the procedures we had talked about, consulting the diagram Paul was holding from time-to-time to make sure I was doing it right. I found myself zoning out, half confused and half embarrassed, over the distinctions between gray and black water, but in the end—armed with rubber gloves and a determination not to make an idiot of myself or get the DNR in on the act—I managed with a little help to disconnect and store everything in the proper side panels.

"Brava," Paul grinned when I finished.

"Yeah, well, I'd have never gotten that valve to budge on the water spigot if you hadn't intervened."

"Did your husband have. . .there must be a tool box around here somewhere," he said. "I should have suggested you try putting a wrench on it."

I felt a sudden twisting in my gut. *Dan.* Taking a deep breath, I forced myself to move past it.

"Next?" I said.

"The keys. You need to lock up all those exterior storage bins."

When I looked at my watch, I realized we had just blown an hour. I was frazzled, sweating and we hadn't even given a thought to getting that rig itself on the road. With some difficulty, I fished in my jeans pocket and hauled out a wad of keys of various sizes for everything from the ignition to the side panels and various doors.

Dan had a coding system for it all, colored tabs that slid around the ends of the keys. Problem was, I had never bothered to learn what any of them meant.

"I don't even know where to start."

"No problem." Paul fought a smile. "We'll just experiment."

It took a good ten minutes to lock everything up and make the motor home interior shipshape. Paul left it to me to decide what to stow and what to leave in place, but I sensed he was silently double-checking everything I did.

"Nothing like heading down the road and having the computer land on the floor," Paul said as he tested the bungee chords anchoring my laptop. "But everything looks good to me. Okay, Lib, it's showtime!"

Breathing hard from all that crawling, hauling and battening down of the hatches, I steadied myself against the open driver side door. "You're telling me I actually have to drive this thing out of here—through all these trees?"

Why on earth hadn't I picked a site as bald and devoid of vegetation as a billiard ball, instead of this Zhivago-esque birch forest? I didn't say it, but it didn't take a rocket scientist to figure out I was on the edge of a meltdown.

"Think pull-through," Paul said gently. "I made sure when you picked this spot in the first place that you could get it out of here alone if you had to."

"O-h-h-h."

"So, if you slide in behind the wheel," he suggested, "I'll take the passenger side."

When I didn't move, Paul's eyebrow arched. "Unless," he said, "you'd prefer that I walk alongside the camper while you ease your way out of here."

"Sounds like a plan. If I'm close to clobbering anything, just bang on the passenger door and I'll hear you!"

Teeth clenched, I shut the driver's door behind me, and after a few false starts, worked the key into the ignition. For what seemed like a long time I just sat there, my hands clutching the wheel in a death-grip and staring out the windshield. Any way I cut it, easing that rig from pad to access road seemed impossible.

Outside the motor home, Paul stood there, patiently watching me with what I took for a go-for-it smile. Okay, I muttered to myself, time is passing. Start the blasted engine. As the motor rumbled to life, I saw Paul flash a thumbs-up. He didn't have to tell me to go slow. Lip caught hard between my teeth, I literally inched my way forward, stopped.

I was never going to make that curve. Paul gestured casually with both hands in an arc as if tightening the turn. Though I still had no real sense of just how the rig would respond, I did my best to oblige.

Against all odds, I made it on to the access road without major backing up—though it took fifteen agonizing, sweat-drenched minutes of maneuvering and one heck of a lot of improvised semaphore gestures from Paul. Finally he signaled he was going to get into the passenger seat. I just sat there, my hands shaking on the wheel, waiting.

"You done good," he grinned. "Great."

"I hit a couple of branches, something up there anyway—stuff was scraping against the roof."

"Nothing major. Arvo and I should trim some of those limbs back anyway, one of these days."

"So, n-n-now what?"

Paul smiled. "We go. You still game for a run up to Tahquamenon?"

"Are you insured? I'll probably fall asleep at the wheel."

At that he laughed out loud. "If you get us there, I promise I'll take the home stretch."

"That's a pretty big *if* . . . !"

"Lady, you've got more stamina than a Himalayan sherpa. I've seen you at work. And you're going to master this, too, if you give yourself half a chance."

"Gee, thanks—I think."

I looked down at the steering wheel. Well, there was no time like the present. Releasing the brake, I began to drive. At least we were heading, so to speak, in the right direction. The access road was wider than that RV pad and the campground entrance road and highway beyond it even wider. We were no longer moving at an absolute crawl.

Once we turned west on Route 2, I actually found myself recovering a little. Traffic was light and when we hit the turnoff going north, ours was the only vehicle to head in that direction.

"At this rate," I sighed, "adding in an hour a day for takedown and another for hookup, it would take me a year to get from here to Florida."

"Cheer up," Paul said. "Practice makes perfect. Just before you get us to the Falls, I'll buy us lunch. Nothing like a little adrenalin to work up an appetite."

"Yeah, well, right now I'd settle for a handful of antacids. I may never eat again."

Paul laughed. "Seriously, I know this terrific restaurant—all natural ingredients. Fiddlehead fern salad with dried cranberries and local goat cheese. Venison with morels. Indian bread pudding for dessert. Fabulous."

"Sounds pricey—"

"My treat."

If anything, the guy was persistent. "I'm not dressed for it," I said. "Besides, I don't feel comfortable with mooching. After all, you're the one giving up a whole day here to—"

"Lib, in case you haven't noticed, you're overworked and underpaid," Paul said quietly. "Just let me even the scale a bit, that's all I'm suggesting here. It would be criminal to settle for burgers someplace with that five-star cuisine just off the road."

When I didn't respond, he chuckled. "Anyway, the place also has an enormous parking lot, so you don't have to worry about where to put this thing."

I took my eyes off the road long enough to glare in his direction. "Low blow," I said.

"Probably. But I convinced you, didn't I?"

I didn't dignify that with a response. Still, when he started giving me directions to pull into the restaurant, I just followed them—too worn out and famished by now to protest.

The parking lot was as advertised. Without a word from Paul, I aimed the motor home as far from anything resembling another vehicle as possible and killed the engine.

"You okay?" Paul said.

"I'm not sure I can stand up any more."

He chuckled. "Stay put. I'll come around and help you get down."

I still had some pride left. Pulling myself together, the keys clutched in my hand, I slid out from behind the wheel and cautiously made my descent to terra firma. As Paul rounded the front of the motor home, I already was standing on the asphalt.

"All set," I told him.

I could tell from his face, whatever his reservations about my skills as a driver, once again I had won kudos in the sheer chutzpah department. Gently he pried the keys out of my hand.

"How about I take custody of those, for the time being," he said.

Pocketing the keys, he escorted me across the parking lot toward the elegant canvas-canopied entrance to the restaurant. Somewhere along the way, the smells emanating from the kitchen at the back of the sprawling log building began to work at reviving my flagging spirits.

"I hope this is all-you-can-eat," I told him, "because I suddenly feel like I've just been felling timber for a week."

"You're in for the treat of your life," he said.

After squinting at the road for so long, the dark interior of the restaurant momentarily rendered me immobile. I couldn't see a darn thing and quietly said as much.

His hand at my elbow, Paul steered me along behind the hostess as she showed us to a window table overlooking a lovely mixed forest that encroached on the rear of the rustic resort complex. When my eyes adjusted to the light, I looked around me to find sheer elegance, from the crisp embossed tablecloths and crystal stemware to the gigantic, antique-antlered chandelier overhead.

"I feel like a grub, Paul," I muttered, fiddling awkwardly with my silverware as I sized up the mostly professionally dressed guests scattered around the enormous room. "Here I sit—in jeans, no makeup to speak of. I obviously have something better than this getup in the motor home. You could have warned me . . ."

I wish you could see yourself," he said evenly. "You have the look of woman who just conquered Everest, Lib. Glowing—"

"Sweating like a field hand."

"You did great out there with the rig, really great. Crowding the centerline a bit, but you handled the curvy stretches like a pro. Not a whole lot of over-steering."

I found myself starting to protest, changed my mind. True, he was my boss—but what was it about this man that made me so insecure, so blasted deferential? It was time to cast off for less turbulent waters.

"You've eaten here a lot?" I said.

Paul shrugged. "Lately, every couple of months, if I'm lucky. The place has been around a long time. Ginny . . . my wife and I used to come here regularly when we summered in the area."

I couldn't miss the way Paul skittered around the edges of his past. It was not unlike my own reaction when my life with Dan came up in casual conversation. We were wary, the both of us, but determined to get beyond it.

"Favorites?" I said.

"The menu changes with the seasons. But if they have the chilled tart cherry soup, it's got my vote. I've never had a bad entree here."

I took his advice about the soup and the fiddlehead salad, but stuck to an item off the appetizer menu for an entree. Paul had no such qualms—with a touch of envy, I listened as he chose a combination of items that would have fed a small country. The waitress left to log our order in the computer and we found ourselves adrift in one of those strange seven-minute pauses.

"I thought you said you were hungry," he said finally.

"I couldn't manage an entree—not if I have my heart set on that Indian bread pudding you were touting."

He laughed. "As you probably guessed, I seem in my old age to have developed the metabolism of a hummingbird. Since Arvo and I started all that major construction over at Northern Lights, I've dropped thirty pounds despite the fact I'm packing in the calories like there's no tomorrow."

"I wish," I said. "If I even smell a wine cork, I gain ten pounds."

"Well, if you get bored to tears waiting for me to finish off this obscenely Epicurean spread I just ordered, you can always go take a nap in the motor home."

"I love food," I told him, "even when somebody else is eating it. But thanks for the offer."

The waitress had just returned with a bread basket full of everything from focaccia to a five-grain bread dense enough to double as a doorstop. One bite into it and I knew, there went any pretense of self-restraint.

"Wow—this is heavenly! I haven't had that kind of real honest to gosh multi-grain since I gave up buying the Whole Earth Catalog in 1979."

Paul looked way too pleased with himself. "I'd say, I told you so—"

"But then you'd have to walk home. Not a bad idea with everything we've ordered."

"Ouch," he winced. "Why do I think I'm going to regret encouraging you to drive that rig of yours? Next thing you know you'll be heading for Mackinaw and I'll be trying to figure out how the heck to follow through with all that commotion you've got going at Northern Lights. Even the locals are sitting up and taking notice."

He fished in his wallet and pulled out what, from the look of it, had to be a recent newspaper clipping. Carefully unfolding it, he handed it across the table toward me.

"Read," he said, "hot off the press . . . "

I did, out loud at first, but quickly embarrassed at what I was encountering, quietly to myself:

Well, folks, in case you haven't noticed, the new owner of Northern Lights campground, Paul Lauden, has landed himself a dynamo out there on Route 2. In just a few short weeks, that crackerjack go-getter Elizabeth "Lib" Aventura has conjured up primitive Viking solstice rituals, sent Arnie's inner tubes on more than one voyage down the Pipe Stem and is plotting our very own Yooper version of Second City starring Pastor Bob. Local merchants are laughing all the way to the bank.

Somebody ought to warn Lauden he better give that woman a raise or he's going to start a bidding war that could get pretty ugly before it's over. Atta girl, Lib! If you decide that curmudgeon boss of yours doesn't appreciate your efforts, feel free to e-mail centerlinechamberofcommerce.com. We'd hire you in a heartbeat.

Red-faced by now, I handed the clipping back to Paul, doing my best to avoid eye-contact in the process.

"Keep it," he said, "courtesy of the Chamber rag, *U-P NORTH,* a window on our little corner of the world. I suggest you tack it up somewhere, just in case you're tempted to start putting major miles on your rig in the foreseeable future."

"Meaning?"

"The Northern Lights season ends late October."

There it was again, pushing the envelope. I drew in a thoughtful breath, let it out just as slowly.

"Paul, I really hadn't bargained for staying that—"

"I realize that. At first I just thought maybe, at most, you would be able to put a few catchy events together, then wind it down again in early August. But you started all this and I hope to goodness, you'll finish it."

"I told my kids I would be heading down to Florida at the end of the summer."

"In those additional months we could have the next season in place, restructure the on-line and media advertising. All of it."

"I appreciate that."

"But—?"

"It's nothing personal, Paul. You've been wonderful and I enjoy working with you. But I came here having spent the past twelve months clinging to the life raft of my children. And frankly . . . ?" I hesitated, carefully weighing my response, "I've kept myself so busy here, I haven't even had time to give any thought to what I want to do—"

"So you're afraid you're just substituting one lifeboat for another. The job. Northern Lights. The whole cast of characters that you've roped into your programs . . . "

We just looked at each other. I couldn't have expressed it better myself. A smile had begun to crinkle around his eyes, his tone half-teasing, half deadly serious.

"Is it really so bad to be needed, even if it is just a down-at-the-heels campground in the middle of the nowhere?"

When he put it that way, I found that hard knot of anxiety in my chest loosening a little. "No. But then all of this seems a bit . . . sudden, overwhelming."

"Fair enough," Paul said. "So, no arm twisting. All I'm doing is upping the ante a little, asking you to think about it. I could throw in a small salary without losing my shirt, if that's what it would take to keep you."

Fortunately, the waitress had appeared with the soup—creamy but with a sweet-sour bite, deliciously cool to the tongue. We ate in silence, savoring the moment.

"For the record, how did *you* wind up at Northern Lights anyway?" I found myself wondering out loud. "You were in radio . . . I think I remember reading it in those PR files you gave me."

The question caught Paul mid-bite and for what seemed like a long time, he chewed on the notion. Clearly, I had caught him off guard.

"By default, I guess you'd say. At first when my wife . . . when Ginny was diagnosed, I worked partly in the Detroit office and partly at home. But eventually it got tougher, impossible. I wasn't about to leave her to face all that with a revolving door of care-givers. Those last six months, I took a leave of absence from the station, just tried to be there for her round the clock."

"It must have been—"

"In a word, *hell*. As only cancer can be. Finally, when she couldn't take it anymore—the chemo, all of it—she pleaded with me to pull the plug. No more treatment. God help me, I had no choice . . . "

I waited, sensing there was more. Paul's face was like stone.

"When she . . . after she was gone, I went through the motions of getting back in the game with the station, but I had been away enough

108

that the board of directors had moved on," he shrugged, "did me a favor really. Somewhere along the line I realized my heart hadn't been in it for a long time."

He was staring out the window now, the rise and fall of his breathing the only sign of how raw and painful the memories were—even now, two years later. I was grateful I couldn't see his face.

"Worse, my son was having all these . . . issues dealing with his mother's death. They pretty much drove a wedge between us. . ."

Wife, career, family—all gone. What do you say after something like that?

"I'm very sorry. I didn't mean to pry."

"Don't be—and you weren't," he said. "Whoever said life is simple. I did the only thing I could. It's over."

Only it wasn't and we both knew it. Slowly shifting in his seat, Paul looked across the table at me. I had opened this wound, it was up to me to close it again as best I could.

"You miss her," I said.

"Every day. But then you've been there."

"Some days I miss Dan so much it hurts." My voice was low. "I'm walking across the campground to the office and it's almost as if I can . . . see him, standing there in that grove of trees at the far end of the picnic area, watching the sunset."

"It took a lot of guts for you to come back here."

"What choice did I have?"

Paul's eyebrow shot up. "For starters, you could have stayed with your kids. Sold the motor home."

"It's what they wanted."

"Still want, if I'm not mistaken—your daughter anyway." He hesitated, softened his tone. "But you didn't go that route."

"No, and won't. Not as long as I . . . "

As long as I what? My experiences over the past month were enough to convince me of one thing for certain—that I couldn't go back.

"I came here determined to prove I could survive alone in the rig, get from one place to another, live on my own," I told him. "Working at Northern Lights is making that possible for me beyond my wildest imagining, though I'm not naive enough to assume that I can do this forever either."

For a split-second I was envisioning myself with a walker, trying to crawl up those steps into the motor home. In the meantime, there were certainly dumber places in the world to think through where my road trip into the unknown—and my life, for that matter—was taking me.

A strange smile played at the corners of Paul's mouth. "Having second thoughts already, I hope . . . ?"

"Constantly," I laughed. "Which is why I think it's only fair to warn you, that as employees go, I'm not the best risk right now."

"How about you let me be the judge of that!"

Our salads arrived, followed by our entrees. Savoring one exotic and unbearably delicious flavor after the next, we found our conversation drifting from work, to our taste in music, to a shared interest in lighthouses and northern Michigan lore. In the end, our taste buds sated, we both passed on dessert. Paul paid the tab and this time I didn't object.

Out in the parking lot, the sunlight was warm on my face. Summer, it seems, was finally here to stay. The Fourth of July was next weekend and beyond it, we already would notice the days becoming perceptibly shorter. How fleeting it all is.

"You up for more?" Paul said, extending the keys in my direction.

"Sure, why not?" I told him. "I got us this far."

He laughed. "Yes, you did. But when it's too much, you'll let me know."

"Of course."

"None of this I'm-going-to-pull-my-weight-or-else nonsense."

"No."

"Good."

He opened the passenger door for himself, then passed me the keys. As I walked around the front of the motor home, I found myself taking in the tiny nicks in the fiberglass, the various winged creatures that had met their demise on the grill. Time to give the old girl a wash and wax job.

"What's so funny?" Paul watched as I slid into the front seat and started fiddling with the shoulder harness.

"Me," I said, "this whole driving thing. Believe it or not, I was just thinking to myself how much smaller the rig seemed than I remembered. But then I haven't tried to back the thing up by myself any distance either."

Paul chuckled, shook his head.   "Feet, yards, months, decades . . .I guess our perception of how intimidating a thing is pretty much depends on where we stand—or are sitting—at the time."

"Well, trust me, behind the wheel this morning, that rig felt way out of my league."

Ten

The three hours we spent at Tahquamenon Falls were magical, way too short but a quiet respite in what had become my self-imposed routine of the past few weeks. After dutifully paying homage to the Upper Falls, the largest east of the Mississippi if you discount Niagara, Paul suggested we move on to the nearby Lower Falls. I was so glad he did.

The Lower cascade all but called out to us to shed our shoes, roll up the cuffs of our slacks and get our feet wet. Wistful, I stood at the water's edge, caught up in the sunlight sparkling in tiny star bursts on the water as it danced over the layers of exposed rock.

I kept seeing the look on my granddaughter Louisa's face last weekend as she threw her hands upward toward the sky, the ribbons of her garland wreath swirling around her—euphoric, totally caught up in the moment. "What the heck, let's do it!" I said. "We've been working our butts off. Payback time."

Barefoot now, laughing and teasing one another at our awkwardness, we began to wade along the ribbon-like sandbars that wound among the craggy boulder-field of the river bed. The currents were strong but the water shallow. Our toes sank deep into the sand as schools of tiny fish darted around us in the crystal water. My jeans were getting wet, but I didn't care.

"The river looks like liquid amber," I sighed, "enough to take your breath away. Dan and I came here several times, but I had honestly forgotten how incredible it is."

"Nature's tea, one of the park signboards describes it," Paul said, "but I like your version better. Apparently that unique pigment comes from tanin in the cedar and hemlock tree roots along the river banks."

Putting down roots. Like the shock of the bracing eddies that tugged at my ankles, I realized that was exactly what was happening in my life—tentative as tendrils go, but roots all the same. I shivered.

"The water's too cold to stand and wait for me," forehead creased in concentration, Paul was adjusting the zoom on his camera. "Just go on ahead while I fire off some shots of that back-lit stand of trees along the river bank."

I went, although when he didn't immediately rejoin me, I half-turned to see what was holding him up. In the process, I caught him shooting downstream away from the falls, camera aimed in my direction.

My hand shot up to deflect his lens. "Hey, cut that out . . . I'm not part of the flora and fauna, thank you very much!"

He chuckled, fired off several more shots for good measure. "Scale. Without some sort of human reference point, this could be Pipe Stem Creek"

"A likely story! I'll expect you to turn over those negatives—"

"Sorry, they're digital."

"You don't use film, then—even for those incredible pieces you have hanging in your apartment?" The question popped out before I had a chance to consider how it might be interpreted.

Paul's smile faded. "You saw them."

"That day you sent me hunting for your to-do list," I said evenly. "You've got to admit, they're pretty hard to miss . . . I thought you told me you were an amateur."

His face had a closed and shuttered look. "Double degree in business and art," he shrugged. "Ancient history. I've been using digital for quite a while now."

An awkward silence settled in between us. As he rejoined me on the sandbar, I noticed he had turned off the camera again.

"I can't help wondering," I said finally, "after all those years in a place like Detroit, was it very difficult . . . adjusting to life out there on Route 2?"

Paul stifled an unintelligible expletive as he momentarily lost his balance. In the process, his ankle apparently connected with a jagged edge of one of the dense purple sandstone rocks jutting up out of the river bed.

"Man, that . . . *smarts!*" he muttered under his breath. "Good thing there aren't piranhas down there. It felt like that razor edge hit bone."

"Sorry. I didn't mean to distract you."

"My own fault," he said. "I'll live."

Still favoring that foot, Paul headed for deeper water and an even larger sandbank mid-river. "I'll admit Northern Lights is about as far from Grosse Pointe as you can get, but then that was the idea, I guess. After Ginny died, there were just too many memories in that house—the bad *and* the good. I just knew if I was going to ever get on with my life in any meaningful way, I had to do something pretty drastic."

"And your house?"

"I basically gave it to my son. He grew up there. It seemed right. I like to think Ginny would have wanted that, rather than just sell it. Then too, it had been in her family."

"It's hard for our kids to process their own grief," I told him, "much less come to grips with how we, as their parents, struggle to cope. When I finally told my daughter that I could no longer hang on like a voyeur at the fringes of her world anymore—or her brother's either for that matter—she took it hard, personally. It was like I was rejecting her, my family."

"In the end she let you go. What finally brought her around?"

"I'm not sure I did, bring her around, that is," I gasped, half-

114

stumbled as I stubbed my own toe against something rising out of the sand beneath me. "I told her that her father wouldn't have wanted me to live like that. Mercifully, that seemed to hit home—that I was an adult with needs of my own, not just *Mom* or funny old *Grama Lib*."

"Still, most of us connect home with house, a place," he said. "Josh certainly did. I've been guilty of it myself, can see where your kids would find it tough to think beyond that—especially if they're picturing you all alone up here in some bus of a camper."

"Six oversize tires and no mailing address."

Paul wasn't laughing. "I've said it before, meant it," he said. "You've got a heck of a lot of courage, lady. Whatever I've done pulling up stakes as a way of getting my head on straight again, at least Northern Lights had a mailbox."

"Little do you know."

Embellishing a little along the way, I told him about that first day in Owen's Shuttle, bracing myself for a collision with the truck traffic and fretting about the driver's blood-alcohol level. So long ago now.

"And to top it off, there I stood with that pile of suitcases like I had just ordered Scotty to beam me down on that concrete slab." I shook my head. "No wonder you were ready to send me packing—though you've got to admit, a wilderness campground has got to be one of the stranger places to come across a red light district."

"You would have to remind me of that," Paul's smile was sheepish, "although you'd be surprised at what turns up. Not at Northern Lights so far, but then I've been to a campground owner's conference or two and the war stories are enough to curl a guy's hair."

Our laughter floated across the water, the echoes playing back at us from the hillsides along the banks. We were letting go bit by bit, both of us, allowing the sheer beauty of the day to ease an awful lot more than just the stresses we faced in putting that campground of his on the map.

"So, you and Dan hung your hats in East Lansing," he wondered, "before you took to the open road."

I told him about the engineering firm, its clients from Lansing and Detroit to London and Capetown. "One year I tried to keep a calendar ticking off the days Dan was home and the days on the road—gave up after about six months. It was just too darn depressing."

Paul chuckled sympathetically. "Holding down the fort alone and your job at the travel agency must have kept you plenty busy."

"Too busy, sometimes. The job and the balancing act got easier after Danielle and David were away at college—and lonelier. When Dan retired and we finally had time to spend together, I let it go readily enough."

"Ginny and I talked the same talk, grandiose plans about chucking it all and checking out those places we just read about," he shook his head. "She was a geography teacher . . . ironic, huh? Over the years she plotted out runs down the inland waterway, even an extended planes-trains-automobile jaunt around the globe. Unfortunately, we never made it."

A familiar knot had begun building in my chest as I listened. "I would be rich with a nickel for every time Dan or I said it. *When we retire . . . then we're going to.* So many things over the years, lost to us forever. If I had to give young couples one piece of advice at the altar, it would be, *Don't postpone,* because life doesn't wait for us—"

"If we don't grab hold of it when it comes," he finished for me.

"Something like that."

Paul had stopped dead-still on a relatively narrow bank of sand—so abruptly I had to shift gears hard to keep from plowing into him. My hand connected with his shoulder to steady myself. As he turned to face me, his smile was thoughtful, sad.

"You ready to call it a day?" he said.

It was getting cold in that water as the sun began slanting toward three o'clock. My teeth were chattering. All good things, it seems, run their course.

Reluctantly, though still with a fair amount of splashing and jostling, we made our way out of the river. If we intended to make it back before dark, it was time to get going.

"I feel like a kid again," I sighed as we dried off on a bench near my motor home sitting there all alone now in the RV section of the parking lot, "twirling around like one of those kids at Sonja's garland workshop. This is just what the doctor ordered."

"And *you drove us here*," he said.

"Yes." I was astonished at how simple that sounded now. "Yes, I did."

"Good for you!" On impulse as we sat there, he wound an arm around my shoulder, gave my shoulder a supportive squeeze.

Boss or no boss, it felt good, right—friends sharing the moment. I shifted on the bench, looked up at him, flashed a tentative smile. Just that fast he was on his feet, looking out toward the motor home.

"So," he said, "I guess it's time."

He was right, we had to get going. Deer would be out soon, potentially dangerous in the waning light. I struck out briskly and we had just about reached the vehicle when Paul seemed to hesitate—started to raise his camera, stopped.

"Scrapbook time," he said casually. "How about we document the moment, you and that rig of yours? That way if your kids don't believe you can be out after hours on your own in this thing, you can always send 'em hard evidence."

I laughed, half-heartedly protested, but in the end I gave in and let him grab his shot. Smiling at first, then vaguely annoyed, I stood there alongside the motor home, feeling more foolish than like the king of the world. Paul casually had shifted position several times to catch the moment and I noticed his fingers move repeatedly on the shutter.

"Great," he kept saying. "The light's really good this time of day. Warm and low."

"Enough already!"

Chastened, he took one last shot and slipped the cover over the lens. "Spoil sport."

"You're the one watching the clock."

"Anyway, I'll need the keys," he said.

"You really don't have to—"

He stopped me with a look. Grumbling under my breath, I fished in my pocket for the unwieldy ring, but made no further protest as he opened the passenger door for me and then walked around the vehicle to take the wheel.

The tension of driving and all that fresh air had taken a toll. Suddenly exhausted, I settled back in the bucket seat alongside him, silent—watching the landscape unfold around us.

I was glad I let Paul take over. The wind had kicked up and I sensed even he was having to concentrate to keep from overcorrecting as periodic gusts slammed against the side of the vehicle. A front was coming through. The clouds were thickening, the forecasts all predicting rain.

"I really appreciate this," I told him finally. "More than you know."

In profile, his eyes fixed on that road ahead, Paul's mood was hard to gauge. "My pleasure," he said.

I had no reason to doubt he meant it. Still, as the miles ticked themselves off on the odometer, I also got the feeling he was using the silence, subtly, to distance himself. For all the wonder of the day, we were ending it as we began—boss and employee on our day off, the friendship springing up between us cautious and totally within acceptable bounds.

But then, however briefly, I had seen a very different Paul Lauden out there, his guard down and vulnerable—the two of us helping each other to avoid a soaking or keep from taking a header in the swirling river. I didn't need a character reference to tell me this was a kind, sensitive man, one courageous enough to take personal responsibility for helping his wife face a devastating illness. Not many men would have done that. And it seems I was lucky enough to have found in him not just a boss, but a friend.

I closed my eyes and with them, shut out the present along with the memories. It hurt too much, just another reminder of the terrible hole

Dan's death had left in my heart and the unthinkable necessity of redefining my life without him.

Apparently I must have slept. Next thing I knew, I felt the motor home braking and heard the faint click of the turn signal. Up ahead I saw the sign and access road for Northern Lights.

"You're awake," Paul said. "Good."

Just inside the campground entrance, he suddenly pulled to the edge of the grass and stopped. Throwing the motor home into park but with the engine still running, he climbed down from the driver's seat, walked around the front of the vehicle. He opened the passenger door and stood with a foot on the internal running board.

"Problems?" I said.

"No. You're going to park this rig on the pad."

Paul looked at me, smiled. I was still groggy, not prepared for yet another traumatic encounter with branches and tight turning ratios.

"Just like that?"

"Just like that," he said. "When you get to the site, I'll be out there watching your back if you need it. It's a pull-through, remember, so you don't have to worry about backing it up."

I unhooked my shoulder harness, and momentarily hyperventilating, began to work my way across the narrow cab to the driver's side while Dan resumed his spot in the passenger seat. As I got close to that familiar little birch grove, Paul told me to stop, got out and shut the door behind him. Once again, I was alone.

The engine was still running. Releasing the hand-brake, I started to pull forward, with Paul walking alongside me every foot of the way. A branch scraped lightly against the roof as I navigated the turn into the site. Gritting my teeth, I tried to ignore the sound and eventually it stopped.

Whenever I looked out through the windshield at Paul, he just smiled, flashed a thumbs-up. *Okay*, it was going okay.

As I approached the end of the pad with the nose of the motor home, Paul raised a hand, palm out, signaling I had come far enough.

With a sigh of relief, I shifted into park, cut the engine and threw on the emergency brake.

"Not bad," I breathed as I climbed out of the cab and went to meet him. "No screaming, yelling or anxiety attacks. Not nearly as bad as this morning."

Paul grinned. "Congratulations."

Without thinking about how it might be perceived, I just seized the moment and hugged him, flushed with the incredible joy at how far I had come. I could tell that I had caught him by surprise, but after a split-second hesitation, his arms came up and held me.

It had been a long time since anyone except family had drawn me deliberately close like that. Suddenly shy, embarrassed—worried about his response, I began to pull away.

The look on his face told me quick enough what he was feeling. My breath caught in my throat. Those smoky eyes of his glittered with a quiet fire.

"This has been . . . you're incredible, Lib," his voice was charged with emotion.

I felt a slow flush spread across my upturned face. Confused and shaken at what I had unleashed, I dropped my gaze, trying to get us back on safer footing.

"I owe you so much," I stammered, my eyes riveted on my sandals, still covered with a dusting of gritty particles from that riverbank. "Anyone else would have just taken over today, but you just stood back . . . let me work it out as we went along. I don't know how to—"

My awkward attempts to express my gratitude died on my lips. *What was I trying to say?* My husband repeatedly had done just that—had taken charge, intervened rather than encouraging me to confront those scarier moments in life on my own. It was Dan's way, a natural dynamic of his loving me all those years. And I had loved it, loved him, with my whole heart.

Yet suddenly here I was, factoring Paul into that equation? It was unthinkable even to entertain that kind of comparison. Disloyal. Repugnant.

I closed my eyes, blinking back tears—something, anything to shut out any thought of Paul Lauden and our day together. Hardest of all to dismiss was how much I enjoyed, even welcomed the easy confidence that was building between us.

My expression must have been an open book. Before I could say a word, Paul shot a glance over his shoulder toward the office. His tone was brusque, all business.

"It's getting dark. I'd better get going," he said. "But if you run into problems with the hookups, don't hesitate to ask for help."

"Paul, I—"

"Glad to help. Enjoy the rest of your day."

The man could have been talking to a tourist he had just escorted to the right campsite. Abruptly and without waiting for a response, he turned on heel and headed back toward the double-wide. I watched him go, hands trembling as I clutched the motor home keys.

What on earth had I been thinking? All I had wanted was to thank a friend for being helpful. Instead, I had panicked—spooked by what I discovered about myself and my marriage as a result of his simple acts of kindness. My boss must think I'm some kind of nut-case.

Worse, even now as I named it for what it was, the truth about the state of my head and heart both disturbed and frightened me. I had put Dan on a pedestal, in life and in death. In my grief and loneliness, I had idealized beyond recognition our life together, his presence in my life.

I told myself it was just my desperate way of trying to live the rest of my life without him. But in fact, I had been unfair to Dan, unfair to myself—and dangerously short-sighted. Much as I loved our years together, built my world around my husband, that world no longer existed.

As I felt the house of cards I had built crumbling around me, it was almost like losing him all over again. And this time, I had only

121

myself to blame.

The motor home was sitting just feet away where I had left it in the morning, perfectly aligned on its pull-through pad. I was going to have to retrace the sequence of hookups to make my home habitable again. Gritting my teeth, I forced myself to do what had to be done, too distraught now to worry whether or not I was hooking things up right. *Just do it.*

Across the campground at the Mini Winnie, Gunnar and Inga were about to head out for their sunset stroll. Spotting me standing there alongside the motor home, they waved a cheery greeting. I responded in kind, but then quickly turned and headed for the coach side door.

Once inside, I blindly threw the switches. Everything seemed to be functioning.

I wasn't in the mood to celebrate. Going on autopilot, I downed yet another dinner of soup—this time cold and out of the can. I tasted none of it.

By now it was dusk. My laptop was still bungeed in place where I had left it. Drained and unable even to hold my head up any longer, I just slipped into that sweatshirt of Dan's and crawled into bed. After what seemed like a long time, I fell into a fitful, dreamless sleep.

Somewhere around midnight I woke to the sound of raindrops against the roof—one of those tentative summer showers, not the driving, howling storm I encountered my first night back in Northern Lights. By the time I slept again, the first gray of dawn had begun to filter in through the window blinds.

I didn't even look at my watch when I got up. Skipping breakfast, I dressed and dragged myself over to the office, half-fearing what I would encounter there.

As it turns out, I found Arvo sitting alone at the registration desk, clad in his meet-and-greet wardrobe of navy work pants and gray polo shirt, munching on a sandwich. Lunch. He flashed a quizzical look as he saw me come in. My watch read Noon, long past time to relieve him.

"Not much of a day, girlee—gray pea soup, like it could rain any minute," he said.

"Maybe it'll get it out of its system now and we'll have a decent weekend for the Fourth. We can hope anyway!" I paused. "Have you seen Paul?"

"Not here." Arvo shook his head. "Gone. Boss left crack of dawn to drive down to Detroit."

I seemed to be having trouble breathing. "Did . . . did he tell you, why?"

"*Business*, boss said. Looks like you and I are holding down the fort."

Eleven

The day passed, then another—in fitful waves of sun and showers. Paul still hadn't returned. Nor had he called to check in.

I tried as best I could to help Arvo finish more of the sites that he and Paul had targeted for upgrading. Most of the work was beyond me and I found myself reduced to stepping and fetching, apologizing repeatedly for how clueless I was.

In mud-streaked jeans, boots and work shirt, one of Dan's faded ball caps covering my sweat-drenched hair, I watched as Arvo eased the tractor off the last of the sites we had targeted for completion. He climbed down and stood alongside me, looking out over our handiwork.

"Tomorrow ya might wanna take that rake and clean up all them branches and trompled greenery," Arvo suggested gently. "And somewhere in the office there's a pot of paint and a brush, too, so you can touch up the numbers on the site posts a bit."

"Sorry I haven't been more of a help," I mumbled, flexing my blistered and aching palms.

"Can't fault ya for trying, Lib-girl. Ya done good, real good—nobody could complain about that."

"Still, two sites aren't the half dozen you and Paul wanted by this weekend."

"They sure beat none! " Arvo scowled. "Ain't like that man to just bail like that, with nary a word or by-your-leave . . ."

It seems I wasn't the only one confused and troubled by Paul Lauden's behavior. As the week went on, without a word, my sense of unease grew exponentially.

Thursday the weather finally cleared and guests started piling in for the long Independence Day weekend. I was pleased to see a number of them made a point of cashing in on the two-fer multiple weekend coupons we had been salting around the area.

I had packed the weekend calendar chock-a-block with jovial silliness, notably a decorate-your-camper contest and a kiddie Yankee Doodle hat workshop and parade. Arvo wrestled a borrowed flatbed on a hitch behind the tractor for a makeshift parade float. Once again Arnie was coming with his inner tubes for a Sunday river float, a lot easier now with the water temperature in the Pipe Stem approaching humane levels.

Thursday night arrived with still no sign of our boss. Tired and jittery, needing the company, I strolled over to Arvo's Airstream to propose that we share a pizza.

"It's just straight out of the box, but edible," I told him. "An anticlimax, I'm sure, after what Paul's been feeding you every Sunday night."

He chuckled. "Right now, Lib-girl, you could dish up that round hunk of cardboard they pack under those things and I would never know the difference. Give me ten minutes and I'll be over . . ."

The two of us settled in around my dinette table, chewing in silence on the shoe-leather crust and meager slices of pepperoni scattered over it—a concoction only marginally improved by all the leftover cheese salvaged from my refrigerator. Arvo finished off the last of the charbroiled crust and shoved aside his empty plate.

"Doggone that Lauden," he growled. "That man's got 24 hours before I climb into that SUV and head down to Detroit, track him down and haul him back."

"And leave me all alone up here?"

My laughter didn't sound convincing, even to me. Arvo flashed a crooked little grin.

"Wouldn't do that to ya, Ma'am," a knot of a frown had settled in between his shaggy unibrows, "but then suppose if anybody oughta cut the guy some slack, it oughta be me. Ain't much of a future for an old drunk around these parts . . . "

I just looked at him. Arvo's gnarled fingers were tracing the subtle grain in the veneer of the tabletop.

"Ya ain't the only one tossed up here like the lone survivor of a November gale," he said. "Had pretty much hit rock bottom when Lauden gave me this job and a roof over my head—all on just my say-so when I was bunkin' on the floor in a bar outside of Centerline. Swore I'd stick with Northern Lights as long as Boss was runnin' the place. Been sober ever since."

"Life can set us adrift in some pretty strange ports of call," I said. I kept coming back in my head to all those suitcases of mine out there on the concrete slab.

"Six months," his grizzled jaw tight. "My little gal and I had six months before she passed. Just a sweet little bit of a thing . . . never figured out what the girl saw in a big old lunk like me—"

"Oh, Arvo . . . "

"Kinda went nuts after that," he shrugged. "Quit my job at the lumber mill and shipped out on a string of freighters after that. Mouth of the St. Lawrence to Chicago and back again, 'til I got to know the inside of a bottle way too close and my name wound up on a list someplace. Shut me down cold, so I spent summers doin' odd jobs after that, winters holed up in a wreck of a cabin on Superior. Not much to show for seventy-four years."

I suspected it wasn't a confessional that came easily, but a lot suddenly made sense to me—the faded tattoo on his wiry forearm, for starters, with the bleeding heart and the initials. A romantic for all his gruff bluster, Arvo had almost gone under with the worst life had to

126

offer. Yet here he was, still doggedly trying to reshape his life, one day at a time.

"You'll not find me pointing fingers," I told him quietly. "I lost a whole year after Dan died . . . and if it wasn't for this job, I can't vouch for where I'd be either right now!"

True enough, all of it, and it felt strangely good in this context to admit it. I saw Arvo's eyes begin to mist over at my take on the respective journeys that had brought us to this place. For a long time he just stared silently out the window of my dinette at the campground settling down for the night. We weren't, it seems, so very different after all.

"Smart man, Boss, to hire ya, that's for sure," he muttered, suddenly awkward. "Classy lady like you. Ain't seen so many folks turnin' in here since I went to work for the place. Boss thinks the world of ya, Ma'am . . . is saying all the time ya really know yer stuff!"

By way of response, I quickly began to gather up the dishes. "Funny, I was thinking the same thing about you and that tractor of yours."

"That's me, all right—just this crazy old Yooper cowboy," he grinned, "like ridin' out those mountain swells on the Big Lake. Yee-haw! Nuts, huh, what a guy winds up doin' when he really puts his mind to it."

It was about to get nuttier. My co-worker eventually wandered back to his Airstream and I spent a more or less sleepless night punctuated by dreams about wave-tossed freighters and crowds of unfamiliar faces streaming toward me through the trees—part Freud and partly, it turns out, a preview of the weekend to come.

TGIF was not a concept in this business. Mid-morning Friday, Arvo and I suddenly found ourselves slammed. While he ran himself ragged out on the grounds playing the host in his own backwoods fashion, I coped as best I could behind the desk. At one point, the line waiting to register stretched half-way to the door and the vacant sites were getting few and far between.

Frantic, I started assigning spots in the overflow picnic area to self-contained units willing to put up with a lack of electricity and sewer connections. At least there were several water taps out there, if everybody shared. Finally enough was enough. Arvo gave me a desperate heads-up as he passed through the office yet again, this time to retrieve a specialized wrench he needed to get the last of those faucets functioning.

"Lib-girl, those crazy hoses out there already look like a snake pit," he growled. "Lord knows what this is doing to our water pressure—like spittin' on a bonfire by now . . . !"

He ran out of breath before he ran out of calamities. "That's it. Ya gotta pull the plug here, so to speak. From now on, doggone it, *tenters only.*"

Not a politic pronouncement since there were still several RVers in line waiting to register. Judging by the chorus of protests and groans, I was about to have a riot on my hands.

"Yes, *sir . . . !*"

My hiccup of a nervous laugh ended on a rising note. For an awful moment, I thought I was going to cry.

Arvo scowled, softened his tone. "Sorry . . . I know I ain't the boss of you. This ain't your fault. Where the heck is Lauden?"

A good question. While Arvo tore back out to deal with the crisis over in the picnic overflow, I tried as tactfully as I could to steer the disgruntled motor home campers elsewhere. Phone tucked under my chin, I began dialing up every off-the-beaten-track campground I could locate in a thirty-mile radius, looking for vacancies.

That left an elderly couple from Minnesota en route to Maine, still patiently waiting for a tent site. Highlighter pen in hand, I had just begun to trace a shaky access route to their site on the campground map when out of the corner of my eye, I saw a flash of movement in the office doorway.

I looked up, did a double-take. *"Paul . . . !"*

My smile of relief began to flicker, fade before it really got started. The man looked like he hadn't slept in days. Though his jeans and the rest of his wardrobe were professional enough, there were dark smudges under his eyes and a rakish stubble along his jaw. He stopped short, just inside the screen, his hands balled awkwardly into fists at his side.

"You've had your hands full here," he said.

That was an understatement. Still, to his credit, he looked and sounded taken aback—even chagrined—at what obviously had been transpiring in his absence. *Make nice*, I kept telling myself. For starters, we weren't alone.

"We're near capacity."

"I see that," he said. "Sorry to leave you and Arvo in the lurch."

It was a matter-of-fact disclaimer, revealing nothing. I forced myself to respond in kind, flashing what could have passed for a smile.

"No problem!"

All this while, the elderly pair had been standing at the counter overhearing the entire conversation. Curt and cryptic as it was, strictly business, one thing they couldn't mistake was that the tension in the room had ratcheted up considerably.

"So," Paul squared his shoulders, suddenly all lord-of-the-manor charm, "what can I do to help you good folks get settled? I gather Lib's assigned you a site."

I didn't wait for the new campers to consult their map. "Eighteen," I told him, "I put them in eighteen."

Hand extended in greeting, Paul was already taking charge. "Paul Lauden, the campground owner," he said. "If you follow me, folks, I'll walk ahead of you to your site."

The couple scurried to gather their belongings—the map and several brochures the woman had snagged from the tourism racks, one of my activities schedules, an umbrella, plus the small bag of groceries they had just purchased from the camp store. At the door, the campers close at his heels, Paul half-turned and shot a pointed look over his shoulder in my direction.

"We need to talk," he said quietly.

What was all that about? I felt the air rush from my lungs in an involuntary sigh—though not of relief, that much was certain. I couldn't tell if he was angry, upset, depressed, battling a hangover or some inexplicable combination of emotions I couldn't even begin to name.

But then I wasn't about to find out either any time soon. I barely saw hide nor hair of the man the rest of the day. Arvo scurried in at regular intervals, harried and out of breath, looking for equipment. The low point of the culture came when he came tearing in with orders from the boss to whip up a NO VACANCY sign to tack up on the Northern Lights signboard along Route 2.

"Boss says you can crank one out in no time—like you're just sitting around over here twiddling your thumbs. . .doggone that guy anyway," Arvo grumbled. "First he comes roaring back looking like death and now he's hustling out there fixing and checking what ain't broke, like a man possessed. Darn near took my head off when he saw my patch-jobs over in the picnic area!"

I fought the irrational urge to laugh. By now I had typed in the text, sized the lettering as a banner and was waiting for the printer to spit out the result.

"Try the phone ringing off the hook," I said, "the store running out of firewood, then the blasted cash register malfunctions . . . "

My co-worker stood watching me like he was half afraid I was going to brain him with the mouse still clutched in my hand. "What the heck's wrong with the guy?"

"Beats me," I shrugged as I handed Arvo the banner.

That wasn't entirely true. Heart and gut I sensed it had something to do with that afternoon at Tahquamenon. But beyond that, I hadn't a clue.

"So, how about it . . . ya wanna cut outta here," Arvo said, "tell the man to take his crazy job and shove it? I'm with ya. . .all the way to Ishpemming . . ."

"Tempting," I chuckled, "but then somebody would have nabbed my camp spot, and trust me, there isn't another vacancy between here and the Soo."

Arvo snagged the sign, my stapler and headed for the office door. "I'll tell you this," he said by way of thanks, "whatever Boss is paying you, Lib-girl . . . it ain't near enough!"

I wasn't going to argue with him. It pretty much went on like that all day as our guests tried to get settled, wandered around checking out the camp store and ransacked the tourism racks by the door for things to do and see.

At four o'clock Friday, my lunch still sat virtually untouched on the counter where I had left it, inedible. By six o'clock, I had *had* it.

Cleaning up the registration desk as best I could, I flipped the Open sign on the door to Closed and locked up the office. Relieved, I saw Arvo and Paul were nowhere in sight.

My feet were killing me and my head was pounding, no surprise after standing there fielding questions all day—did we rent canoes, where did we keep Smokey the Bear and when were we planning the fireworks? All that when I half suspected the fireworks would cut loose any minute, only not the kind the tourists were expecting.

Even with the motor home's door open most of the day, my usually cheery living space seemed stuffy, closing in on me. I had been nursing a bottle of merlot for a couple of days now and before I changed into something more comfortable and did something about dinner, I poured myself a glass—better said, a tumbler. Drained it.

So much for a headache! And so much for my boss and his disappearing act.

Emptying the dregs from the bottle into the glass, I rummaged around in the motor home wardrobe and retrieved a knock-'em-out power-red embroidered caftan that Dan had liked so much. I was so sick of running around in slacks and boots and so badly in need of a genuinely scalding hot shower, that I had to do something.

The silk felt cool against my bare skin. I shed my shoes and padding barefoot over to the kitchen area, popped the last of my heat-'neat dinners into the microwave. Before I settled down on the sofa to wait for it to do its thing, I switched on that CD again by the Drovers—their very name conjuring up images of the open road. Nothing left to lose, the music urged, no future in looking back.

The driving Celtic rhythms resonated like a call to arms in my tired heart. If that didn't keep me moving, nothing would. I knew if I closed my eyes, I'd be out for the duration.

The microwave had just dinged when I heard a tentative sound at my screen door. Startled, immediately cautious, I swiveled around on the sofa, then stood so I could see who was out there.

On some level, I already knew. Although the sun still hadn't set, I reached up and clicked on the motor home's porch light.

"Paul," I said.

"May I come in."

It wasn't a question and he didn't wait for my response. He stood with one foot poised on the lowest carpeted stair. It was too late to object now.

"Sorry if I'm not in the mood for welcome mats. Arvo and I sure could have used your help."

Paul's eyes narrowed and from the way he paused to knead at the knot of muscles at the back of his skull, I sensed I wasn't the only one battling a headache. "I don't blame you for being . . . upset," he said.

"You could call it that." I hesitated. "I'd offer you some wine, but I just finished the last of it. Sorry."

"That's about the last thing I need right now." He exhaled sharply, then just came out with it. "I spent the week down in Detroit."

"Arvo told me. *Business*, he said."

"I went to see my son."

My mouth felt stiff. "You're under no obligation to tell me what you do or where you go."

"Maybe. But I'm going to."

Apparently whether I wanted him to or not. I was too tired for a scene. "Be my guest," I said, stepping back enough to let him into what passed for my living room.

The maneuvering room was too tight just to stand there, glaring at him. Settling down on the bench seat of the dinette seemed like the safest bet. Paul gingerly took up residence on the sofa. At least we had a good three feet of floor space between us.

Paul was looking down at his hands, his expression so bleak that it physically hurt to witness it. "Hopeless as it seemed, I decided to give it another shot—to talk to my son, clear the air, mend fences . . . "

He didn't need another word to tell me what the outcome had been. This was a man clearly unused to failure, yet for all his sacrifices and determination, he had lost his wife to cancer, and in short order, his career and his son. To admit defeat, about anything, would not have been a viable concept in Paul Lauden's emotional vocabulary.

"Your son wasn't expecting you . . . ?"

"When all else fails, try the element of surprise," Paul said. "It was hard to go over the same old ground, but I was determined to do it—that whole sordid saga of how opposed Ginny's father was to her marrying me in the first place, a huge part of the problem."

He made eye contact and I saw the questions in his eyes, the tell-tale muscle working its way along his jaw. "I told you once I was prepared to listen . . . meant it," I said. "If that's what you're wondering."

"More than my son was willing to do, unfortunately," he smiled but there was no humor in it. "Partly his grandfather's doing, I'm sure, but then Frank Dender was always used to calling the shots. When I met the guy, he was hell-bent on deciding who his daughter was going to marry—certainly not some summer intern on his payroll, an art major scraping by on a scholarship from a state university. Fortunately for me, Ginny drew a line in the sand, was fully prepared to elope if he balked."

"And her father never got beyond it?"

"An understatement. Frank gave in to the marriage, but not without a price. At his insistence, I bit the bullet and shelved the idea of a studio of my own, went to work for my father-in-law in the art department at the radio station. Problem is, his notion of keeping me in line backfired . . . big time, for both of us."

Paul broke off, stared off in the distance. "After fifteen years of grinding my teeth every time he threw me yet another bone of a non-project while he rode the place into the ground, I was pressured by key players on the Board to lend my name to a palace coup. The plan was to go for broke and try to overhaul the staid, antiquated programming before the place tanked entirely. Frank was livid, but in the end the Board prevailed—started giving me stock options and free rein to run what was becoming a mega-communication network."

"Leaving Ginny *caught,* between the two of you."

"If she had been anyone else. . .it could have destroyed our marriage, easy enough. But to her eternal credit, she never let her father or the situation drive a wedge between us."

"All that must have been tough on Josh."

Paul grimaced, shook his head. "Eventually, where Frank failed with the parents, he more than succeeded with the son," he said. "Josh was always an impressionable kid, more than happy to ride off to Yale on Granddad's nickel and snap-to-attention when Frank offered to bring him into the business. I should have seen what was happening, but there was this strange, hostile . . . *father-son* thing going on between us—"

"Classic. We've all been there," I told him quietly. "Every parent on the planet can dredge up one moment or another when his or her offspring thinks good old mom or dad are pretty much too stupid to live. And if someone outside of the dynamic chooses to use that—"

"Frank certainly had plenty of help," Paul shrugged. "By then Ginny was desperately ill and I was rarely in the office, home with her more or less 24-7. Ever since she was diagnosed, her father was casting about for someone to blame. If she just hadn't married beneath her, hadn't spent all those years as a teacher instead of just taking care of herself, none of this would have happened—sounds plausible, right? Unfortunately, Josh was so devastated by, angry over his mother's illness . . . let's just say, granddad and grandson *really* bonded over that one."

134

"So even now your son . . . blames you somehow."

"As he sees it, I let Ginny die, should never have let her stop treatment. But then in all fairness to my son, as ill and frail as my father-in-law was himself in recent years, he apparently had been busy. A week after Ginny died, the Board informed me that my son was taking over as CEO at Dender Broadcasting—with the backing of the former Chairman of the Board, my father-in-law."

"Oh, Paul . . ."

"I have to hand it to the old man. After resenting me all those years for having *stolen* first his little girl and then his business, as he supposedly in jest liked to describe it, he finally evened the score. With a vengeance."

"It must have been—"

"Strangely anticlimactic, as far as the business goes. I had never wanted the job in the first place. But it poisoned things between me and my son. And I won't lie, that was and is . . . gut wrenching hard. I came up here originally on a whim to lick my wounds, to the one place we had been truly happy as a family all those golden summers in Hemingway country. I left six months later with a campground. When I went downstate again, it was just long enough to clean my stuff out of the house and move up here, into that double-wide. That was a year ago."

"You haven't seen Josh since?"

"Rarely. And then, most of the time, with a battery of lawyers between us."

"So why now?"

A hint of a smile tugged at the somber lines of his mouth. "You, Lib."

"I . . . I don't understand."

"Neither do I, not entirely," he said softly. "But Monday at the Falls, standing out there in the middle of that gosh-awful-freezing water, when you talked about your daughter, talked about losing your husband—you said something I'll never forget. *Don't postpone*, you said."

"Paul, I'd feel . . . I couldn't handle it if I believed you alienated your son even more because of something I—"

"You had the courage to tell it like it was with Danielle, came up here all alone without a clue as to what you were going to do. There are worse ways to go through life. I've been walking circles around my son's utter contempt for how I handled his mother's death and everything since. No more."

I hesitated, finally pressed the issue. "What really happened down there in Detroit?" I said.

"Things got rather ugly, though at least Josh didn't have me thrown out of the house. I had some business to take care of, a buffer of sorts. Still after a few days of trading glacial silence and shouting matches, I finally told my son flat-out that while I understood he wasn't interested in reconciliations, it wasn't going to change what I intended to do one iota."

"Your life up here, running the campground?"

"Partly, and suffice it to say, he wasn't much interested in that either. So I got quickly to the real bottom line. Once again, *you*."

"*M-me . . .?*"

"What we're trying to do here, of course. But also that I wanted to start . . . *seeing* you, dating—outside of work. That it was my intention to tell you that. And while there were certainly no guarantees, I had to hope that you would at least consider it."

Stunned, I just looked at him. "You're . . . you *can't* mean that!"

Paul winced. "Almost word for word what my son said. Only not quite as polite."

I blinked. This man had just told me he was attracted to me, had risked ever making peace with his son by telling him how he felt. And by way of response, I pretty much laughed in his face.

"Paul . . . I didn't . . . I can't even imagine what a mess I'd be in right now if you hadn't helped me . . . ," my voice shook, steadied again. "You've been a great boss—a good friend. But no way on this . . . earth am I ready even to *think* about what you're . . . "

As I watched, a smile began to flicker at the corner of his mouth. "I think you really believe that," he said evenly, "though it's hard to dispute the truth when you see it in black and white."

It was only then I noticed the slim manilla envelope lying beside him on the sofa. Carefully opening the flap, Paul retrieved several sheets of white photo paper, leaned forward and slid them on the table in front of me.

I found myself face to face with an 8 x 10 black and white shot of myself in front of the motor home in the Tahquamenon parking lot. I hadn't remembered Paul kneeling on the asphalt to take it, but he must have. From that angle the motor home appeared larger than life, almost ominously so, rearing up behind me. Undaunted, I was looking off into the distance, as if all the mysteries of the universe were somewhere out there, for the taking.

It was the most emotive and introspective portrait of me anyone had ever taken. That image cradled carefully between my fingertips was a glimpse into my very soul.

"Oh, Paul . . . it's—"

"Keep looking," he said.

I did. Beneath it lay a print of me untangling the ribbons on the garland of that young girl at the crafts workshop. The sheer joy on both our faces needed no caption.

Swallowing hard, I moved on to the photo below it in the modest stack. It was one of those grab shots Paul had taken when we were wading in the river at Tahquamenon—a tranquil landscape in graytones, the tiny human presence intended only to establish a sense of scale.

"There's more, Lib . . ."

The final print was a closeup cropped from that same river scene. With the image enlarged like that, I could see the real focus of Paul's lens was anything but a pastorale study of water and sky. In the process, he had captured that split-second moment of subtle recognition in a woman's life when she begins to recognize her own power.

Feisty and playful, that smile was aimed beyond the plane of the photograph straight out at the person behind the lens. And miracle of miracles, that woman in the photo was *me*.

The mood was a lifetime removed from that grieving, desperately uncertain Lib Aventura who had commandeered Owen's Shuttle on her way to Northern Lights. The expression on my face fell short of flirtatious, but close enough! *Sensual*, I realized to my shock and chagrin, unabashedly so.

"But I didn't . . . I wasn't . . . "

"The camera only records what it sees," Paul shrugged.

"I didn't know you were . . . you *manipulated* me—"

"Not intentionally. And whether you recognize what is happening in that shot or not, I would be the worst kind of fool to let all that just . . . *slip away*. Not twice in this one man's lifetime."

My breath caught in my throat. I laid the photo down on the table with the others.

"Do the math, Lib!" he said softly. "Even upset, confused and exhausted, you hooked up the motor home alone on the pad, first time out, like you'd been doing it all your life. By next week—if you ever go out in that rig with me again after this—you'll be backing it up like a pro. If and when the weather cooperates, you'll learn to handle crosswinds and slick asphalt. *Parking* . . . now *that*, I'll admit, might take a little longer. . . "

He slowly leaned back on the sofa, shook his head. "And meanwhile, here I sit watching you calmly begin to put together next year's calendar, whether you're still here in October or not—"

"Paul, I never promised you that I'd—"

"No, you didn't. And you can't blame me for being acutely aware of that. Face it, time is *not* on my side here . . . ," he hesitated, suddenly seemed to be weighing every word. "Unless I somehow get your attention, give you time to think about what we may be . . . *losing* here if you go? Let's just say, before either one of us knows it, you're going to get out there on Route 2—aimed east and south in that rig—and we'll *never see each other again*. Am I right?"

His gaze was steady, boring right through me in its intensity. He had gotten my attention, all right.

"And so you risked a . . . blowup with your son. You told him about me, before you even knew what I would say, how I would react?"

Paul didn't even flinch. Compared to that, the chance he took abandoning Arvo and me for a week at what had to be the peak of the season was chump change.

"What else do you suggest I could do to convince you I'm serious," he said quietly.

At that, I felt a roaring in my ears. Disbelief bordering on indignation crackled in my voice.

"I *saw* that photo of your wife, Paul . . . the one over your desk. Can you look me in the eye and tell me that you don't still . . . *love* her?"

For a split-second his jaw hardened and he stared past me into the distance. His eyes flickered shut and when they opened again, they were as clear and unclouded as the Michigan sky after a hard rain.

"Whatever my faults and whatever my father-in-law believes," he said, "disloyalty is *not* one of them. I loved my wife deeply, a part of me always will. But I like to think she . . . that Ginny would understand, be *glad* that our years together taught me to recognize, how to fight for a good thing when I—"

"Love isn't . . . interchangeable, like a pair of socks you just—"

"*No,*" he said quickly, "it *isn't!* Any more than I'm trying to convince you I can ever replace what Dan meant in your life."

"Paul, we don't even *know* each other. Not really."

He ran a hand thoughtfully over his tight-cropped salt-and-pepper hair. "Through all the collective grief and loss, I believe we know enough. We know what it means to be happy with another human being . . . trust me, not everyone in this world can say that, Lib!"

I felt as if I had just been felled by a timber. Jaw clamped tight, I dropped my gaze.

"For the record," he said after a while, "before I left Detroit, I gave that portrait of Ginny to my son. For better or worse, he knows I'm trying to move on with my life, and that as repugnant as it is to him, I still want him to be a part of it."

"You realize," I said slowly, "you've taken one awful, terrible chance . . ."

"From the look on your face right now, I'd say *two*!" he hesitated, his expression unreadable. "Though on some level, it always comes back to the same thing. What have I got to lose. . . with either one of you!"

Light-headed, I clutched at my now-empty glass and just stared at the man. What he had done was so outrageous, so desperate, that words failed. Paul just let me chew on it, that half-smile still playing at his mouth, giving me the space—the time—to respond.

"You really *did this* . . . really meant it?" I breathed.

He nodded. "Yes."

"And your son?"

"Pretty much what you'd expect," he said. "Furious, bitter, disgusted—though I've got to hope he can grow beyond it. If that photo doesn't convince him how much his mother and I loved each other, then nothing will. *You* saw it in a matter of seconds . . . I've got to hope with time, granted maybe an awful lot of it, he will get there on his own."

My hands were shaking as I retrieved that last photograph again from the table, and for what seemed like a long time, just stared at it. Whether the wine or the shock or the potent brew of emotions his confessional had triggered, I found the tears trailing unchecked down my face.

Paul was coiled tight, as if about to close the distance between us. He didn't, but his voice was hoarse with emotion. "Lib . . . Lib, honey, don't . . . !"

"I can't believe that you . . . you've turned my whole life upside down," I whispered.

"God, I certainly hope so. Because if some morning you just take off onto that highway without even—"

To his credit he caught himself and stopped short, as if pressuring me was the last thing in the world he was intending to do. Either way, stay or go, I knew my life would never be the same.

"This is *unfair,"* my voice was low. "I didn't come here to . . . never thought . . . never intended . . . "

"Fair or not, neither did I," he said. "Believe me, neither did I!"

Time was passing in the steady drip-drip from the faucet in the kitchen, still leaking for all my efforts to repair it. By now the tears had dried on my face, stiff and uncomfortable.

"So, what are you . . . suggesting . . . ?"

"You finish out the season, Lib. I keep up the driving lessons. We go out to dinner, take in a movie now and again, prowl the Michigan and Superior lakeshores to scope out some of the great lighthouses around here, spend time together," he said. "We wait and see."

"That . . . *simple?"*

"That simple."

"No strings?"

He shook his head. "No strings."

Hard to argue with someone, when all he was asking was for me to do my job, keep an open mind and let tomorrow take care of itself. "And in October?"

"It's just the Fourth of July," he shrugged. "We've got Labor Day and Columbus Day and Halloween, All Saints—I'm sure I've forgotten *something*—before anybody has to answer that question."

He chuckled quietly to himself. *"Whatever* it is, I'd be willing to bet you'll think of a way, somehow, to celebrate it and tack it up on the Activities Board."

"And if I decide—"

"To *go,* Lib . . .?" A shadow darkened his all planes-and-angles features and his voice lowered to a whisper—raw, intense. "Then, I'll spring for the rig's first fill-up," he said, "all 75 gallons. Reluctant as hell maybe, but I'll do it."

My heart was beating its way out of my chest, but somehow I stayed clear-headed enough to listen to, trust my instincts. It was either change the subject, try to keep it light—or panic, make a dash for the exit. And regardless of the outcome of all this, we both deserved better than that.

"I gather, then, you've decided not to *fire* me," I teased, willing my voice not to sound as shaky as I felt. "Even after that mess I made over-booking the place."

His gaze never wavered, for all the questions in his eyes. I had risked an answer of sorts, if he chose to read between the lines. Whatever I felt, working for him mattered to me—enough that I wasn't about to tear out of the campground the minute he headed out the door.

"Fire . . . you . . . ?" he breathed, as a flicker of a smile began to warm his eyes. "Fat chance—though, I'll admit, just to cover our bets Arvo and I are going to make one last swing through the grounds together tonight. You can hear the air-conditioners rumbling out there in all those rigs, a disaster in the making."

It wasn't the only damage control in order right now. Tired to begin with, I suddenly felt emotionally drained as well—desperately in need of some quality time alone to sort through everything Paul had told me.

As he stood, I awkwardly joined him, close enough quarters in that living room I could sense the rise and fall of his breathing. Not quite understanding how, I found myself in his arms—in a chaste, but badly called-for hug. Whatever drew me there was not about passion or love. It was about honest "like" and the need to open the windows in my airless void of a world, whether I was afraid of the fresh breezes out there or not.

"Lib, I have really got to go. We could be blowing circuit breakers all over the darn place."

"Go, then," I told him.

So fleeting that I could have almost imagined it, I felt his lips brush against my temple before he levered enough distance to make eye contact. From the look of it, he was far more anxious about my reaction than he let on.

"It's . . . you're really okay, then . . . ?" he said.

"No, but I'll live—long enough anyway to help the petting zoo folk get settled in at nine o'clock tomorrow morning."

"The . . . what . . . ?"

"Baby farm animals decked out in red, white and blue for the Fourth. Some local 4-H kids were looking for a project and volunteered. I guess I forgot to tell you . . . sorry."

"You're hopeless," he chuckled, letting me go, "absolutely incorrigible. You know more people around here than I do!"

Point was, I was only beginning to know this man for whom I was working, know myself in the process. The tension-releasing sound of our laughter washed over me like the waters of Tahquamenon plunging over those stony outcroppings.

"Duty calls," he sighed, "unfortunately. "

I frowned, "It'll be black as pitch out there soon . . . no time for either you or that sidekick of yours to be messing around with electrical boxes and water connections."

"You're a fine one to talk," he winked, already at the door. "Do us both a favor—try to stay out of trouble and *off* that blasted computer, for once!"

As I watched, he disappeared into the twilight around the end of the motor home. His laughter floated back at me from the half-darkness.

Going on autopilot, I shut the door, locked it. As I looked out over the tiny living area, I found myself wondering what I had been intending to do with my evening before Paul Lauden had showed up on my doorstep.

First things first. I clicked on the CD player again, needing the company. By sheer chance the vocalists began a gritty ballad that kept coming back to the same unsettling refrain—love won't be the thing that does us in, the end of the world as we know it.

Not exactly reassuring stuff under the circumstances. Shutting out the words and just letting the rhythms carry me away, I forced myself to concentrate on setting the timer on the microwave. My dinner had been sitting there for almost an hour on that turntable, stone cold by now.

The future would keep. Right now, my motor home was sitting in the middle of a beautiful birch grove, the smells emanating from the microwave smacked of basic comfort food. For the moment, that was enough.

Twelve

Moving on. In a single night at Northern Lights, the ground under my feet had shifted. If Paul Lauden and I were going to continue working together in that new landscape, knowing what his agenda had become, it was going to have to be a deliberate choice on my part. Small comfort, I could pull the plug any time. Paul reassured me of that loud and clear, and heaven help me, I believed him.

After a more-or-less sleepless night, part of my brain still was urging me to start wildly disconnecting hoses and keying routes into my portable GPS. Instead, I took an extra five minutes with my makeup repairing the ravages of all that midnight tossing and turning and showed up in the office just after nine.

Paul had beat me to it, was checking out the answering machine messages from the night before. The 'call-back' list on the counter in front of him appeared to fill a fair number of stick-em sheets. Up-coming reservations, I had to hope—for the Fourth, forget it, there wasn't a square inch unclaimed.

An awkward moment ensued as we made eye contact. Then he quickly scrambled to his feet and moved out from behind the reservation counter. "Sorry, I wasn't expecting you this early—the computer's all yours."

"No problem," I took a deep breath, forced a smile. "Right now a caffeine-fix is first priority anyway. How did the batten-down-the-hatches tour go last night?"

He chuckled, shook his head. "The twilight zone out there, but those jerry-rigged shared water connections over in the picnic area held. No blown fuses. All in all, a darn lucky night, I'd say. As for the caffeine . . . way ahead of you!"

With some difficulty, I got my hands around the steaming mug of coffee he was extending in my direction—striving for minimal hand-contact in the process. If I hadn't been half-watching for his reaction, I would have missed the faint tightening along as his jaw as he watched me sipping at the potent brew.

"A peace offering, I hope."

"Not entirely," he said. "It occurred to me maybe the . . . politic thing to do would be to whip up an IOU for those guests in that picnic overflow—something clever, guaranteeing them a prime spot next time."

"Done. I'll come up with something within the hour. At least I didn't hear a lot of restless natives out there last night, illegal fireworks or marauding teens. But then all that merlot was enough to put me out for the duration. Thank goodness for once I set the alarm!"

"You?" his eyebrow arched. "I don't believe it. I gather, those petting zoo folk of yours showed up—"

"Shamrock Farm. They were twenty minutes early, knocking on my motor home door. We rolled out their little snow-fence corral and kids are already gathering."

"Anything that would give our insurance people a headache?"

"A lamb, a baby alpaca and a pet pig, housebroken and with a stars-and-stripes ribbon on its tail—nothing that seriously bites, tramples or mutilates."

"Supervision?"

"A local 4-H leader and four assorted young assistants. We've got it covered . . . *Boss*!"

Paul's eyebrows shot up at my calculated choice of vocabulary.

146

"So we're back to that, are we?"

"No. Just reminding you who signs the checks around here. I promised our young volunteers a modest donation to their pizza kitty."

"Modest, as in?"

"Ten bucks. You don't want to embarrass them either!"

He made it fifteen, his expression guarded as he handed me three five's from the petty cash drawer. "I suppose I should be relieved you aren't asking for two weeks' severance pay, while I'm at it."

It was thrown out there casually enough, half in jest, but a question nonetheless. "As in my cutting and running, you mean," I said. "Hard to slink out of Dodge in a 34-foot rig. Anyway, as you can see, I'm still here."

"Yes," he let out a long, slow breath—smiled. "Yes, you are."

Win, lose or draw, the worst was behind us. The rest of the weekend flew past in a blur of crepe paper streamers and newsprint origami tri-corner hats, requests for bug spray and sunblock 50, the pungent smell of campfires and bags of marshmallows disappearing from the shelves of the camp store. Bottom line, we gained 30 additional repeat reservations spread more or less evenly over the remaining months of July and August.

"Incredible," Paul said, "wildly better than anything I hoped or expected."

Fighting a smile, I handed him the breakdown of ZIP-codes hot off the printer tray.

"Wisconsin, Ohio," he read, "Illinois, Ohio, Texas . . .you forgot Hawaii—"

"Missed that one!"

"I was on the desk when they came in. A rental, the big rig with the TRAVEL AMERICA decal on the side. Tough to miss . . . but then, apparently it's the only thing you missed. By Tuesday we may be down to bare dirt in spots in the picnic area where all those rigs were parked, but your quick reflexes in using that as overflow was a stroke of genius!"

"Blind dumb luck."

Flipping forward through the reservation book, he came to a halt at what had to be next weekend's entries. "At the risk of sounding like an ingrate, how's the Yooper Weekend programming going?"

"Hilarious," I chuckled, shook my head. "We've lined up a retro teen polka-hip-hop band, as weird as that combination sounds. Plus, a spa dealer from St. Ignace is bringing over a portable sauna and hot tub full of shaved ice for winter-in-July polar bear demonstrations, complete with raffle giveaways of *loofa* sponges."

"G-rated I hope."

"I'm told it's a hoot—get on your swim suit and pretend it's mid-January. Harmless enough. Although, I *am* a bit nervous about the karaoke event in the evening. It's right after that pastor Annie recommended does his Up-North humor thing, definitely no four-letter Anglo-Saxonisms, but still . . . "

"You forget, I was in radio," Paul said. "Find me an air-horn I can use to bleep 'em and I'm all yours!"

I laughed. "Well, one thing's for sure, I haven't had this much fun since I directed my daughter's fifth grade talent show when the theater arts teacher was out on pregnancy leave," I said. "And to think I'm actually getting paid to come up with this stuff!"

"Is that a hint?" Paul's eyebrow arched as he thought about it. "That I haven't said a *word* about fitting in time for your next driving lesson?"

"No problem. With all that stuff in the works, I thought maybe we better bag it this week."

"A deal's a deal. I'm game to go if you are," he shrugged. "We've got a break Tuesday when this Fourth-of-July crowd thins out. Only this time I thought we'd head farther west, over to Escanaba—give you a chance to handle a bit heavier two-lane highway traffic."

"The weather's supposed to be marginal. You're sure I'm ready

148

for that?"

"We get a later start and give the worst of it time to clear. Take the trip slow, maybe visit a couple of lighthouses on the Michigan shoreline around Manistique."

"On one condition," I told him, "lunch is *my* treat. Getting ready for the weekend, I picked up some quick-fix gourmet goodies that I could heat and put together in the motor home and—"

"Aha!" he teased. "A great excuse to pull over somewhere and learn how to start the auxiliary generator."

I had forgotten that. We would be on the road sans electrical hookups. Vague memories surfaced of Dan not-so-quietly grumbling about how cranky that back-up power supply could be. Something else I had to look forward to.

It turns out, the weatherman lied. What was billed as spotty downpours clearing by mid-day on Tuesday turned out to be thick overcast and a prolonged gully-washer that started drumming away on the roof of the motor home around dawn. I woke to find the lower-lying spots in the campground already transforming themselves into sizeable wading pools.

So help me, I wasn't going to punk out. Opting for a stand-up breakfast, I quickly scanned the motor home tech manual. Then donning my head-to-boot military surplus rubberized poncho, I started unhooking the vehicle from the campground systems.

The downpour made it hard to see what I was doing. Even so, I finished the job in just over three-quarters of an hour, fifteen minutes less than it had taken me last week, *with* help. Things were soggy, but looking up.

By the time Paul showed up at nine-thirty, I had changed into a dry blouse and jeans, towel-dried my hair and managed to get the worst of the mud off my boots. Half in the dark to keep from running down the auxiliary batteries, I took a break and tried to revive myself with a hefty jolt of cold coffee left over from breakfast.

"You must have been at it since crack of dawn," Paul said, "monsoons and all. Even the ducks are running around in waders out there!"

I laughed. "You should have seen me when I got done. I looked like a drowned rat."

"But you did it. I'm impressed—*and confused.* Wasn't the plan to sleep in?"

"The rain woke me," I shrugged. "With that downpour, I figured it might take me longer, so to be on the safe side, I just got up and went at it. You were right about putting a wrench on that faucet connector. Otherwise, no problem."

"You're sure you still want to do this?" he said slowly.

"After slogging around out there unhooking this thing—of course. Unless you're getting white knuckles at the thought of riding with me."

The attempt at humor sounded forced, nervous even to me. He looked at me thoughtfully before reacting.

"Nobody says you need to be a martyr about this, Lib. Or expects you to prove anything."

"I know that."

"Okay, then. But only if you're sure . . ."

By way of answer, I slipped on my rain gear. It seemed prudent to ask Paul to double-check my prep work, but that done, it was too wet to let anyone stand out there in that downpour watching for the overhead limbs and branches. While he monitored our progress from the passenger seat, I managed to maneuver the motor home out on the access road with the minimum of scraping sounds and stifled expletives.

With the motor home on idle at the campground entrance, I looked in vain for any signs the storm had run its course. Instead, rain seemed to be gusting sideways now, blinding sheets of it whipping across the asphalt of the highway.

"You know," Paul made eye contact, frowned, "it's not too late to change your mind."

I flashed what I hoped was an optimistic smile in his direction. "No problem. I just need a minute to clear my head. Would you believe, I don't even know where the headlights are? I never drove this thing at night—which is exactly what it looks like out there!"

"Try to the left . . . that cluster of dials on the dash."

Squinting in the shadowy light, with some difficulty I found the switch. "Bingo!"

A hint of a smile softened the tense planes of his face. I sensed it wasn't my driving but the weather that had him spooked.

"Congratulations," he said "you've officially survived your Cinderella permit—no dings, dents or even near misses."

"We aren't in Escanaba yet, either."

And weren't likely to be if I thought about it any harder. Flexing my hands on the wheel, I clicked on the turn signal, checked for traffic and then eased the vehicle out on Route 2, once again headed west.

Five minutes on that highway was all it took to convince me that I had blundered into a perverse replay of my outing with Owen of Owen's Shuttle, charging off into the unknown in that van of his. Only this time I was at the wheel, stone cold sober.

"Talk to me," Paul said quietly. "You haven't said a word in ten miles, though that death grip on the wheel speaks volumes. Lib, if this rain keeps up, I vote for cutting this little junket short. These road conditions would wear down even a seasoned driver."

"Point taken. But I'm fine. Really."

As if giving a lie to that assessment, a gust shook the motor home so hard that I gasped and momentarily took my foot off the gas pedal. Fortunately, we had just come to one of those periodic slow-vehicle turnout lanes and even the enormous semis had begun passing me. Gritting my teeth, I held on for dear life as the water from their tires surged up over my side window like an ominous, gray wall.

I didn't have the nerve to look at the speedometer, didn't want to know what miserable progress we were making. The landscape around me was reduced to an unrecognizable blur of rain-lashed trees and that empty strip of grass mown along the shoulder to minimize collisions with the burgeoning deer population.

The final insult was hitting a construction zone in what passed for a several-block main drag of one of the tiny villages strung along Route 2 at random intervals—really little more than isolated collections of diners, gas stations and motels. I found myself caught in a terrifying squeeze between the oncoming lane of traffic and a seemingly endless trail of orange highway department cones.

"You're right . . . at this rate, forget about Escanaba," I muttered through clenched teeth as a cascade of murky water surged over the windshield from the pavement below. "We're never even going to make it to Manistique!"

Without my asking, Paul calmly began to talk me through the morass. "Forget about speed limits," he kept telling me, "no one in their right mind is trying to go that fast. Just take it slow, Lib . . ."

Fat chance I'd do anything else. Between the drop-off to the right of me and the semis coming at me from the west, it was like threading a needle with a bulldozer. There hadn't been one of those stretches with passing lanes lately and I was trying not to panic at the long line of headlights piling up behind me.

Sixty more miles of this. The thought was appalling, even though the traffic seemed to be thinning out again.

"In a couple of miles on the left," Paul said evenly, "you'll see a sign for the Seul Choix Light. I suggest we get off this speedway, take a county road for a while. Nothing in the world says we need to make it all the way to Escanaba in this mess."

"You'll get no argument from me," I said. "Just tell me when—oh m'gosh . . . the shoulder . . . !"

With a terrible, gut-wrenching thud, first one, then two of the motor home's wheels slid off onto the gravel. Paul didn't even flinch.

"Steady," he said evenly. "Steady, don't brake, just ease off on the gas, ride it out and gradually steer it back on the pavement."

I knew better than to panic and jerk the wheel hard to the left. But Paul's voice gently cuing me to respond was like a precious mantra as I maneuvered the rig slowly back on the asphalt. I was so tense from the effort, my shoulder blades felt as if they were fused to the base of my skull.

"Hang in there, Lib! The end is in sight. I'll give you fair warning when we get close so you can begin to plot your exit strategy."

"Thank heavens," I breathed.

The rain gods must have been listening. By the time I reached the turn-off, the downpour had begun to subside a little and even the winds were not slamming us quite as ferociously. I waited as a string of oncoming traffic cleared, then turned south on the secondary road heading toward Lake Michigan.

I couldn't even imagine how grateful those other drivers behind me were to have me out of there. It took every bit of willpower I had not to stop the motor home mid-lane on that county road, climb down and kiss the asphalt to celebrate.

Thirteen

As if someone had thrown a switch, within a mile toward the lake on that deserted secondary road, the sun came out. Thready dark clouds were still scudding fast across the sky, but beyond them it seemed to be clearing. *Seul Choix*—from my memories of pondering road atlases over the years, I conjured up impressions of a tiny lighthouse symbol perched on an isolated bump of a promontory sticking out into Lake Michigan.

At least Paul had the tact not to laugh when I tried to pronounce it. "The locals call it Sis-shwa," he said.

"What ever . . . after what we just went through, I'm not sure anything named 'last chance' is really a good idea."

"Worse. It's *Only Choice*," he chuckled.

"How did a lighthouse wind up with a name like that?"

"Beats me," he said, "though legend says the light is haunted, apparently by some past keeper with a penchant for cigars and rattling the silverware. Otherwise, it's really a . . . "

His voice trailed off. Up ahead about a block from us at the edge of the narrow county blacktop, a large deer had stepped out of the tall grass alongside the roadway and was poised half-on and half-off the pavement.

"Where there's one, there are more," Paul said quietly. "It's how John Stavros had that accident a couple of years back . . . "

I shivered, remembering. Instinctively I had eased my foot off the gas pedal, trying not to over-brake and send us into a skid. By the time the doe and her two fawns had ambled on to the asphalt, I was able with some effort to bring the rig to a full stop, waiting for them to cross.

We were so close, I could see the beads of water glistening on the animals' sleek, rusty coats. For what seemed like a long time, the mother deer just stared out at us, curious and wary. Then looking back at her brood, she nonchalantly continued her crossing, with the fawns scampering behind her.

"Humbling," Paul said, "how precarious life can be—and so very beautiful."

I sensed his gaze flicker in my direction. After the hellacious obstacle course behind us, I needed any pep talk I could get.

"You're a good man, Paul Lauden. I've given you a lot of guff, just thought you ought to hear it," I told him. "Nuts for riding with me, I grant you . . . "

I heard him clear his throat. He was staring out the windshield again, so I couldn't read his face.

"And you wonder why it occurs to me to just take those keys of yours and toss 'em into the woods," he said, "if that's what it would take to ground you here, permanently."

Something in his tone told me he wasn't talking about just my driving. "And yet you're in that passenger seat," I said, "aiding and abetting this cockamamie quest of mine for mobility."

He chuckled softly to himself. "All the more a fool, I. . . right?"

No, it occurred to me, anything but foolish. If I were free to go, I was also free to stay. Somehow my gut told me Paul Lauden not only understood—but maybe even was counting on that.

"Time to get moving," I said.

Easing my foot off the brake, I resumed driving but with a weather-eye now on the undergrowth on either side of the road. We were coming to another turn-off and to my dismay, the turn marked Lighthouse deteriorated abruptly to rutted gravel—as near as Paul could tell from the map, four teeth-jarring miles of it.

I slowed to a crawl again, uncertain that water-logged, unpaved surface would even hold the rig. "Am I going to take the bottom out of this thing? We could find ourselves in mud up to the axles. Four miles is pretty far if—"

"Really not as bad as it might seem," Paul said, "and at least the weather is finally cooperating. What say, once we get there, you park this rig and then we hike for a while along the lakeshore before pushing further west?"

"Right now even standing on solid ground for a while sounds just great to me."

After what seemed like the longest four miles in history, in the distance through the trees, I caught a glimpse of the white-capped blue of the lake. Off to one side, half-obscured by a grove of mature hardwoods, stood an enormous white tower attached to an unusually large red-brick keeper's house.

The parking lot was deserted, not surprising given the morning's deluge and the fact it was a Tuesday coming off the busy long weekend. I pulled in and immediately cut the engine. The silence was eerie, the calm scarier than the road noise and the sound of that storm.

"We . . . actually . . . stopped . . . ," I whispered.

Inexplicably, my hand couldn't seem to work the key out of the ignition. Paul finally took pity on me, leaned over and with a deft movement of the wrist, retrieved it.

"Eureka," he smiled, "we found it."

"Pretty darn hard to miss an 80-foot tower sitting out in the middle of the woods . . . !"

Already half-way out the passenger door, Paul shot a quizzical frown in my direction. "Are you okay over there?"

I was still clutching at the wheel with both hands, knuckles as white and rigid as if epoxied in place. It was difficult even trying to catch my breath, much less speak.

"No," I stammered, "yes. . . I really don't know."

"Stay put," he said.

I did, staring like a zombie out the windshield as he picked his way around the puddles to open the driver door. When I still didn't budge, he leaned in and gently coaxed me down from the driver seat. Shaking, barely able to stand up, I stood there in his arms, willing myself not to break down and start wailing like some scared kid who had just tried to skateboard and had wiped out against a telephone pole.

"Now, that wasn't so bad," he said evenly, "was it?"

"Awful. Hair-raising. I've never been so terrified . . . "

"But you handled it like—"

"I was a menace, criminally irresponsible, could easily have killed us both . . . dodging those trucks, dropping down on the shoulder like that. Did you see what I did to that . . . construction cone . . . ?"

That desperate debrief was all but incoherent. Paul's hand was tracing gentle arcs between my shoulder blades, like someone consoling a hysterical child.

"It's okay," he said, again and again. "It's over."

"But it's not, that's the point. What if I had been all alone out there in the middle of nowhere in that rig . . . ?" My voice trailed off in a hiccup of sound. "Danielle was right—I was *certifiable* to think I could do this . . . "

I felt his quick intake of breath. His hands tightened around my shoulders, forcing eye contact.

"Listen to me, Lib . . . this isn't your fault, any of it! If I hadn't been sitting there next to you in that passenger seat—unintentionally escalating this outing to some kind of crazy game of chicken—you would have pulled over a long time ago."

I started to protest, but he cut me off.

"Admit it. You would have taken shelter in some parking lot, or whatever you could find, have waited out that storm. And when you felt comfortable, then and only then, you would have gotten back out there

. . . *under control, Lib.* Absolutely safe."

With a terrible shock, I realized that he was right—*and* wrong. In fact, none of that mattered. I was here, at a destination I had never sought, never anticipated, with this man, Paul Lauden. Anything but safe, common sense told me, on so many fronts—yet, for all the uncertainty of the moment, I wouldn't have it any other way.

At that the tears finally came, hot and stinging. With an anguished little cry, I burrowed my face against his rain slicker, pouring out my fear and frustration, a bitter and toxic brew of emotions that left me drained, disoriented, vaguely embarrassed at how totally vulnerable and out of control I felt. My head throbbed like it was in a vise and I could hardly keep my eyes open.

"Change in game plan," Paul said quietly. "You're going to do what I should have insisted you do this morning, before we even started all this. I'm going to turn down the covers in that motor home, tuck you in, head out for a good long walk and let you sleep this off before we move one more inch—"

"No," I felt my chin thrust out as I faced him, "I'm good . . . fine. Really."

"Nice try, Lib, but forget it! I should have never, ever have let you take that rig out in—"

"And how do you think you would have stopped me?" My voice came out high-pitched, half on the verge of my losing it again. "Don't you think I knew it was probably foolhardy to take the rig out in that awful deluge? Only I was so proud, so stubborn, so . . . utterly *stupid*—"

Chuckling softly now, Paul was holding me at arms-length, taking in what had to be an absolute train wreck as fashion statements go. I felt and knew I must look a fright after all that crying, my hair wildly out-of-control from the rain hood of my parka.

I bristled, felt the anger rising in my voice. "I fail to see what's so . . . blasted funny?"

"Us," he said gently. "Unless I'm very mistaken, Lib, I think you and I have just had our first genuine knock-down, drag-out fight."

"Well, I'm glad you find it so amusing!" I snapped. "You've got your nerve to think that we . . . that I'm . . . "

Groping for words it finally dawned on me, what I couldn't bring myself to express was already out there, mirrored back at me in Paul Lauden's eyes. I broke off mid-rant and just looked at him.

"You're *what*, Lib . . . ?" he said softly. "Because in case you haven't noticed, I'm falling in love with you. It needs to be said, God help me, and there it is."

He had put a name on it and there was no taking it back. *Love* was not a word either one of us used lightly. Something in my upturned face must have given him his answer.

I saw him begin to lower his head, knew he was going to kiss me. And I just let it happen, fleeting and achingly gentle, but quite enough to convey the absolute truth of what was happening between us.

Then he was smiling down at me, his strong artist's hands still cradling my shoulders. I blinked, half thinking I had imagined the taste of that kiss, the look that went with it. For a split-second I felt the insane urge to get back behind that wheel and go tearing out of there, spewing gravel behind me as I went.

"Forget it, Lib!" his voice was low. "I've got the keys."

Was I all that pathetically transparent? His answer was to draw me to him again. Only this time as he fit his mouth to mine, I sensed a heightened insistence, deliberate, willing me to respond.

I closed my eyes, light-headed, swaying against him as every fiber in my body cried out for him to hold me. Even as I surrendered to the moment, a barely audible voice inside was telling me it couldn't last. Lurking in the dark recesses of memory were realities I couldn't will away, images that froze my heart.

Dan. My daughter. The grief-stricken faces of my family, saying goodbye to what had been the love of my life, along this very same wild and desolate lakeshore. The past was asserting its claim on what I needed and felt. I was powerless to stop it.

Mercifully, Paul was astute enough to sense what was happening.

159

He caught the subtle mixed signals in my body language even before I could bring myself to raise a hand to stop this, utter a simple, very ambivalent, *no*. As he began to let me go, his voice was raw with emotion.

"Lib, Lib. . .sweetheart, the last thing on earth I intended was to frighten you like that, push you beyond your . . . comfort zone," he said, "not out there on that godforsaken highway, not here and now, trying to show you how very much I—"

"I k-know. And you didn't . . . weren't out of line, weren't encouraging me to do anything I didn't want to do. Not behind that wheel, not here, now when you . . . when we . . . ," the words trailed off in a whisper of sound, only it wasn't just my voice that was trembling.

My reaction wasn't about him or us, any of it, I realized. It was a conditioned response to four decades of loving another human being. I had never been unfaithful to Dan in life, never even looked at another man with feelings like the ones I found suddenly so close to the surface.

Yet, here I was. Here we were.

As I forced myself to look at him, Paul looked so devastated, I couldn't help it. Laying a hand tentatively along the planes of his face, I stood on tiptoe and before I had time to think about it, kissed him full on the mouth. The look of utter astonishment on his face was priceless.

"Good . . .now that's settled," I exhaled fiercely, plunged ahead so there was no time for more second thoughts from either one of us, "I'm giving you fair warning. First I raid the medicine cabinet for something to knock out this monster of a headache. And then, if you recall, we had a plan. We're going to work off all that excess adrenalin—among other things—on those hiking trails you were talking about!"

"Lib, you aren't in any—"

"Non-negotiable. Seul Choix. We're going."

Paul just looked at me. "Did anyone ever tell you, you are . . . one . . . *tough* lady . . . !"

I laughed. "You have *no* idea."

160

But then neither had I, not until this very moment. For better or worse, I was grabbing at life again, shaking in my muddy boots, but taking hold of it with both hands.

"Well, at least we ought to ditch all this crazy rain gear," he muttered.

The light in the motor home bathroom was unforgiving and the mirror even more so. Still, I went to work with brush and tube, trying my best to repair the ravages of that mega-crying-jag Paul had just witnessed.

This man had seen me, if not at my worst, then darn close to it. Eyes red, nose dripping and totally hysterical. But miracle of miracle, even while I may have been entertaining thoughts of flight, he had only drawn me closer.

It was all there in the face staring back at me from the glass—my doubt, the anxiety, the quiet awareness. I was glad Paul was out there waiting for me, glad that somehow of all the campgrounds in the world, I had found my way back to his.

"You okay?" he said.

"Coming. There's nothing wrong here that a little calculated pill-popping won't fix."

I had left a half-empty bottle of water stashed inside the refrigerator door, enough to chase down the tablets. Flashing a smile, I stepped out of the bathroom, headache tablets in hand. Paul had been waiting on the couch, stood to meet me.

"Human again?" I said.

He grinned. "Beautiful. But then that was true all along."

"You're delusional," I laughed, shook my head.

But then, I wasn't really complaining. For the next half-hour instead, I power-walked my way along the lakeshore like a woman in training for a half-marathon. I was running on empty, every single minute of it, but on some level I hadn't felt this empowered and confident in so long, I couldn't even remember.

Paul let me take the lead—stopping occasionally to let his

photographer's eye linger on the sunlight sculpting a hillock of sand and beach grass, dancing along the foamy crests of the breakers. It seemed strange to see him without his camera, understandable enough considering the pea-soup weather with which the day began. I could tell he missed it, couldn't resist teasing him about how hard he had to work at catching up.

"There may have been some shaky moments behind the wheel of that rig," I said, "But on solid ground, buster . . . watch out!"

"Should I interpret that as a threat," he laughed, "or a promise?"

He was just giving back as good as he got. Still, for a split-second, I just stared at him, suddenly dead serious.

"Maybe a little bit of both, Paul Lauden," I said evenly. "Just maybe a little bit of both."

Fourteen

I had told my daughter I wasn't looking for another relationship—true enough when I said it. But then with all her fretting about my going to work for 'some guy' at Northern Lights, as she saw it, Danielle had done her share to awaken me to that possibility. Paul Lauden had simply nudged that particular door open the rest of the way.

It is possible to learn a lot about someone working for and with them. I knew my boss had a long fuse when it came to people and problems, was capable of both spontaneity and the ability to zero-in on a task with formidable tenacity. He was willing to take enormous risks to fight for the things—or people—he loved. And I, it seems, was now one of them.

We were becoming a team, Paul and I, matter-of-factly relying on each other for even the most minute decisions that impacted the image and future of the business, from the colors chosen for a brochure to the lumber selected for the observation platform for the bog. When I suggested networking to get the campground involved in some of the widowed-singles RVer support programs, Paul gave me a resounding thumbs-up. We were walking in those shoes ourselves, knew how challenging it could be.

As if by mutual agreement, for the next few weeks there was no overt repeat of the tentative intimacy that had so abruptly surfaced between the two of us outside my mud-streaked motor home in the Seul Choix parking lot. Still, to my dismay, I was finding it harder and harder to ignore that undercurrent of physical attraction as we worked together, often in very close proximity.

We were installing new slat blinds on the office windows, fraught with a lot of awkward touching of arms and bodies. I tried to hold the blinds while Paul secured them in the brackets over our heads, when out of the blue he suddenly laid down screwdriver, took the unwieldy blinds out of my hands and laid them down across the top of one of the nearby shelves. As if mentally calculating, deliberately setting the distance between us, he took my two hands in his.

"I know you feel uncomfortable talking about it," he said, "but I can't go on like this, sensing you flinch or stiffen every time we even come within ten feet of each other. Lib, I spend the better part of any given day thinking about you . . . enough, by the way, to wring the stuffings out of a guy over time. I would give anything to be able to show you how much I care, even a simple hug without—"

"Paul, you know that I . . . it's not intentional on my part." I had learned to make an art form of evading his gaze when the circumstances seemed to call for it.

"The hell of it is, I can sense you wanting to respond," he said quietly. "Until you remember that I'm not Dan."

"It feels, somehow, as if I'm . . . being unfaithful."

Paul hesitated. "To a memory, Lib."

"Still living for me."

"I understand that. But I can't believe Dan would want you to lock all those powerful feelings inside, any more than Ginny would want to be remembered either as some . . . dark, guilt-ridden voice in the back of my skull telling me it's wrong to love or feel or touch. We learned those precious things together, she and I, over our lifetime. I cannot believe she would want her legacy to be I . . . buried them with her."

A hard knot was beginning to form in my throat, but not from

164

grief. There was a profound, deeply honest truth in what Paul was saying.

"I . . . *want* us to be close," I whispered, "I do . . ."

"If I know that, I can be as patient as I need to be, have to be," he said. "I love you, Lib."

His hands gently framing my upturned face, Paul leaned down and kissed me, as if sealing the promise. He didn't have to reassure me again how he felt. I already knew.

Change had ceased to be my enemy. I was seeing life with new eyes, deliberately channeling into my work what I felt and saw going on around me. Though the possibilities were infinite, the events on my infamous Activities Board were becoming more and more focused now on the unique character of this community—on the people, like me, who found themselves drawn to this very special place.

Our Yooper Culture weekend was an enormous hit. I sat there in the picnic area with the crowd of campers and heard Pastor Bob, a relative newcomer to the area himself, regale us with his commentary on the state of things in our little corner of the world.

The audience loved him. I, for one, found myself taking away from the night more than I had anticipated.

"Some folks say nothin's going on up here in the U.P.A., five hundred miles from just about anyplace on a map that has enough people to support a professional sports franchise," Bob said by way of getting started. "Except Green Bay and . . . hey, man, we all know about those Packer fans . . ."

That triggered shouts of approval from our Cheesehead contingent and a few catcalls from the Michiganders. Bob chuckled, shook his head.

"Nothin' happening up here, folks?" he said. "Ya hear it all the time. Don'tcha believe it! How many things have to happen before we get smart enough to know that *something's happenin'* . . .? Robert Frost said that—smart guys those poets. He'da liked it up here, sure enough, 'cause he knew folks up here would have an answer."

"Wh-a-as happenin' . . . we are!" he would roar. Quickly the whole crowd caught on, tourists and locals, chanting that mantra along with him.

"Life isn't a four-letter word in the old dictionary up here either," he said. "Takes the whole darn alphabet to spell it out. Only a guy's gotta be there—gotta be present, gotta be *attending,* be paying attention to figure life out. Yoopers, even we wannabes, may not have a lot of things, but we're here. Not many of us as numbers go, but *being someplace* is something we sure know something about."

Gotta be there, gotta be paying attention. I hadn't been or done either for a long, long time—had taken so much in life for granted. Even my journey to Northern Lights began as a stopover not a destination.

Traumatized by the reality of love and loss, I came here wanting nothing but to move on. When I blundered into a job, it was only to buy me time to get back on the road. But in spite of myself I stayed, and miracle of miracles, things started happening.

Paul and I were lunching together at Annie's an unsettling number of days a week now, fixtures in our own right on the local scene. Though I still flinched on our weekly road trips when the back-up alarm on the motor home began to beep, I could now maneuver in reverse for a good fifteen feet on my own without hitting anything, progress of sorts. Paul and I had drifted together in a borrowed inflatable kayak down Hemingway's beloved Two-Heart River on a rare day off. There was poetry in life again.

My days were so chock-full and compelling, I genuinely forgot to worry about what I was going to do when the season ended. Without fanfare or over-thinking it, I had begun tentatively to look ahead—playing with a calendar for next season that would mix up favorite events from the past months and some creative new ones. How lucky we are when we find something to do that makes us so happy, we feel guilty even calling it *work*.

Labor Day at the campground was billed as a Fifties weekend, complete with improvised poodle skirts and an Outdoor Movie Night. Arvo helped me string up a huge bed sheet for a screen and I commandeered an AV-aide from the local high school to turn the picnic area into a classic walk-in theater at one time so popular in these isolated rural areas. We screened that celluloid Mackinac Island classic, "Somewhere in Time". Even the local band boosters got into the act, thrilled when I asked them to sell the popcorn and vintage era concession treats we scrounged from the internet.

To top off the holiday, Arnie used his rattle-trap school bus to drive all the campers who were interested east to the Mackinac Bridge—an engineering masterpiece from that same kinder, gentler era—for the fiftieth birthday Bridge Walk. Sonja and I made custom tee-shirts for the occasion and Paul even closed the office long enough to join in.

I was there . . . participating, a lump in my throat, as our little contingent gawked its way across the five-mile long span, while camera in hand, Paul captured the moment. On all sides of us we saw families transporting kids in strollers, a gang of Red-Hat ladies pushing their frailer members in wheelchairs—tens of thousands of people all headed in the same direction, no grander plan than to walk dead ahead from one side of the Straits to the other.

My certificate at the finish line read 25,204. I memorized the number with the same awe as if I had just won the lottery, one in a million. Being there was its own reward, priceless.

Safe at the Finish line on the southern I-75 off-ramp, the bunch of us from Northern Lights cheered and hugged each other as someone over the loudspeaker sang a wonderfully sappy version of "Happy Birthday, dear Bridge", then we boarded the bus for the trip home. Trolls and Yoopers, campers from parts east and west and the good folk from Centerline and Bentley—they all came together that day. Watching them from the back seat of Arnie's shuttle, Paul and I surreptitiously held hands, like two teenagers cuddling in the back of the school bus.

"I love you," he said.

"Ditto," I whispered and for once I didn't blush. Still, with a heavy heart I couldn't bring myself to reciprocate, name my own feelings for what I knew them to be either, *love*.

It was Annie, in fact, who finally pried the word out of me. The Tuesday after Labor Day as she showed Paul and me to our usual booth in the back of the diner, I couldn't help but sense that for all her cheery proprietress banter, her smile stopped short of her eyes. On a powder room run, I took a detour past the cash register to suggest that the two of us plan a girl's night out sometime soon.

Annie wasn't a complainer. From the little she shared over the months about her husband's accident and the difficulties of his care, I knew her family was coping as best they could, but it was certainly not easy. Their kids were ten and thirteen, and between their helping out at home and at the diner, my friend worried constantly they were losing their childhood in the process.

"Mondays, you're closed in the evening," I said quietly, "aren't you?"

"We will be more often soon when we cut our hours, but for now that's it."

"Good. We'll have a girls' night out next Monday . . . my treat."

"Oh Lib, that's really sweet," she sighed, "but I don't think —"

"Annie, you *need* this. You know you do."

She hesitated, forced a smile. "Thank you," she said. "Yes . . . you're right, let's do it. What time?"

"I'll pick you up around four. We can hit some of your competition west of here, let somebody else do the cooking for a change."

Annie was waiting for me on the front porch of their

immaculately kept ranch on the outskirts of Centerline, had shed her ubiquitous slacks and official Diner tee for a lovely sun-dress and cardigan. The nights were already getting cooler now and along stretches of Route 2, some of the maples were getting a jump on the color season—urged on by the exhaust from all the traffic as families got in their last vacation weekends.

"You look beautiful!" I said as Annie clambered into the passenger seat of the Northern Lights SUV.

So help me, I caught the tinge of color rising in her cheeks. "I don't get to do this much," she admitted, "haven't worn a dress all summer. It's just not practical in the diner and outside of work we really haven't been going anywhere."

"I can't even imagine how difficult it has been."

Annie was silent a long time. "Things have been looking up . . . really," she said. "Still, sometimes I get so angry—how unfair it is."

"If it would help to talk about it, you know I'm here."

Instead she started rattling off the names of several out-of-the-way bistros down the road where we could hang out for a couple of hours. "Some other time," I told her, insisted on taking us up to that gourmet-heaven to the north of us near Tahquamenon. I had called ahead and they were open. At first Annie put up a fuss, but I wore her down.

The miles sped by with a lot less stress in the SUV than Paul and my trip in the motor home. But something was on Annie's mind and after a while I just gave up on small talk, tried to give her the space to say it.

"The worst of it, Lib . . . ," her voice shook, steadied again, "John was such an active man, always out in the yard with the kids, playing ball, taking them fishing and mushroom hunting, coaching those teams of his. Sometimes after the accident, he would look at me with that quiet desperation that makes you wonder out loud when life is no longer really . . . *living*."

"Paul says he went through the same thing with his wife," I said softly.

"I know. We . . . Paul and I talked about it a lot when he first came to Northern Lights . . . "

Annie broke off and stared off into the distance. An uncomfortable silence settled in between us as I hoped against hope that I wasn't misreading the situation—a bond between these two that went beyond people facing the same personal crisis.

Finally I forced myself to say it. "Paul said the two of you became . . . really good friends."

"Talking to that man kept my sanity when John was at his lowest—butting his head against the reality that medicine can do only so much."

She let out her breath and I could hear the deep well of pain in her voice. "There were times when I felt so terribly . . . disloyal" she said, "even *guilty,* to be sharing all that with a relative stranger. What I really wanted was to shake John out of it—that or take the kids, get in that beat-up truck of ours and never come back. I just felt so . . . damn lonely, desperate. Getting to know Sonja helped . . . and now you. You have no idea how good it feels just to have a girlfriend's shoulder to cry on once in a while."

I processed in silence what she was telling me, chagrined and angry at myself for how off-the-mark I had been. *"Oh, Annie,* I'm so sorry . . ."

"Trust me, when it came to feeling sorry for myself, I didn't need any help. And then out of the blue, Paul shows up at the house with this experimental retina-directed equipment that lets quads place phone calls, even write. Lord knows how much it cost, where or how he got it, but he did—hauled it back from Detroit over the Fourth. Next thing I knew, Earl Forester and the local emergency response team started helping my husband organize what he's calling a Neighbor-Net phone bank—"

"One of those odd-job services?" Apparently time with his son wasn't Paul's only agenda on that run last month to Detroit. He hadn't said a word to me about any of it.

170

"With a twist," Annie said. "It connects volunteers with families facing long-term problems . . . losing homes to fires, extended illness, you name it. John's been so into recruiting his volunteer bank that lately I've had to tell him to lay off—he hasn't been watching the clock and his calls are getting people out of bed at all hours!"

I hadn't seen her this excited since we first talked about working together. "Annie, you must be—"

"Beyond grateful. You can't even imagine what all this is doing for John's self-respect, his morale . . . to say nothing of our marriage."

"I'm so glad, really and truly glad for the both of you," I told her, meant it. "I had no idea."

Annie's voice sounded tentative, almost shy. "You know, I'd really like to have you meet John—come over for dinner sometime. He still isn't quite up for it, seeing people socially like that, but—"

"We'd love it," I said quickly. "Only make it a potluck, a lot less stressful after you've been feeding half the U.P. every day." I hadn't been watching my pronouns.

"*We . . . ,*" Annie said thoughtfully, "as in you and Paul? It's official then. I thought there might be what folks would call *a little courting* going on out there on Route 2."

The best defense, I decided, was just to keep my eyes on the road and my mouth shut. Annie shifted in her seat, shot a glance in my direction.

"Unless I badly miss my guess," she persisted, "I think Paul Lauden is falling in love with you, Lib—has been for a while now. You're very lucky, both of you."

Small towns, God bless 'em. I weighed my words carefully before reacting.

"You're not the only one who owes Paul Lauden a lot," I said. "That job at Northern Lights has filled an enormous hole in my life. Paul is teaching me to handle that rig, giving me my independence—"

"And you're afraid all that is coloring your feelings, twisting how grateful you are into something else entirely?"

171

"Pretty much," I said.

"Love isn't convenient or programmable. Would that it were, huh? It was never in *The Plan* for this Polish girl from Chicago to wind up in a north woods icebox with a hunk of a gym teacher from a close-knit Greek family either. And still, despite everything that happened since, I don't regret one single bit of it!"

My voice was low. "Annie, when Dan died, it was as if my heart died with him . . . "

"All the more reason to take a good, hard look at what life is offering you," she sighed. "In his blacker moments, John kept making me promise that if and when I would be alone, I wouldn't shut my heart away with him in some plot of earth. It would be an insult, he said, to everything we had and felt, the good times not just what came after."

Life is meant to be lived. In so many words, Annie was just replaying my own carpe diem manifesto when I left Madison, what Paul himself had told me when he talked about his wife and our relationship.

I shifted in my seat, my hands flexing impatiently on the wheel. "Annie, be realistic . . . it's barely September. I moved here in June. We're only talking months since Dan— "

May. He died in May, *over a year ago.* With a shock I realized somewhere in the months since I came here, I had ceased to calculate my life around that milestone. It had to be *sixteen* months now, give or take, since my world had collapsed in ruins around me.

Annie's voice was knowing, sad. "Where is it written that there's a timetable for these things? I've seen how fast life can bring us to our knees. I've also seen how unexpectedly it can help us find a way to stand again—even if the phone bills it takes to make that happen at the moment are downright . . . scary!"

It wasn't phone bills I was worrying about. Even an unlimited calling plan on my cell and the land-line in the Northern Lights office hadn't given me the courage to level with my daughter about what was going on in my life.

"I'm afraid my kids would never forgive me," I said. "Not my

172

daughter anyway. She loved her father, and somehow feels it's her job to perpetuate that. Even my coming here was enough to send her into a tailspin."

"You haven't told your kids that you and Paul—?"

"Are an *item*?" I finished for her. "I haven't even put Paul and my name together in one sentence publicly anywhere, except as boss and employee or as very good friends. Because if I let myself go down that path, Annie—"

"Then you're afraid you'll panic and run for cover."

"Try this recurring urge to disconnect the rig and go tearing down to Florida alone," I told her. "Believe me, I thought about it a time or two."

Annie chuckled softly, shifted in her seat. "Who knew? If you caught me at the right moment, I'd have gone right along with you."

"I'm on the downslope of sixty," I told her. "My summers of adolescent romance are ancient history. Can anybody truly know someone in just a couple of months?"

"I can only tell you Paul Lauden is one of the most decent men I've ever met. Witness what he did to break my John out of that prison he's in, without fanfare, without—"

"I never said Paul wasn't generous, considerate . . . "

"There's love and then there's *Love*. What you see in that man's eyes each and every time he looks at you—it's the real deal, I'd stake my life on it."

"All the more reason to be sure that I don't take advantage of how good he's been to me."

"Oh Lib . . . I wish you could see your face when the two of you are sitting together in that back booth of my diner. Girl, you absolutely, positively . . . *glow*!"

In the gathering darkness, hands clutched tight on that steering wheel, I suddenly found myself trembling. "Annie, you are really *not* being helpful here!"

"What's the worst that can happen if you admit you're starting to care about him, Lib—really care?"

"When did this all suddenly become about me?" I said. "I suggested this night out to cheer you up—not start a major debate about my love life, such as it is!"

Annie groaned in mock disbelief, hand theatrically shielding her forehead. "Love . . . *you finally said it . . . !* "

I laughed, but there was really no humor in it. True enough, I said it all right . . . but to *Annie*. Said it half in jest, trapped in the pitch black confines of the SUV speeding away from Northern Lights. At that rate, I couldn't even imagine what it would take before I ever admitted it to Paul, much less admitting it to my family.

Fifteen

It was bound to happen and it did, the second weekend in September. At least this time my daughter gave me fair warning.

"Mom," she announced in the course of her nightly phone call, "we're coming—Friday. The kids have a day off from school and if we leave Madison by noon, we should make it before dark. That way we can have a nice long weekend together before we all settle back in the grind again."

"Terrific!" I told her, all the while struggling to get a handle on the fact that summer, at least from my family's point of view, was over. "First thing in the morning I'll pen in a reservation on the board in the office and hang a Reserved sign on the post at one of the nicest sites."

"The kids really enjoyed it last time," Danielle said. "They've been telling all their friends how cool their Camping Grama is."

I chuckled, thinking about the near meltdown I had a couple of days ago trying yet again to fix the leaky faucet in the motor home. In the process I damaged the threads so badly, the faucet wouldn't go back together at all and Arvo had to come over and help me replace it.

"Some days Grama seems a heck of a lot 'cooler' than others, kiddo . . . trust me!"

Silence followed that disclaimer from my daughter's end of the line. "I know it can't be easy," she said. "But I hope you also know how proud I am of you, glad that you're starting to feel safer, more confident handling the rig by yourself like that. Much as we miss you, it's good to hear you're enjoying yourself, happy with what you're doing. You deserve it!"

"I . . . thank you for that . . . "

My daughter wasn't finished. "To tell you the truth, Mom, the last couple of weeks I've even started going on-line looking for info to help you plan your trip south. I'll bring it with me Friday, so we can have fun thinking about making reservations, plotting the best routes."

My mouth felt dry, and for the life of me, I didn't know what to say. Beating a path to Florida or parts south was the last thing on my mind right now.

"Isn't it a little premature, honey? I mean it's only September—"

"Time flies, Mom. You don't want to wait until the weather gets too dicey to figure out at least where you're going to hang your hat down there."

True enough. And much as I hated to admit it, I seemed to be mastering the art of avoidance on a lot of fronts these days, including that one. With the close of the season right around the corner, I saw my options narrowing by the minute. And if not this weekend for a heart-to-heart with Danielle, then when?

With folks in our little corner of the north woods beginning to suspect the turn my relationship with Paul was taking, I had to believe that after a long weekend watching the two of us interact, my daughter wouldn't be far behind. By the time Friday came, I was a quiet basket case, slugging down the caffeine and watching the day crawl past on the office clock—worried sick about what I was or was not going to do when my daughter arrived.

Around two-thirty, I suddenly looked up to see Paul standing outside the office screen door silently watching me. Startled, I called him on it.

"No spying on the help, Boss! Bad for morale."

I could read the worry in his eyes as he joined me at the desk, stopping only long enough to grab a mug of that high-test for himself. The two of us routinely nursed the same pot the better part of a day and by mid-afternoon like this, it was strong enough to peel the paint off the side of a barn.

"Something's bothering you, Lib," he said in between cautious sips of the toxic brew. "I've sensed it all week, hoped eventually you would talk about it."

"In a word—*Danielle*."

His eyebrow arched. "She still wants you to come back to Madison."

"Actually, there's been a change in battle plan. All my small-talk about our excursions in the motor home have pretty much convinced her that it's time for me to play snowbird, head south before the rig is up to the windows in sleet, hail and other nasty stuff."

"It's only September."

"Tell that to my daughter! She's been on-line researching routes, campgrounds, even plans to bring the stuff with her this weekend. Her way of showing her support, I can't fault that . . . *but still . . .* "

Paul's frown deepened. "Ouch . . . !"

"My sentiments exactly. If I keep dodging the issue as I have been, Danielle's bound to connect the dots," I said, "figure out that the reason I'm still here has *nothing* to do with me or that motor home—"

"And everything to do with us."

I felt my heart-rate accelerating just thinking about it. "The word's already out there locally, Paul. Annie Stavros said last week that you and I seem to have become *the* hot topic of conversation down at the diner. I can't even imagine how my daughter would react if she suspected that I'm . . . "

The rest of the sentence hung there between us unspoken. "That you're . . . what, Lib . . . ?"

"That I'm . . . falling in love with you."

Silence greeted that pronouncement. It couldn't have escaped notice how tough it was finally to come out with even that conditional declaration.

"It's understandable why you've hesitated to tell your daughter," he said finally, "especially battling dropped calls over a cell phone. You're worried she's going to react like she did when you first came here or worse, like my son did when—"

I sighed, shook my head. "I can picture the whole thing already."

Paul was looking down into the depths of his mug, as if somehow there he would find a solution to the impasse. Finally he shoved it aside, made eye contact.

"They're going to be here in a couple of hours."

"You were the one who said it—that time is not on our side, Paul," I sighed. "There are so many question marks, and I've been running scared, avoiding them all. Maybe Danielle has a point. We're shutting down the water and other utilities at Northern Lights by the end of October and after that, what the heck *am* I going to do . . .?"

"It depends on what the operative word is, Lib. Is it still *I* . . . or is it genuinely *we*."

Was this my problem or ours? On the answer to that question hung an awful lot more than just what I was going to share or not share with my daughter in the next 72 hours.

"For the record, if it were up to me," he said quietly, "I think it's time to let anyone in a hundred-mile radius—Arvo, Annie, and yes, your kids—know flat-out that whatever the future holds for me, you are part of it. And figuring out how to make that work before Northern Lights closes for the season is more important than running this campground, filling Activities Boards, deciding where or how we choose to live, any of it . . . "

He broke off, giving his blunt declaration time to sink in. "If the love is there, everything else is only logistics. Nuts and bolts. We're both good at that. I think you're telling me, finally, that you're ready to talk about it—and if that's true, we'll make the time, sweetheart. Trust me, we'll make the time."

My throat felt tight and I had that scratchy feeling behind my eyes that signaled a crying jag in the making.

"Right now, Paul, I'd just settle for a hug."

I didn't wait for him to come to me. Setting down my coffee mug, I met him halfway, slipped into his arms without a thought for anything but the need to know he was there.

"Better?" he said after a while.

"Lots."

"Lib, I can't tell you what to say or not to say to your family," he sighed. "Fortunately or unfortunately, depending on how you look at it, you've got a long weekend ahead of you. Whatever you decide to do, I'll support you. You know that."

Unfortunate timing, all of it. As we stood there holding each other, I thought I heard the screen door open. My back was to the door, but from the way Paul stiffened, I sensed immediately that he heard it, too.

We were no longer alone. In the first flush of embarrassment, I assumed it had to be Arvo. Three words from Paul were all it took for me to realize just how off the mark I was.

"Danielle," he said, " you're *early*."

I didn't have to see her face—the tension in Paul's voice spoke volumes. Thank heavens he was still holding me or I think I would have sunk through the floor.

"*I see* that!" she said.

By now I had managed to shift enough so that we could make eye contact. As I watched, the shock and disbelief imprinted on her features were quickly giving way to something far more ominous.

"You made it, honey . . . good, great," I stammered, "it's wonderful to see you . . .!"

"I suppose you expect me to say the same—?"

At that I quickly closed the distance between us and gave her what had to be one of the most awkward, painful hugs of my adult life. My daughter stood unresponsive in my arms, all but thrusting me from

179

her in her haste to sever the contact.

"I see you two have been . . . *busy!*"

My insides were churning at the undisguised hostility in her voice, as calculated and forceful as if she had slapped me. Paul just stood there, his jaw set and his hands clenched at his sides. His face was terrible.

"Danielle, honey—"

She cut me off. "And when do you think you were going to get around to telling me, Mom? We call back and forth on a regular basis . . . and not a word. Not a . . . damn word!"

"Honey, I can understand you're—"

"What, Mom? Shocked. Confused. Madder than hell. Disgusted. Take your pick, because—"

"That's *enough*," Paul said quietly.

Danielle just looked at him, her eyes crackling with anger. "I don't . . . believe. . .this . . . !"

"Whether you believe it or not," he said, "just before you walked in that door, all morally outraged, your mother was standing here tearing herself to pieces because she loves you. She loves you so much that she was, probably still is, fully prepared to throw away her own life and happiness with both hands rather than lose—"

"My respect?" Danielle laughed, her contempt for the both of us all too apparent. "Too late to worry about that one, I'm afraid."

"I was going to say, your *love*," he said softly. "Although, frankly, I'm not seeing a heck of a lot of evidence of that right now."

My daughter's face turned a fiery red. "*You . . . you, of all people,* have . . . *absolutely* no right—"

"Dani, stop it! Stop right there, before you say one more word."

My daughter's face swam in and out of focus. She really hadn't answered to that nickname in years. It was the one Dan, her father, had conferred on her as a little girl.

Although I was shaking like a leaf, my voice was suddenly strong and sure. "I can live with whatever you think of me, if I have to. What

I cannot and will not tolerate is you taking that out on Paul Lauden. He's been nothing but kind, patient . . . unbelievably supportive of me, while I've vacillated and fought the obvious until I just couldn't any longer."

"Which is . . . ?"

"I think I love him, Danielle. And if you can't find the compassion, the simple humanity to at least . . . try to understand that—"

"Then . . . *what*, Mother?"

"You would break my heart."

I could tell instantly that was not what my daughter was expecting. Not at all.

"But, honey, as far as my feelings for Paul Lauden are concerned," I told her softly, "it wouldn't change one single solitary thing . . . !"

For better or worse, Paul had taken that at his cue to move alongside me, with his arm wound around my trembling shoulders. It was so quiet in that office, I could hear the rise and fall of my daughter's breathing as she processed what I told her.

"Mom, how . . . could . . . you?" she whispered. "Daddy would never have . . . he never, ever . . . "

Her face started to crumple but before I could react, she pulled herself erect and bolted out of that office as if escaping a raging inferno. She never once looked back.

I couldn't say a word, couldn't move. Every nerve ending was on high alert, as if I half expected any second to hear the sound of my son-in-law's van tearing up the gravel drive toward the highway. But except for the vicious slamming of a car door, only a deathly calm prevailed out there.

The seconds passed, then minutes. I don't remember asking, *what next*. But I must have.

"Sweetheart, we're going to walk out of that door together," Paul said slowly. "And if your family is still out there, which I've got to hope and trust they are, we're going to greet your son-in-law and those grandkids, business as usual, like we're both thrilled to see them. You're going to give them the map marked with their campsite, then stand back . . . and pray!"

Paul knew by now how I worked. On autopilot, I retrieved my family's site information materials from where I had stashed them in the camper registration book.

"Good," he smiled as he gently took them from my hand.

"I'm not sure I can do this," I said softly.

"I'll be there."

"You . . . she was . . . horrible to you, Paul."

I saw a grim smile play at the corner of his mouth. "Understandable, totally, under the circumstances."

It was one of the longest walks of my life, through that office door out into the afternoon sunshine. Something was ending here. Either way, if we survived this, my relationship with my daughter would never be the same again.

Just outside the door, Paul stopped and made eye contact. "Your hand," he said gently.

I felt his close around mine, warm and sure—knowing from one minute to the next we had become a couple, matter-of-fact and public about it. Circumstances, it seems, had made all my agonizing and what-iffing moot. There was no longer any point in pretending anything else.

But then Paul's intuition hadn't failed us, either. The van was still there, nosed against the concrete slab with my son-in-law Chris behind the wheel.

At our approach, I could see my son-in-law fumbling with the button that lowered the glass for the side window, finally turning the ignition key to activate the mechanism. At least I had to hope that was his intent. It wasn't until I saw the window lower that I allowed myself to breathe a tentative sigh of relief.

"Chris," I said, "I see you're using the neighbor's camper again. It's really great to see you—you remember Paul, I'm sure . . . "

"Lauden, right?" Chris said.

Paul nodded. "Welcome back to Northern Lights."

In the back seat, Louisa and Peter's faces—solemn and wide-eyed—had the look of children suddenly thrust into an adult situation with no clue how to react. They obviously had gotten an earful.

"Hi, guys!" I waved in their direction. "You set for a fun weekend?"

Paul meanwhile was casually extending the map in my son-in-law's direction. "Campsite twenty-four," he said. "Lib's got it marked. We're heavily booked this weekend, but she set aside this spot the minute she heard you were coming. Lots of trees and fairly level. Should be no problem getting the pop-up in there. If you like, I could even walk you over there . . ."

"Thanks," Chris said. "We should be able to find it."

"So then, why don't we just let the bunch of you get settled," I offered. "Paul and I will come over later with a bottle of wine."

"Give us an hour or so," my son-in-law told me. "With any kind of luck we should have figured out this crazy setup by then."

"Great, honey. We'll look forward to it."

Paul and I stood there together on the porch, holding hands, watching while my son-in-law put the van in gear and cautiously set off for the access road I had traced on the campground map. Through all of this, Danielle was staring straight ahead out the windshield on the passenger side as if we weren't even there.

"They aren't leaving," I breathed. Not for now, anyway.

"Give your daughter time to cool off, Lib. Your son-in-law isn't going anywhere. Good for him!"

Paul frowned, glanced down at his watch. "Three o'clock. I'd say give them until five and we'll wander over there."

When Arvo came in to the office to tell us he was calling it quits for the night, he found us together at the registration counter. At the sight of Paul's arm around my shoulder as we double-checked the site availability, he just shot a knowing wink in our direction.

"Have a good night, kids!" he chuckled.

Little did he know.

Sixteen

I was getting used to the reassuring feel of my hand in Paul's, the way our strides subtly adjusted themselves as we strolled over to my family's campsite that evening. A last-minute influx of new campers had delayed our arrival by a good half hour. Also good, I decided. Even from a distance, we could see that Chris had mastered the cranky pop-up. From the signs of movement inside the canvas, my grandkids were having a great time bouncing on the beds.

As for my daughter, body language pretty much said it all. She and her husband had taken up vigil on camp chairs at opposite extremes of the clearing around their fire pit, watching the flames eating away at the wood Paul had stacked there earlier for them.

It seems Danielle and my son-in-law had quarreled. I could guess the cause.

"Hi, guys!" Chris said, getting up from his camp chair to come to greet us. "We've been expecting you . . . but then we saw that string of rigs pulling in—"

"Slammed," Paul laughed, shook his head. "We hoped you'd figure it out. We got here as quick as we could."

Danielle was staring at him, as if *never* would have been just fine with her. Forcing a smile, I settled into a canvas chair set up next to her.

She didn't even look at me.

"Nice fire," I said. "Paul brought the wood over, hoping you would use it. We've got some chardonnay and local maple cheese for munching, marshmallows for the kids from the camp store."

"Thoughtful, we appreciate it!" Chris frowned. "Glasses, though—a problem. Will plastic tumblers do? The pop-up has a kitchen of sorts, but we're stretching the resources here."

"Anything's fine," I told him. "After that last minute stampede of new campers, it feels good just to sit and enjoy."

"So, Paul, you're from this area?" my son-in-law said as he made the rounds filling our glasses. Mine had the cartoon of a penguin on it.

"Detroit," Paul said. "I worked in radio for most of my career. After my wife died I sold my share in the business and moved up here."

"Quite a change, I should imagine."

Paul laughed. "Not for the faint of heart, that's for sure! Radio can be pretty stressful, especially live on-air programming. But between leaking water systems, power outages, gas prices and unreliable weather forecasts, I sometimes think this tourism business is worse."

"I can imagine," my daughter said pointedly, "you never know *who* is going to show up on your doorstep!"

It was a thinly veiled slam, but at least she wasn't just sitting there in stony silence. The scowl her husband shot in her direction summed up his take on things.

Paul chuckled softly to himself, shook his head. "I will say, your mom sure threw us for a loop that day she turned up here," he said, as nonplussed as if he were recapping the pre-season football standings. "It was the first and last time anybody arrived without a rig and toting a pile of suitcases. I almost chased her off the grounds—not exactly an auspicious beginning."

"It's never too late," Danielle muttered. "I understand she's a whiz bang driving the motor home these days."

"I'd close the place first, barricade the exit," he said evenly.

185

"Lib's been a breath of fresh air, the luckiest thing that's happened to this place . . . and me, in a long time."

I had been holding a zip-seal bag with cheese and another with tiny rice crackers. As my son-in-law finished pouring the wine, I reached out and offered the improvised hors d'oeuvres to my daughter. Pitiful, as peace offerings go, but something.

"Do you have a plate or something for these, honey?" I said.

My heart bled for her as I caught sight of the tears welling up in her eyes, her desperate struggle to regain her composure. Even seated across the campfire from each other, I could read the love, the compassion in Paul's eyes.

"I'll scare up something," Danielle mumbled as she took the munchies and headed for the camper. "The kids are going bonkers anyway . . . it's time I shooed them out of there."

Subdued, unusually shy, Louisa and Peter joined us at the camp fire, though it took considerably longer for their mother to do the same. I had to take the initiative and coax the kids to share a hug, then offer a simple, hello, to Paul. They greeted his offer of marshmallows with solemn expressions of thanks and then wandered off with their dad to scare up fresh sticks on which to toast them.

That left the three of us—Paul, my daughter and I—sipping at our wine and staring into the fire. Awkward, to say the least.

Danielle broke the silence. "Mom says you live here all winter?"

"Last winter, anyway. I have an apartment in the back of the office," Paul nodded, "small but adequate. And it makes it easier to run the place, living on site. Arvo moves into town after the season is over. The quiet out here can be nice."

My daughter didn't look convinced. "I can't imagine it's particularly hospitable, with what . . . sixty inches of snow a season, winds howling off Lake Michigan. Even getting out of that campground entrance has got to be a major deal."

It was so obvious a change in tack, that I found myself stifling a smile. Why live in an icebox when Florida awaits!

186

"I use the camp grocery shelves to store supplies for months at a time. Plus, it's amazing what a pair of cross-country skis can accomplish by way of mobility," Paul told her. "Still, the previous owner made a point of heading down to Florida or points south in the worst of the weather. I've been considering it, once I'm sure the place is ship-shape enough to leave it unattended."

I tried not to look surprised. In fact, although I had shared my intentions to migrate south early-on in my stay at Northern Lights, I had never heard Paul discuss his own seasonal plans.

From the distance, we could hear the children's high-pitched chatter. Headed our way with their dad, they were toting an impressive collection of sticks for the marshmallows. I had to smile. It looked like they had found enough for half the neighboring campsites as well.

My daughter's face froze in an anxious frown. "Chris is expecting me to apologize," she said stiffly, "to you *both*, which is what I'm doing. When we were dating, his parents treated me like . . . trailer trash and I vowed never to be that way to—"

"To your *kids*?" I finished for her softly.

"It never occurred to me it might be my *mother* calling my bluff!"

I could sense how desperately hard this was for her. About as tough as it was for me not to intervene, just to let her finish what she had to say.

"I . . . I would chalk my behavior up to how rough it's been to handle Daddy's death. But that's really no excuse—"

"I can't fault you for being upset, honey." I hesitated, but it had to be said. "I wasn't honest about what's happening in my life—and I regret that. When the kids are in bed, let's go over to my camper for a while, leave the guys to mind the store . . . talk."

Danielle forced a smile. "Yes. Good. I'd like that."

"For the record, Dani, I love you."

It was a precarious truce, but a beginning anyway. As Louisa and Peter proudly recounted their foraging skills, I caught Paul's eye. There was hope.

By now he had retrieved his all-in-one fix-it tool from its leather case and was giving Peter and Louisa a crash course in how to make fire sticks. I was relieved to see them move in close, peppering him with questions. Paul was making an art-form of stripping the smaller stems and leaves from a promising branch and then using the jackknife blade to whittle a point at the end.

"Scouting 101, kids," he said. "Leave sharp objects to the adults."

My grandson laughed. "That's what my dad says."

"Smart man, your dad!" Paul winked.

About a lot of things, I found myself thinking. I was absolutely convinced that were it not for Chris, we wouldn't even be having this precious time together. Remind me, I told myself, to find a way to thank him, big time.

The marshmallow roasting progressed quickly to contests to see who could get the most gooey centers without turning the outsides into charcoal briquets. Paul tried, then quickly abandoned a flick-the-wrist technique to extinguish the occasional rush of blue flame after the entire marshmallow went sailing in a flaming arc into the woods.

"Not recommended," he grumbled, "unless I want to spend the off-season hosing down the undergrowth to get rid of the mess."

Peter and Louisa were laughing hysterically at how chagrined he looked. My daughter was taking it all in, I noticed. Even as darkness closed in around us, I could sense her visibly beginning to relax a little.

Whatever her reservations about Paul and my relationship, Danielle was amassing plenty of evidence that he cared about me enough to relate to my family. And they were seeing up front what I had, an interested and interesting man struggling to build a new life for himself as surely as I was. Right now, as common denominators go, that was a lot.

"Aw, Dad, do we hafta?" Louisa led the chorus of protests as Danielle put the brakes on the sugar consumption with the announcement that it was time for bed.

Chris was subtle about it, but I noticed he shot a reassuring glance in my daughter's direction. "Absolutely. But if the two of you get in your PJ's and crawl in your sleeping bags, I'll wander over and tuck you in."

Without being coaxed, the two of them came over and gave me shy little hugs. Then with long faces and a lot of looking back over their shoulders toward the campfire, Peter and Louisa set off.

"Typical," Chris chuckled. "We polish off the marshmallows just in time for the coals to hit their prime."

A small pile of logs was still lying alongside the grate. As I watched, Paul got up, stretched the kinks out of his back and knelt down to add some reinforcements to the embers in the fire pit.

"One log a fire never makes," he muttered as he expertly revived the blaze. For tinder he broke up some of the unused branches the kids had gathered.

"Can't complain about the service around here," Chris said, "when the campground owner takes it upon himself to make sure the fire pits are stoked."

Paul grinned. "On the house," he said. "It's going to get chilly quick now that the sun's gone. Lib's got that effective little furnace over in the motor home, but out here and in your pop-up, this is it!"

It may not have been a hint, but I took it. "How about we wander over to the motor home, Danielle, and brew up some espressos. I even think I have some biscotti squirreled away over there."

Together the two of us wandered along the access road to my RV pad. Once alone in the motor home, an awkward silence reigned as I began to haul out coffee tins and the espresso pot. Perched stiffly on the bench seat of the dinette, Danielle stared out the window into the darkness.

"I've been out of line," my daughter said after a while. "Chris tells me all the time to lighten up, to stop micro-managing everybody and everything. Two years ago it almost came to. . .blows. . ."

I straightened from the task at hand. "Blows, as in—?"

"Metaphoric, of course," Danielle hastily explained. "But Chris actually moved out for a week—stayed with friends somewhere. The kids were distraught. We've been talking and I've been trying . . . really trying . . ."

"Honey, nobody's perfect. Not even close."

She stared down at her hands, toying with the placemat fringe on the table in front of her. "I find myself . . . lip-synching to that voice in my head—vintage Dad. *Don't bother with that, Lib, I'll do it. Sweetheart, you're going to wrench your back trying to lift that . . . let me. . .*"

"I never minded," I told her quickly. "Your dad was gone so much, it was kind of . . . *nice* to let him take charge, see that he felt needed."

"Well, I just assumed that was the way it was supposed to be and that Dad was *the guy*, the one responsible. Plus, I was the oldest—poor David still complains about how bossy I was."

I chuckled softly, shook my head. "He idolized you, for all that, honey. When the other kids were taunting him, there was Big Sister out on the porch, threatening them with murder and mayhem."

"Scary."

"And your way of loving. He understood that."

"Most of the time," she sighed. "Yeah. But I can tell you, my husband was getting pretty darn sick of it. I'm really, truly sorry to have thrown such a hissy fit in front of the kids. When I came storming out of the campground office like that, they just sat there in the back seat like pillars of salt—"

"Kids don't demand perfection of us, just honesty. You were upset, you stayed. We're working things out as a family."

Danielle turned on the bench and met my gaze. "I wonder if you understand how really, really hard it is to see you . . . relating to somebody besides Daddy," she said softly. "I'm not sure I'll ever . . . totally get used to that."

"If it's any consolation," I made myself say it, "neither am I."

"Paul is . . . I have to admit he seems really . . . nice. And good to you, that's the main thing."

I didn't tell her how much her own prodding and poking had contributed to raising my awareness of Paul Lauden as a man, not just a boss or colleague. She already was feeling guilty and confused enough as it was.

"I would understand if you thought all this was too much and way too soon," I told her. "Believe me, I've strolled that particular avenue on almost a daily basis."

"Is there *ever* a right time?" she sighed. "You'll remember, Chris' parents thought we were way too young, 'unsuitable' seemed to be their favorite word—made no bones about telling us to our faces. If you decide to stay up here over the winter, I'll try not to cluck or fuss. Just promise you'll drive down once in a while and thaw out."

I laughed. "I just heard on the radio last week that thanks to global warming, we're now a climate zone warmer up here, a dubious consolation, but there it is."

"One less thing to worry about, you mean," my daughter grimaced. "I guess I'm at it again, a royal pain . . . "

"I'll live," I said. "Besides, it's kind of fun to live long enough to see the tables turn . . . to start to scare the heck out of your kids, now and again."

We hugged each other, laughing, holding the moment as much as each other before we headed out to the campfire carrying our goodies. God bless her, Danielle made a point of shining the flashlight ahead of my feet, so I wouldn't trip. In the process, at one point she almost landed head-over-teakettle herself.

Mid-Sunday afternoon my daughter and her family packed up, headed home. Sad as I was to see them go, I breathed a sigh of relief—what easily could have been a disaster had viscerally deepened the relationship between not only Danielle and me, but Paul and my family as well.

"Hate to punk out on you," he said as he stood alongside me on the office porch, waving until they were out of sight. "But Arvo left a message on my cell about problems with one of the circuit breakers. I'd better check it out."

"No problem," I said. "I was just planning on vegging, heating up something and turning in early. It's been a long weekend."

"But a good one."

"Yes. Thanks to you and Chris."

Paul smiled. "You and your daughter are going to be fine, Lib. I hope you believe that."

I nodded. "I couldn't believe she actually got out, ran over and hugged me one last time before they left."

His relief was apparent. "I noticed that," he said. "Good for her . . . and you."

"Anyway," I stifled a yawn, "duty calls and you look dead on your feet."

Paul laughed. "Not the only one apparently," he said, "but first things first."

With a smile, he coaxed me into his arms. His mouth was warm and insistent, prolonging the moment. And then he was striding across the lawn toward Arvo's Airstream.

Still shaken from the roller-coaster ride of the long weekend, I decided to bail on dinner entirely and instead settled down with that novel I had been nursing. Around nine I heard a faint tapping on the door, went to open it.

"Saw the light was still on," Paul said. "Thought maybe you'd be up for a nightcap."

In his hand was a half-empty bottle of Chardonnay. My merlot supply had turned out to be less than a half glass.

"Tempting," I said.

"I know you prefer the reds."

"Any port in a storm, when it comes to vino. But then the company is definitely a step-up from listening to that leaking faucet and the same dozen tunes on autoplay."

He laughed. "Glasses?"

"Real crystal, no less, in the cupboard over the stove. I can't bring myself to settle for plastic. Just a tad too close to Thunderbird out of a Mason jar."

As we sat on the sofa together, snuggling and munching on raw veggie chunks left over from my family's visit, I told him about my conversation with Danielle, her struggles to give me the independence I needed, much as I had once done for her.

"Funny, how hard it is to adjust to new normals," I said, "like who is doing the mothering at any given moment. At least my daughter and I can laugh about it now."

"Danielle wants the best for you. It's hard to fault her for that, Lib."

Hard, too, to keep skirting questions of just what that "best" might be. I shivered.

"You're cold." Paul made eye contact and his hand closed around mine. "Want me to get some heat going?"

"Stay put, I should check the vent—the furnace hasn't been on in a while."

The bracing air felt good against my flushed cheeks as I stepped outside to make sure creatures hadn't been nesting where they shouldn't have. That done, I set the dial on the thermostat and felt the immediate rush of air as the furnace came to life.

Paul was on his feet, waiting for me to finish. "You remembered the drill—well done," he said.

I forced a smile. "Nothing to it. Chalk it up to your Survival 101 Road Tips for the Technically Challenged. I can't keep bugging you on the cell phone, from goodness knows where, every time there's a shift in the wind direction."

A frown flickered between his brows and he just looked at me, hard, without comment. "We're back to that," he said finally. "Trust me, Lib, I'd be hot on your trail in the SUV before you even hit the end of the campground driveway in that rig!"

"Then just what . . . *do* you propose I do? My daughter had a point—we're going to be up to our ears in white stuff soon enough."

"You stay. We move in together, figure things out together as we go along."

I was trembling harder now, only this time not from the cold. Small comfort that he didn't use the M-word or I think I would have lost it entirely.

"Live with you . . . just like that?"

"This *is* the new millennium. Plus, I do have heat over there, if that's what you're wondering."

"And that is going to solve exactly what . . .?"

By way of answer, Paul gently pulled me into his arms and with a groan of unspoken passion and longing, buried his face against my hair. "Lib, there is no way on this *earth* I am going to let you go," he whispered, his hands moving against the small of my back, fitting my body to his.

After all the tension of the weekend, finding ourselves outed so unceremoniously and everything that came after, we had moved light years beyond pretending we weren't both fantasizing about more than just chaste kisses behind the woodshed. Two yards, maybe less, covered a lot of ground in a motor home—in more ways than one.

Without knowing or caring who was initiating it, I found myself lying in Paul's arms on top of the quilted sleeping-bag coverlet on my bed. I was aware of one thing and one thing only, the overpowering need to be touched and held, to love and be loved.

Heart thudding, I felt his mouth tease its way along the column of my throat. His fingertips began tugging at the buttons to my camp shirt. My body was straining to meet his touch, my gasp of pleasure was meant as an invitation. The impact was anything but what I intended.

For a split-second, Paul inexplicably froze. Then on a shuddering

194

sigh, without warning or explanation, he abruptly half turned on to his back so that we were no longer in contact. Confused and disoriented, I just lay there while he stared silently up at the ceiling. After what seemed like a long time, the ragged cadence of his breathing and my own finally began to steady again.

"We can't do this," he said softly. "Not like this, Lib—knowing where we are and in whose bed. *Guaranteed* you'll be regretting this in the morning . . ."

The sharp twisting in my gut was a brutal reality check. This had been Dan's bed as well as my own, *ours as a couple.* And while my body seemed willing enough to ignore that, my heart and head were telling me Paul was right.

"Suggestions welcome," he said as a muscle twitched along the edge of his jaw. "I suppose there's always a brisk dip in that lake across the road . . ."

"It's going to get down in the thirties tonight," my teeth were chattering at the mere thought of that icy water. "I'll gladly settle for making like two spoons in a drawer, or heaven forbid, resorting to a bundling board. Even my daughter would be hard pressed to object to that one—here or over at your place, though the thought of moving a single inch is frankly gosh awful . . ."

At that almost incoherent outburst, I felt as much as heard the rumble of laughter deep in his chest. "Lib, honey, have you ever got yourself a *date!*"

The rightness, the reasonableness of it all won out. We stayed put, laughing as we awkwardly shed jeans and our work boots. Then nestling together under my thick down comforter, still clad in our skivvies and work shirts, we cuddled and talked about nothing and everything—from the pros and cons of wintering in the U.P. to hooking the SUV to the back of my rig and heading south or west or both.

It was tentative and all over the map as what-iffing went, but enough to both reassure and terrify, in about equal proportions. Long after I sensed Paul had drifted off to sleep, I stared eyes wide open into the blackness, every nerve ending on high alert.

From the extended murmuring and faint bursts of laughter outside, I guessed that the guests in the camper near us were still outside enjoying their fire-pit. But then eventually, I too must have slept because I awakened to sporadic bird calls outside the motor home window and Paul's arm still cradling me against him.

"You're awake," he said softly.

I stifled a yawn. "Barely. And only temporarily, I hope."

It was still dark in the motor home, but as he shifted alongside me, half sat up in bed, I could have sworn that Paul was watching me intently. When I turned in his direction, I saw only the shadowy planes of face backlit by the pale glow from the nightlight radiating from under the bathroom door.

"You said I'd regret it in the morning," I said softly. "Well, it's morning. Almost anyway—"

"And . . .?"

I didn't give myself time to think about it. By way of answer, I reached up and steadied my hand against the strong ridge of his cheekbone.

It was subtle as declarations went, but enough. His astonished intake of breath told me without a word that the time for hesitation had come and gone. I felt his warm breath against my face as slowly he lowered his head, kissed me. This time there were no second thoughts from either one of us.

There would be other nights and days when we would revel in the luxury of sight as well as feeling and touch. But this once I gave thanks for the forgiving power of half-darkness.

Here in this space and time, age and the impact of the years ceased to matter. We were simply a man and a woman, two lovers finding each other in the cold night, with only the love between us as our guide.

Seventeen

Dawn broke on the birches around my campsite blazing away in burnished gold, their true and joyous colors masked all those long months beneath their dark summer green. Snuggled in Paul Lauden's arms, still half-groggy from sleep, I knew how they felt.

Love had led me on an unforeseen and lonely journey to this place in my life—my turning season. There was no going back, only ahead.

We are more than the sum of our years. Still, whatever Paul Lauden was seeing as he looked at me, I knew it was not the girl who had once stood, hands trembling, as her equally young husband-to-be slipped a plain gold band on her finger. For my Dan all those decades, it was partly that girl at the altar he was remembering every time we touched one another. I had sensed it in his smile, the capacity to look beyond the laugh lines impossible to conceal even with the most careful of makeup, the legacy of extra pounds after two pregnancies and muscles that would never quite tone the same again for all my hard work.

Life and death had changed all that. Sadly, that girl in the gossamer veil and seed-pearl embroidered satin was gone forever. And no one would ever know me or see me quite that way again—not even Paul Lauden.

"You've been lying there," he said, "wide awake, wondering what the heck you've gotten yourself into. I've been waiting for you to ask. . ."

There was no easy way to confront it, but I took a deep breath and did, straight out. "You're an attractive man," I said. "At our age, women outnumber men umpteen to one. Sometimes I look in the mirror in that closet of a bathroom of mine and wonder who on earth that woman is I see staring back at me."

I shifted in his arms so that we could make eye contact. For what seemed like a long time, Paul thoughtfully studied my upturned face.

"None of which changes what goes on in our hearts or heads, Lib. You're one of the most beautiful women I've ever—"

"Meaning, we're only as *old* as we think, or feel. . ."

I stopped short of cataloging the state of my crow's feet. A smile tugged at the corners of Paul's mouth.

"Define *old*," he said. "I only know that anybody who had the guts to get behind the wheel of that motor home in a blinding rainstorm doesn't have to apologize to anyone . . . on *any* scale that matters . . ."

"Tell that to my cellulite."

He shook his head. "Okay, Lib, if the name of the game here is comparing stats and vitals . . . I couldn't finish a 10-K any more without CPR and an oxygen tank either."

My laughter sounded forced, even to me. "Double standard," I said. "There are guys your age out there who refuse—on principle—to date anyone over forty . . ."

"Their loss."

That familiar muscle along his jaw had begun to twitch as he turned something over in his head. "By the way," he said slowly, "it's you I was making love with last night, if that *really* is what you're wondering here . . ."

Caught off guard, I just looked at him. "I wasn't . . . at least I don't think so, not in so many words. Still, I'll admit, it's good to know."

With his fingertips, Paul gently began to trace the curve of my mouth. I shivered, dropped my gaze.

"You never told me, by the way," he said finally, " how the two of you met, you and Dan."

"College. Senior year. At an honors reception. He was a magna and I was a summa. He never stopped teasing me about it. But then I didn't have to take calculus or physics either."

"Love at first sight," Paul guessed.

"Not exactly, but close. We spent that next summer together working out on Mackinac Island before we settled into our careers. He thought I had this 'thing' for a political science major from Buffalo raking in humongous tips at the Grand Hotel. I disabused Dan—and the guy from Buffalo—of that quickly enough."

Paul chuckled softly, shook his head. "My Ginny was pinned to an Alpha-dog law school grad with every expectation of a seven-figure future when we met. Three months later we were engaged."

"Hopeless romantics," I found myself thinking out loud, not the only common ground between us. "Mercifully it never occurs to us at the time, how hard it might be to reconcile that instinct to grab at love with two hands and what comes after—when reality hits, how precious and short a lifetime can be."

Paul's face was a study in emotions too complex to pigeonhole. "And yet, in spite of all of that," he said slowly, "maybe even because of all that. . . *history*, realizing how it ends, you have to know, have to believe that I love you, Lib."

There wasn't a question in his voice as he said it. But the man deserved to know what I felt, even if I wasn't at all sure I could begin to pretend to tell him. "Paul, I . . ."

That split-second hesitation was all it took—the words froze in my throat. Outside, close from the sound of it, a vehicle door slammed, then voices. Our neighbors were stirring. With a sigh of frustration, Paul quickly glanced down at his watch. Last night I had left my own on the shelf above our heads.

"What is it . . .is there something—?"

"Busted," he chuckled softly. "Right now we're officially a half-hour late for work. Unless I miss my guess, not just Arvo but by now your hyperactive neighbors two sites down are bound to take notice."

"You're kidding!" I shot up in bed alongside him, fumbling for my watch in total disbelief. "I haven't slept in that long since that first wild night I showed up at Northern Lights."

Paul was right. My watch read nine-thirty and ticking.

"Well, one good thing," I told him, "at least there's no more point in skulking around. I guess we've got Danielle to thank for that. First dibs on the bathroom . . .!"

Paul had slept on the side nearest the door. With a muffled groan of protest, he slid out of bed and began to climb awkwardly back into yesterday's jeans and polo shirt. "Take your time," he said. "I'll head home, shower and change—get things cooking over at the office. Our sidekick's going to be wanting his marching orders."

"Great . . . you realize we'll never hear the end of this . . .!"

Paul stopped, hand on the motor home door, and looked back at me, still sitting there tousle-haired amid the bedding. "I certainly hope not," he said quietly, didn't even crack a smile.

For the next three precious days, I found myself burning the candle on two ends with an elan that I hadn't felt in decades. Paul Lauden and I loved each other. My bed was no longer empty and my heart was making its peace with everything that meant.

Days, we were working our tails off. My daughter and her family, it seems, had caught the last balmy weekend. Forecast was for night temperatures to hover around the freezing mark or lower for the rest of the week—a wake-up call that our opportunity for major projects this season had finite limits. Paul and Arvo decided to concentrate all their energies on the precarious job of creating a solid footing for the boardwalk out at the bog.

"If we're going to get that nature walk up and going next season, it's now or never," Paul said.

With some misgivings, I had to agree. The work turned out to be even more brutal than I had feared.

After three twelve-hour days in a row, the two men were perpetually exhausted, going on reserves. Their work clothes were so muddy that Arvo made a run to the laundromat in Centerline instead of trusting them to the stackable washer-dryer in the bathroom of Paul's apartment.

"And you accuse me of being obsessive compulsive," I scowled as the two of them headed out yet again late afternoon on Friday. "You're killing yourselves out there."

"We're gainin' on her, Lib-girl," Arvo chuckled. "Like a mud pit, not fit for man or beast, but we're gainin' on it."

"See you for dinner?" Paul had popped back through the office door one last time to check. "My place for a change. Steaks . . . if you promise not to mess up my carpets with those boots of yours. And yes, we *will* take tomorrow off . . .!"

I kept replaying in my head the sound of his laughter as I checked inventory lists for the camp store. Much nicer, I decided, than all those rows of numbers, totals and subtotals I was crunching hunched over the computer.

My back finally signaled loud and clear that I had been sitting too long. I had just struggled to my feet, taking a break while I cleaned up the registration counter, when I heard muffled shouting outside.

Seconds later, Arvo flung open the office door—red-faced and out of breath from running, He leaned on the door frame for support, barking out instructions in that raspy voice of his.

"911. *NOW* . . .!"

I didn't ask for explanations. Hands shaking, I punched the numbers on the phone keypad, heard a woman's voice come on the line and identify herself.

"Northern Lights," I said, "that campground on Route 2. We've been . . . it's a—"

"Tractor roll-over," Arvo gasped.

My heart stopped. *Dear God . . . Paul.*

"Miss, I can't hear you," the operator said. "Are you at the campground now . . .?"

My knees didn't seem to want to support me. With a stifled cry, I let myself down quickly on the stool alongside the counter. Trying not to panic, I began to communicate over the phone what Arvo was telling me, filling in the gaps as needed.

"Paul Lauden. It's Paul Lauden, the owner. He's pinned under a tractor . . ."

Where exactly? I pictured quickly enough where Arvo and Paul had been working, but none of that would make sense to the operator. As coherently as I could, I tried to put into words not just the geography but the logistics the first responders would encounter. Among other things, I warned the woman that the road to the bog was more of a path, muddy and almost impossible to navigate with heavy equipment.

"Please," I finished, "dear God, *hurry* . . .!"

The operator quickly confirmed the directions, then recited a short list of things we should be doing on our end until the EMTs showed up. Don't try to move anything or allow him to move. Use blankets horse-shoe fashion to stabilize his neck and spine if possible. Keep him warm, alert and awake.

I clicked off the phone, shot to my feet. Arvo stood just inside the door as if turned to stone.

"Please . . . go and wait by the road for the EMT's," I told him. "I've got to hurry. Paul's all alone out there . . ."

Arvo nodded, his face grim. "I'da never left him but Boss's cell went into that muck with him. Ma'am, I'll warn ya," his voice was raw, pulling no punches, "he's hurtin' bad and gettin' him out of there . . . it's gonna be real *rough* . . .!"

No time for tears. Paul needed me calm, level-headed, no matter what I felt or what I found. Blankets, the operator said. On the run now, I traversed the half-empty aisles of groceries toward Paul's apartment. The door was unlocked. I yanked the throw off his sofa bed then the blanket and sheets I found underneath, tucked everything awkwardly under my arm.

Hurry, I kept telling myself. With night temperatures in the low thirties all week, the ground and water would be bone-chilling. As I flung open the office door, I saw Arvo in the distance, loping toward the highway.

The footfalls of my boots were muffled on the chipped bark path as I sprinted toward the bog and my breath trailed out ahead of me. From a distance through the trees, I caught sight of the beast of a vehicle, lying on its side with its enormous wheels almost parallel to the ground. From the odd angle it appeared something must have broken the tractor's descent, cushioned the impact. Small hope, but hope nonetheless.

"Paul," I called out, my voice breaking. "I can't . . . where are you? Talk to me, sweetheart!"

My voice echoed back at me from the water of the pond. Frantic for any signs of life, I raced around the back of the upturned vehicle.

"Lib . . ."

The stifled moan was coming from under the tractor. *He was alive.* My heart sank as I saw him, half turned on his side with his left arm and upper body free, his legs and lower torso pinned in place with the large wheel of the tractor towering above him like a demonic mushroom. What I could see of his face was ashen, jaw clenched tight from the pain.

"Dear God," I found the words shaping themselves in my head, "not now. Don't let him die like this, here in this awful place."

The only answer was the sighing of the wind in the tamaracks overhead and the terrible, labored sound of Paul's breathing. His right arm seemed pinned under his body, but with his left forearm he was trying to hold himself out of the water, his hand clutching for something solid. It must have felt like he was drowning in all that ooze.

"Sweetheart, don't try to move," I whispered as I sank down alongside him in the mud. "I'm here . . . talk to me."

"Stupid, huh?" he groaned, jaw clenched, as he strained to make eye contact. "So . . . damn. . . fast . . ."

"Don't, Paul—stay still, don't try to pull yourself out of there. I'm going to have to take a chance and ease this blanket under your head, try to keep your face out of that water."

The wad of bedding wasn't much help, but at least he didn't seem to be working so hard any longer at staying above the murky surface. Gently so as not to move him unnecessarily, I began to tuck the throw around him as best I could. Half-way through those efforts, Paul seized my hand, held on so tightly that I gritted my teeth to keep from crying out.

"I'm here . . . I won't leave you," I said. "And help is coming . . . it just takes time, sweetheart. They're on their way. It's going to be all right."

Outrageous as lies went, but I needed as desperately as Paul to believe it. Where was the rescue squad?

Paul started to speak, then teeth clenched, he stiffened as another wave of pain washed over him. His eyes flickered shut. I had taken basic first aid years ago, knew the symptoms, from his cutting in and out to the sweat beads glistening on his pale features. Shock. Hypothermia.

I couldn't imagine how cold he felt. Water and mud were quickly soaking through my own jeans and I had forgotten to put on a jacket over my blouse and wool sweater. With my free hand I awkwardly tried to adjust the blankets around Paul's shoulders.

"I know it's cold, sweetheart. Help is coming."

He made eye contact and I could read the desperate awareness in his face. His voice was so low I had to lean closer to make out what it was he was saying.

"All our . . . hard work . . . ," he began, through gritted teeth, then broke off as a wave of pain hit him.

The campground was the last thing on my own mind right now,

but Paul didn't have to finish. I knew. We both did. Whatever his injuries, it could take weeks, months before he was mobile again, even longer before he could be back on the job, if by then there was still a business to come back to.

"We *will* survive this. You. Me. Northern Lights. Don't you worry . . . not about the campground, not anything. Just think about getting better. Arvo and I will get help if we have to. Whatever it takes, we'll do it—"

"Only another couple of . . . feet, Lib . . .!"

It was dangerous to speculate about what might have been. He could have been free and clear, or just as easily, crushed to death under that enormous weight. Gritting his teeth, Paul shuddered and his eyes flickered, closed.

From the distance I thought I heard the wail of sirens, faint but growing louder. "They're almost here, sweetheart," I said, "just hang on . . . please, hang on . . ."

His grip on my hand tightened. I hadn't imagined it. Paul had heard it as well.

The throaty rumble of vehicles and the sound of shouts echoed through the trees. In that narrow sliver of daylight between the ground and the undercarriage of the tractor, I caught a flash of movement, two rescue workers on foot in full fireman's gear headed our way.

"Here," I shouted. "We're over here . . .!"

"Lib, you've got to get out from under there. We'll take over now," I heard a voice behind me say, "this whole rig is probably unstable."

"I won't leave him."

It was Earl Forester's face I saw under that oversize helmet and hard behind him, Bob, that pastor who had been so wonderful at the Yooper comedy night. In code, with Earl kneeling alongside me in the mud, the two men were quickly deciding which emergency equipment to deploy and how best to maneuver it down the narrow lane, then raise the tractor enough to get Paul out.

Through that terse exchange, I felt a third set of hands loosening my death-grip on Paul's hand. It was the cook at Annie's, bodily coaxing me up and out of the way, while yet another volunteer took my place under the vehicle. His arm around my shoulders, the burly volunteer continued to ease me away from the muddy pit.

Paul's voice stopped me. "Lib . . ."

"Here, Paul . . . I'm not going anywhere . . .!"

But someone had wrapped a dry blanket around my shoulders, and more insistent now, began to steer me back down the lane out of harm's way. The EMT half-dragging, half-carrying me out of there looked like a kid, probably eighteen at the most, except for his eyes.

"You could wind up with hypothermia here, Ma'am," he gasped as he tightened his grip. "It's best if we wait in the rescue vehicle."

I had the feeling he was reading it straight off a card filed somewhere in his head. "I told Paul I would be there," I breathed, "I promised."

"Ma'am, you really don't want to watch that. We have got to let them do their job."

That finally got my attention. Arvo had said as much. I couldn't guarantee how I would react when they tried to raise that monster of a vehicle enough to get Paul out. Instead, numb and helpless, I sat on the open door frame of the ambulance, staring back toward the bog while my young benefactor plied me with tepid, all but flavorless tea.

In the distance, silence was punctuated now and again by muffled commands, shouts and the roar of a chain saw, tangible signs that a rescue was in progress. On the way to the ambulance we had to pass a second tractor that had been brought in to help and as I watched, several of the volunteers cautiously began to maneuver it toward the spot where the rescue team was working. I kept remembering Paul's face, deathly pale, tried not to imagine what he was going through.

Finally I sensed a flurry of activity on the trail. Supported by other volunteers, Earl and several other rescue workers appeared, swiftly maneuvering what appeared to be a back board in our direction.

"Paul . . .!"

Straining to catch a glimpse of him through the hands and bodies at work around him, I slipped past my captor and grasped Paul's hand. Earl and several of his companions already had begun lifting the board, preparing to ease it through the open ambulance door.

I repeated his name. Even with an oxygen mask and an IV in place, Paul had spotted me, was struggling to communicate.

"No . . . wait," his voice was hoarse, insistent.

"Here . . . Paul, I'm right here."

I didn't wait to ask, simply started to climb into the ambulance alongside him. Astonishingly quick for all his heavy gear, Earl intercepted me, pulled me back on solid ground.

"Lib, they're headed for St. Ignace. . .then Petoskey once they stabilize him," Earl said. "There simply isn't enough room back there for the crew to do their job. You have got to let him go."

He wasn't giving me any choice. In the end, it was Paul's voice that got through to me.

"Call my son," he said. "Call Josh . . .!"

We both knew what that meant. "Yes—yes, I promise. Paul, I love you."

At that I saw his eyes flicker momentarily in recognition then close again. The back board secured in the ambulance, one of the EMT's slammed the doors shut behind them and the vehicle started down the lane.

In the confusion, I managed finally to wrench myself free of Earl's grasp. Tears blurring my vision, I stumbled along behind the rescue vehicle, recoiling at every jolt and thud as the driver inched around the potholes in the muddy lane. At the office parking lot, the ambulance picked up speed and the siren kicked in—a high-pitched wailing that hung in the air long after the vehicle disappeared onto the highway headed east.

It was suddenly like everything was moving in slow motion. While the first responders scattered toward their own vehicles with their gear, their pagers crackling with terse news of someone else's heartbreak, I stood rooted on the concrete slab in front of the office clutching at the wet sleeves of my mud-soaked sweater, unable to muster the will to put one foot in front of the other. Instinct was to climb into the SUV and tear out of there behind the ambulance. But there were promises to be kept, a campground to run and calls to make, at least one of which filled me with quiet dread.

Arvo hovered alongside me, stony-faced, his hands balled into fists at his side. "Ma'am, ya gotta get inside," he said. "No point freezing to death out here."

It finally dawned on me that just beyond the parking lot, campers were standing around in little clumps looking over toward the office, their fleece jackets looking all the world like garish blossoms against the dark foliage of the woods. These people were going to wonder what the heck was going on and someone needed to tell them.

"Those . . . Arvo, our guests are going to be worried, imagining all sorts of—"

"I'll take care of it," he was already halfway across the parking lot. "Just a little accident is all, folks—working out in the bog. Nothing to worry about. Everything's under control."

He stood there a while responding to their hushed questions. That accomplished, a hand clamped awkwardly on my shoulder, he half-talked and half-walked me out of the cold into the double-wide.

It was one of those awful deja vu moments as the door swung shut behind us. I found myself looking around me as if I had just gotten off Owen's Shuttle, with no clue where I was or what lay ahead of me.

"Is he . . . what if Paul . . .?"

"Boss is tough," Arvo said. "He's going to make it. Ya gotta hang on to that, Ma'am."

Yes, I did. As we stood there, muddy water was pooling from our jeans and boots on the newly waxed linoleum.

"I'm gonna get out of these wet clothes," Arvo said. "Think ya really oughta do the same."

"Later," I told him. "One of us ought to stay with the phone for a while. It's going to be a long night. No need for us both to wait here—I need to, want to do it. I'm fine, really I am."

Arvo's jaw clamped tight as he thought about it, then grumbling under breath, eventually he wandered out the door toward his Airstream. I was left sitting alone at the counter.

The computer was still running. On autopilot, I began googling every possible multiple fracture combination I could imagine involving hips and lower extremities. It quickly became a depressing journey through lives disrupted, sagas of excruciating pain, drug withdrawal and long-term physical therapy.

Emotionally drained from every worst case scenario imaginable, I wept until the tears no longer came. The room was getting dark and by now the mud on my clothing had dried stiff and hard. I shut off the computer and sat staring blankly around me.

It was nearly dark. Most of the rows of the shelves in our little grocery were half-empty now and the tourism brochure racks had the pillaged look of a retail outlet after a fire sale, despite all my efforts to keep them stocked. After seeing so much action all summer, the lending library with its ever-changing and dog-eared collection of novels looked so forlorn.

Grim and barren as the familiar space appeared, my heart told me otherwise. This was no longer just a stop-over on the way to goodness knows where, not just a space where I chose to work or a campground getting ready to close for the season. It was home.

The sense of futility was overwhelming. I wasn't going anywhere, while out there in the night somewhere, Paul Lauden was on a journey of his own, one I could not share.

I loved him, finally had the courage to admit it—flat out, no hedging or lingering doubts. Pray God, it wasn't either too little or too late for that to matter, for either one of us.

Eighteen

"Kiddo, you there?"

It took a few repetitions of the knocking for me to realize someone outside the campground office was trying to get my attention. I undid the deadbolt and opened the door.

Sonja Forester stood there like some wraith out of a Norse legend, her white hair backlit by the sensor-activated floodlights on the porch. Talking nonstop, she swept me into her arms.

"Oh, Lib, I've been listening to the scanner. . .you must be frantic. Earl's still out with the guys on another run, though I'm sure the plan would be to take Paul to Petoskey. Good folks down there, Earl says. They handle all kinds of accidents—skiing, boating, ATV's. . .you name it—and all the time. Scary how many ways folks can do themselves in around here. Paul will be in safe hands . . ."

She came up for air, frowned as she checked out my muddy clothes and total lack of a response. "Kiddo, you look absolutely . . . awful!"

I wasn't about to disagree with her. "Sonja, what am I going to do?"

"For one thing, you're going to take care of yourself, eventually get a good night's sleep if you can, because you're going to need it. Paul is going to need you with him down—"

"Impossible. There are still campers out there, it's the weekend and I promised Paul I'd look after Northern Lights. He and Arvo have been so busy pulling stumps at the bog, we haven't done the first thing about getting ready to close for the season. . ."

"We'll see about all that," Sonja said brusquely. "Right now, I'm thinking food . . . you haven't eaten a thing."

It wasn't a question. While I hovered near the phone, she insisted on organizing dinner for me, raiding the camp store and Paul's refrigerator for supplies. That done, she coaxed me into poking around at what she had made, though I tasted none of it. She was threatening to draw a steamy bath in Paul's tub and shoe me into it when the phone rang.

"Pastor Bob . . . I was on your 911 run," the caller said. "I've been doing some sleuthing and Paul's in surgery as we speak. The folks down-state were short on details—tough to get the skivvy these days if you aren't next-of-kin . . ."

"Do you . . . did they say what—?"

"Apparently the x-rays and CT scans in St. Ignace showed a femur fracture, for starters, so they sent him straight on to Petoskey. I suspect he'll be in pretty rough shape all over for a while, but they should know more by morning. Earl told me Sonja is staying with you . . . but just remember, if you need anything—"

"I'm fine, thank you . . . really," my mouth didn't seem to want to move. "But if you hear anything else, you'll call?"

"Of course . . . you can depend on it." He hesitated then added, "Folks around here are also praying for you both . . . thought it might help to know that."

It didn't. Pleading for miracles wasn't high on my agenda right now. Through the pounding in my temple, I wanted to cry out the truth—that the only thing I desperately needed to know was, *why*? That, and to vent my disbelief and anguish at having found love and joy in my life again only to see it snatched away in a heartbeat. Choking back tears, I thanked the man and hung up the phone.

I pulled myself together enough to tell Sonja where things stood with Paul, then over her objections that I would "catch my death", I pulled Paul's ski jacket from a coat-rack just inside the apartment door and made tracks for Arvo's Airstream. The lights were on and through the slat-blinds on the windows, I could see he was still up and about. Pounding on the closed coach door, I waited.

"You've heard from Paul," he said as he threw open the door.

I shook my head. "No, but there is news."

Without embellishing, I repeated what Pastor Bob had unearthed. For good measure, I shared an abridged translation of all the medical jargon I had been wading through on-line.

"Which is why I'm here," I said. "Looks like we're going to have to work out the rest of the season, then shut this place down. It could be months before anyone with those kinds of injuries can walk any distance without help, to say nothing of work again. . .not the kind of physical stuff you two do, anyway. I suspect Paul's not going to be able to winter up here alone either . . . so that brings up possible problems of security once we close . . ."

"I thought of all that," Arvo nodded and I could read the worry in his eyes, "though I don't think that man would take too kindly to us hauling him around or shouldering all of this on our own. His wife was sick a long time . . . made him pretty feisty about what he lets folks do for—"

"We can't give him a choice." My heart sank even as I said it.

Arvo wasn't telling me anything I didn't already suspect. From the rare times Paul had been under the weather in the past months, I had seen first-hand his reaction to anything that faintly smacked of coddling. Then, too, there were all my conversations with Annie Stavros about the weeks and months after her husband's accident.

"Well, better you than me, tackling that one," Arvo grimaced. "Worse comes to worse, we just barricade ourselves up here and do what's gotta be done."

212

Sonja was waiting for me on the office porch as I slowly worked my way back across the parking lot. "I assume you want to stay here overnight in Paul's apartment, close to the phone," she said.

"You don't have to babysit me, Sonja. I can—"

"We've had enough drama and heroics for one day," she said. "I won't leave until you're settled in safe and sound."

Truth was, by now I could barely put one foot in front of the other. At Sonja's insistence, I soaked briefly in the tub to warm up, then changed into one of Paul's dress shirts she had dug out for me as a nightgown. The shock of the crisp fabric against my skin triggered a gut-twisting awareness of who had last worn it—where I was and where I really wanted to be, lying in Paul's arms, not alone in his apartment, his empty bed.

"Are you okay, kiddo?" The frown lines were back between Sonja's brows. "I could stay, you know. Old Earl is perfectly capable of spending a night on his own if—"

"No need. I'm just having trouble with these . . . blasted buttons."

Ducking my head, I made a show of concentrating on the task at hand. Through the pounding in my temple, I heard Sonja rummaging around to find sheets to remake the bed I had ripped apart on the way to the bog. That accomplished, she fussed at organizing the phone, tissues and an extra blanket within easy reach on the wicker coffee table.

"Annie is going to try to get out here tomorrow," she told me on the way out the door, "after things settle down at the diner. Meantime, if you hear anything else from Bob or the hospital, give Earl and me a call so we can get the jungle telegraph going. What you don't need right now are umpteen folks calling you every few minutes for an update."

My eyes were heavy with sleep. The last thing I remembered was the sound of her fumbling with light-switches and door locks as she literally shut down the store. Morning, I told myself. I would figure out what to do in the morning.

The dreams that came were anything but benign, full of shouts and sirens and oceans of muddy water swirling around me. When I

213

finally looked at my watch, it was 4 AM—time to give it up and stop straining in vain for the sound of the phone.

Stumbling into the apartment bathroom, I cleaned myself up as best I could, then went about the business of doing the same for my mud-caked wardrobe from the day before. The dryer had just dinged when the persistent ringing of the portable office phone shocked me into action.

"Ms. Aventura . . .?"

My mouth felt packed with cotton wool. "I'm Lib Aventura."

The woman rattled off her credentials too fast to catch it all. I did pick up enough to realize that Paul had managed to authorize the hospital to share his medical status with me.

"He's . . . is he out of surgery?"

"And in ICU," the voice said. "They worked an hour-plus on that femur fracture. By tomorrow or the next day we'll have him on his feet and barring complications, he'll be moved to the orthopedic ward within a couple of days of that. There may be related injuries but they're reluctant to be too aggressive at this point. Time will tell."

"Is it . . . how long will he . . .?"

"They use what they call femoral nailing to treat the break. We'll probably keep him here up to a week, then another week in rehab before he can even think of coming home. Fortunately the break didn't cause any arterial damage or major blood loss, but they'll be watching for clots."

Fortunately. My mind seized on that word like a life-ring in a roiling sea of emotions. It was all I had.

"And infection? He was in that swampy water . . ."

"A continuing concern given the circumstances. If the break isn't healing, that may require a bone graft."

More surgery. I couldn't even allow my brain to go there. "Is he . . . the pain level must be . . ."

"We're managing it as well as can be expected, oral and IV narcotics are usual in these kinds of cases."

All that was a textbook response, no more or less than what I had picked up on-line. "Would I be able . . . are visitors allowed to . . ."

"Right now Mr. Lauden wouldn't . . . isn't necessarily aware enough to appreciate whether or not anyone is—"

"I see." Suddenly light-headed, I braced myself against a wicker chair-back for support.

"Once they move him out of ICU, of course, it's another story."

"You said . . . a day or two?"

"Provided there are—"

"No complications. I understand."

"Ms. Aventura, I appreciate how difficult this must be for—"

"Thank you," I stammered. "For everything you're doing. There are a lot of . . . really worried people up here right now."

The woman gave me a phone number and extension to call for updates on Paul's condition. Long after she broke the connection, I sat there with the phone in my hand, listening to the sound of the dial-tone.

It was tempting just to keep replaying the woman's conversation in my head, seizing on even the smallest hesitation or choice of language to either calm or unwittingly conjure up my darkest fears. But then fruitless speculation was not going to make it any easier to do what I had to do. After slipping into my freshly laundered clothes, I rummaged through the contents of Paul's desk and came up with a leather-bound address book. Cracking it open, I skimmed the entries looking for a name.

Josh. I tracked it down under the L's, recognized the area code as Detroit, the street as a residential address. Punching in the numbers, I got a disconnect notice, guessed immediately that I had misdialed or misread Paul's almost illegible scrawl.

The second time was successful. I counted the rings, five, before I heard the answering machine pick up and almost immediately after it, the sound of a live human voice on the line.

"Josh Lauden."

I had obviously caught him still asleep. It took him a while, and a low undertone of profanities, to figure out how to turn off that mechanical voice droning away about leaving messages.

"You don't know me," I began quickly. "I'm Lib Aventura, program manager at Northern Lights campground."

A suppressed oath followed that pronouncement. "Do you realize what time . . . it's barely—"

"You're father's had an accident," I said. "Serious. Pinned under a tractor at the campground late yesterday. They've taken him down-state."

The silence told me I had succeeded finally in getting Josh's attention. "Where . . .?"

"Petoskey. He's had surgery to repair a fractured femur, maybe other injuries but they are reluctant to—"

Josh didn't let me finish. "I don't know what you expect me to do."

"Your Dad loves you," I said. "Needs you to be—"

"His problem. Not mine."

The phone went still in my hands. Then dial-tone.

Zombie-fashion, I walked back to the Airstream and told Arvo about the call from the hospital but skipped over the one to Paul's son. My co-worker listened without comment.

"We got our job cut out for us, Lib-girl."

True enough and there was no time like the present to get on with it. At my suggestion, Arvo wandered back to the bog to assess what we were coping with in the wake of the accident. With a heavy heart, I threw myself into cleaning up the mess around the computer, updating the campground stats and bookkeeping while I could still reconstruct them. Noon passed and I never noticed.

Suddenly my watch read 2 PM, I had a roaring headache and it seemed like the walls of that huge room were closing in on me like a vice. Knowing only that I had to get out of there, I awkwardly shrugged into my jacket, grabbed the keys from the hook behind the registration desk and headed for the campground SUV parked just outside the office door.

I headed east along Route 2 with no plan except that I needed to talk to someone, not just sit there coaxing search engines for any sense of comfort, however feeble. Annie Stavros had walked in these shoes. I knew she would have gotten away if she could have. I was going to have to go to her.

The first of her Diner signs had just sped past, when beyond it a scant quarter mile a different signboard entirely caught my attention. This one was small with nondescript black-on-white lettering, badly in need of a fresh coat of paint: COMMUNITY CHAPEL. JUST AHEAD.

It had been over a year since I had darkened the door of anything remotely resembling a church. My last deliberate prayers had been wrenched from my heart while holding Dan's hand in that ambulance. I had struck an informal bargain with God in those bleak days after my husband's memorial service, an unspoken laissez faire—expecting nothing, faith a word that seemed to have no relevance in my life.

If I hadn't been watching for it, I could have missed the entrance to the parking area, half hidden by knee-high grass and bushes. At a crawl, I navigated around the ruts and muddy spots until I pulled abreast of a wooden platform and set of stairs seemingly descending to nowhere down the side of a sandy embankment.

For what seemed like a long time I just sat there in the tiny parking lot, hands on the wheel and the motor running, staring straight ahead out the windshield. Finally I cut the engine, unhooked my seatbelt and got out.

The chapel was perched halfway down the slope, tucked between two vegetation-covered dunes, barely visible from where I was standing. I remembered it from the photo in Paul's apartment, the squat tower, devoid of steeple, and the graying clapboard walls that promised nothing remarkable architecturally.

Clutching hard at the weathered handrail, I started down the twisting stairway—ten, then ten again, then another ten. Dizzy and disoriented, I stepped out on a grassy hillock only to find the building even in worse shape close-up than my first impressions from above had

217

led me to believe.

Needing desperately to sit down, I caught sight of a hand-lettered invitation hanging precariously from two eye-hooks alongside the arched doorway. OPEN FOR PRAYER. I cracked open the heavy door, cringed at the rush of stale air against my face.

Whatever I was expecting to find in that deserted sanctuary, it was not this, not this at all. While everything about the exterior spoke of spectacular neglect, inside the oak woodwork was burnished to a golden sheen and each tiny pane of the floor-to-ceiling windows was meticulously caulked and snug. Faded red hymn books were neatly spaced in the delicate wood-slat racks on the back of each pew and on the bare wood of the altar stood a simple antique pickle crock filled with dried wild flowers.

Beautiful. All of it a testament to loving hands at work.

I blinked, my gaze drawn steadily upward by what based on shape alone could have been an enormous leaded-glass window. It wasn't. Centered on the stark white board-and-batten wall of the nave, someone had mounted a series of huge, unframed, what seemed at first like randomly-shaped photographs.

It took me a moment to realize the blocks of images were not in color, because the light reflecting from the glossy surfaces was almost blinding in its intensity. On several photos, luminous shafts of wild grass danced across brooding hillocks of sand. Higher up, starbursts of foam played along the dark shoulders of the waves that swept off into the distance. Above it all, puffy white clouds and sea birds floated across an endless canvas of sky.

I blinked again and the scenes on the deliberately-spaced panels fused into one. It was the Michigan lakeshore facing the dunes on which the chapel was standing. *Paradise.* Or at least our little corner of it.

Paul's work. I would have known it anywhere. A masterpiece. Without color, just subtle gradations from white to black, he had found a way of capturing in visual language and imagery, the essence of the human longing for the Infinite. It was like coming from and walking into the light, the alpha and omega, beginning and end of our life journey.

My throat tight, I had to look away. Desperate for a point of reference, I seized on a sheet of laminated white cardstock lying on a simple oak table behind me just inside the door.

WELCOME TRAVELER AND MARVEL,
THAT EVEN IN THIS REMOTE
AND UNLIKELY REFUGE,
WE ARE NEVER ALONE ON THE JOURNEY.
WE EACH NAME THE GIFTS THAT WE FIND HERE—
LOVE, COMFORT, TRUST, FRIENDSHIP, COMMUNITY,
HOPE OR PEACE,
THE DEEPEST LONGINGS OF THE HUMAN HEART.
THE PRESENCE OF GOD.

Under the text was a shot of the chapel in the mist taken from down below along the water's edge, half-hidden by the steep face of the dunes. The back of the dog-eared card was a Who's Who of my friends and neighbors who had contributed to the chapel restoration. Paul's was near the bottom.

Hands shaking, I slid into the back pew and sat, felt my heartbeat slowly steadying. No words came, only the hot sting of tears as I stared up at the wall behind the altar.

Paul had never spoken of this place. Apparently he was content yet again, as Annie had told me once before, to let his work be his silent witness, waiting to be discovered for what it was. A gift of love and thanksgiving. He had done all this without fanfare or accolades in his search for something around which to reground his shattered world.

Even in the depths of the sea, God is there. Paul's grief had brought him here and now me as well. The possibility of losing him became suddenly both horribly real and unthinkable.

Startled, I heard the sound of the door. As I whipped around on the seat, I saw Annie Stavros standing behind me.

"I came as soon as I could," she said softly, "On the way over the crest of the dune I saw the campground SUV in the parking lot and I knew I'd find you here. Lib, I am so sorry . . .!"

As she eased into the pew alongside me, she reached out and held me. It was an invitation finally to let go, to let the tears I had been battling all day fall unchecked.

"Have you heard anything?" she said after a while, fishing a tissue from the pocket of her jeans jacket.

Haltingly, I tried to piece together the hospital's take on things. "He's had surgery. Lord knows how much more ahead, if even half that stuff on-line is true. There was vague talk of other possible injuries, long-term therapy—"

"Where . . . where did they take him?"

"Petoskey."

I found it tougher and tougher to respond, when they were the same questions stuck on autoplay in my head and there were so few answers to silence them. Where, in fact, was he right now and what was happening to him down there? Was he going to be all right?

"Of course you need to be there, Lib," Annie's voice was saying through the roaring in my ears. " Just take that rig of yours and go!"

My mouth felt stiff. "I don't believe . . . I can't do that, Annie."

"The trip's not that long. You've had a lot of practice driving by now."

"I wasn't thinking about the drive . . . it's what I might find down there," I told her. "It's very possible Paul might not even . . . want me there. I need to respect that."

Annie didn't need me to spell it out. We had talked so much about her own struggle helping her John cope with the aftermath of his accident. They had been married for years before they had to face that moment. Paul and I had only known each other a summer.

"You really love him?"

I nodded. "Yes."

"Then you'll go . . . you'll handle it. And if he can't, you'll find a way to help him get beyond it . . . somehow."

Tears swam in my eyes but I blinked them back. "Annie, this is so . . . horribly, horribly hard . . ."

Her voice was low. "I know. Which is all the more reason why you have to go."

"Problem is, Annie, whatever I want or should or ought to do, Arvo simply can't manage that place all alone."

"Already taken care of," fishing in her pocket, she retrieved a folded up sheet of computer paper.

Silent, I took in a grid of names, dates and times—more complicated than anything I had engineered when planning the program schedules for Northern Lights all summer. Names I knew were there and some total strangers. A lot of them.

"I don't understand."

Annie smiled. "Earl and Sonja have been on the phone, helping John and my kids round up a small army of volunteers to help staff Northern Lights until it closes for the season. Teenagers in the evening and weekends, adults during the day. Earl found a couple of plumbers to help Arvo with the winterizing. . ."

Lightheaded, I felt my breath quicken. The names and dates swam before my eyes.

"Dear God, Annie."

"Yes," she smiled. "Whatever I believe about Higher Powers and miracles, these . . . incredible people are at the heart of it."

I looked down at my hands cradled in my lap. "This is the first time I've even been inside the four walls of a church since Dan died."

Her smile was knowing, sad. "After John's accident . . . trust me, I had a lot of trouble with spouting upbeat songs about goodness and mercy and fortunate sheep. In the end it was the people and the sense of being surrounded by love, not words that brought me back. We break so . . . damn easily, Lib, and yet I'm learning to never, never underestimate the human capacity to heal."

I sensed she wasn't just talking about shattered bones and

wounded tissue. "I've got to hope that," I said softly.

Not just for Paul. But for myself.

Welcome traveler and marvel. My daughter was right and oh-so-dead-wrong when I set out on this journey. Maybe I didn't have a roof over my head in the traditional sense. Not a grain of that sandy ground under my feet at Northern Lights belonged to me. Still, in any way that mattered, I had been going home.

True, I was tracking my miles deliberately by more ephemeral measures now. In hugs exchanged, in glances that signaled trust and vulnerability, the pain and empathy of human joy and sorrow shared.

Love. Friendship. Hope. Forgiveness. Peace. The face of God in the face of my neighbors. Even grieving at the thought of the pain-wracked face of the man I loved, against all odds and reason, I breathed a silent prayer of thanksgiving—for what I had. In spite of the losses.

Annie was right. I needed to go to him. The road was just outside the door, back up that hillside and through the tall grass to Route 2. There are times and places in our lives when a road map just isn't necessary any more.

This was one of them.

Nineteen

I held out one more sleepless night, then crack of dawn disconnected the motor home and headed east and south. The journey was one of those out-of-body experiences that left me remembering virtually nothing of where I was or how I got there.

Things didn't improve at my destination. I stood at the hospital reception desk in Petoskey while a pink-smocked volunteer tried unsuccessfully several times to direct me to the ICU. Wandering the maze of corridors like a sleepwalker, I tried to steel myself for what I would find.

The decor was glass and cinderblock, the ambiance hushed tones, dim lighting. Paul's room, if you could call it that, was served by a central monitoring station that buzzed and hummed with the elusive realities of life, pain and healing. For all the activity going on at the nursing station, Paul was alone.

He seemed to be sleeping. I stood in the doorway, watching him, searching for some clue to what he. . .*what we* had ahead of us. That was no easy business with all the white sheeting and an alarming array of monitors, drips and tubes that all but blocked access to his bedside.

One leg was immobilized in some sort of cast-like contraption and there were ugly bruises on his temple and one cheekbone. Amid the cuts and scratches, I saw a wound deep enough to require stitches. From the tension around his mouth and eyes, despite what had to be mega-doses of drugs to deal with the pain, I sensed instantly he must still be experiencing way too much of it.

Quietly as I could, I repositioned the solitary chair closer to the bed rails, every nerve ending alert. The movement must have wakened him. He stirred, and as I cautiously reached out and cradled his hand in mine—avoiding a disconnected IV still implanted there—his eyes flickered open.

"Lib . . . what . . .?"

I took a deep breath, forced a smile. "Trust me, it's getting colder than heck on the U.P. in that motor home at night without you . . . you never warned me about that. No way was I going to leave you alone down here either."

"But . . . how . . .?"

"Camping, where else? Some tiny public campground—close enough that I can walk over here."

He started to say something. Instead, I saw his face twist momentarily and his breathing became shallow, ragged. He closed his eyes.

I found myself chattering away as if somehow I could will him the courage to ride out the worst of it. "Would you believe, I actually drove the motor home more or less nonstop?" I said. "Left early, got here around ten in the morning, paid for a site and set up. The trip took me way too long, but then no flattened construction workers either and only two close encounters with the shoulder. I can't believe those vicious winds crossing the Mackinac Bridge—"

"Too . . . damn . . . dangerous," his speech was agitated, slurred from the meds, but the gist of what he was saying was clear enough.

I hastened to soften the edge on my derring-do, deflect the worry in his eyes. "No problem, I just took it slow . . . you would have been proud of me. But you were right, though. There were no pull-throughs in the campground and I still needed help parking the rig. The guy in the campsite next door saw me struggling and helped."

The furrows in his forehead deepened as he tried to put that rambling confessional in some context. "The accident," he seemed to be searching my face at every word., "so . . . stupid, Lib."

"Not so good, I'll admit. But point is, you're still here, thank heavens. Unfortunately, a bit the worse for wear—"

"More surgery . . . if the last one didn't take. Therapy for six to eight months. Best case, no more triathlons."

I didn't press him for the worst. He wasn't prepared to go there and I had already googled my own way in that direction. As it was, it was costing him an enormous effort to string together that grim prognosis, one word and phrase at a time.

"You seem . . . those painkillers they've been giving you—is it morphine?"

"A drop in the bucket," his faint rasp of a chuckle ended on a groan. "By day's end those . . . sadists want me out of bed and up on my feet . . . "

It took a split-second to register. The woman on the phone said they would move him to the orthopedic ward and out of ICU in a matter of days. As for the part about him standing any time soon . . . *insanity.*

"*Today . . . ?*" I breathed.

"I had better be . . . ," he never used the F-word but did now, "_____ 'n comatose . . ."

Enough to wring the bejeebers out of anybody. And yet here he was, a desperate smile playing at the corner of his mouth. For a split-second I looked away, trying not to let him see how close I was to losing it entirely. My first instinct was to roar out to that nursing station and punch out somebody's headlights.

"One piece of good news in all of this," I said softly.

I told him about John Stavros and his marathon phone blitz to keep the campground office covered until the close of the season. Paul looked stunned, and for what seemed like a long time, he just stared off into the distance.

"You're . . . I can't let them—"

"Help?" I finished for him. "I beg to differ. Annie told me what you did to help her John get that new equipment, his link to the outside world . . . his Neighbor-Net . . ."

The irony in that couldn't be lost on him, certainly wasn't on me. In all likelihood, Paul himself was probably one of the new Neighbor-Net's first test cases. Whatever else he was intending to say went lost in a strangled half-cry of awareness.

Alarmed, I watched his breathing escalate and he gripped my hand until the knuckles turned white. His face was terrible.

"Paul, don't . . . please don't . . . you mustn't . . ."

By way of answer, he slowly closed his eyes. Tears of frustration slid silently down his face. My own weren't far behind.

"I know how much this. . .hurts, how truly difficult it is, but you have *got* to let go . . . let people be there for you," I told him softly. "You've told me as much ever since I met you. This is his time, John's chance to be strong for someone else."

"He . . . those people don't . . . they have no reason to—"

"I beg to differ. Ever since the accident, I couldn't answer a single phone call without someone sharing some story about what you did for them or someone they knew. For starters that . . incredible window of yours at the dunes chapel. You never told me."

Paul's eyes held mine. "You . . . *saw* . . ."

"Oh, Paul," I whispered, again and again. "I love you. Dearest, you aren't alone in this."

Mercifully, I knew now that neither was I. Gradually I saw his eyes close, his breathing steady and he drifted off into a fitful half-sleep. My own face wet with tears, I slipped quietly from the chair and made my way to the nursing station.

"I can't believe . . . you can't tell me that level of pain is normal, or necessary!" I demanded, hard pressed not to start hurling things randomly at all that expensive hardware.

The head nurse looked uncomfortable. "Lauden, right? You

226

missed the worst. For the first 72 hours after surgery he was more or less out of it. Today is a lot better. But with these long-term injury cases, we need to whittle down the dosages progressively or addiction can become a problem . . ."

I hesitated. "Prognosis?"

"Too soon to tell. But he's a fighter."

I fought a smile, remembering what he said about the upcoming therapy. Apparently they already figured out what and who they were dealing with.

"He'll . . . they're sure he'll be able to . . . walk?"

"No spinal cord damage and though the leg is pretty banged up, therapy can work miracles," she said. "It's a tough road and a patient has got to want it"

Muttering my thanks, I told her I would be back in an hour or so. Quickly she flipped through what had to be his chart.

"Probably not a good idea. He's moving out of ICU within the hour and therapy is scheduled at four," she said. "The first time can be . . . difficult—"

I didn't even want to think about it. As is, I half-expected with all those meds in him that by morning Paul may not even remember I had been there today at all.

The next 48 hours were as close to hell as I ever hoped to get, watching helpless from the sidelines as Paul dealt with a pain-stamped regimen of one step forward and two back, literally, with a walker and retinue of therapists, up and down the halls of the orthopedic ward. Within a matter of days his face was not so ashen and drawn and most of the visible cuts and bruises were beginning to heal and fade.

They were still pumping him full of pain-killers, understandable when the therapy was getting tougher every day. His mood vacillated from resolute to frustrated and angry to rock-bottom, with rare precious moments in between when I sensed the Paul Lauden I knew taking control, the Paul Lauden before the accident.

I tried not to let the emotional whiplash wear me down. That was getting more and more difficult. Things finally came to a head one evening when I was sharing the latest news from up north.

"Arvo and Earl have a plan to shut down the water and sewer systems in two weeks," I told him. "Meanwhile one of the high school students has taken it upon himself to update the web site for next season . . . with something he calls flash graphics. It's pretty amazing. I've been using the WIFI at the campground in the evening to feed him new text and a draft calendar . . ."

Paul's face twisted in a frown. He was never one to avoid eye contact, but he was doing it now.

"Lib, you have no idea how grateful I am," he said slowly. "You . . . I know you've been truly heroic, holding all of this together . . ."

There was a subtle undercurrent in his voice that told me there was a punchline. It was one he was hesitating to share.

"But . . .?" I said.

"I can't let you do this."

I just looked at him, waiting. Sooner or later he was going to have to make eye contact and when he did, I was ready for him. "Meaning exactly . . . what?"

"You didn't bargain for any of this," he said. "Neither did I—exploiting you, Arvo and the rest. I just can't let this continue. Won't . . .!"

My chest suddenly felt tight. Something in his face told me this was nothing new or something arrived at out-of-the-blue. Paul had worked through this whole scenario in his drug-induced Neverland long before I ever popped up at his bedside and nothing in our intervening days together had changed the script one iota.

"Everybody out there on that little stretch of Route 2 knows your turn will come on the giving end of things again some day—"

"Be reasonable, Lib," he bit off one word at a time, as if

228

choosing his words, forcing himself to say it. "You *can't* winter in that campground by yourself. Neither can I . . . even with help, not after this. You made it down here on your own. Good. So, back to Plan A. That crew in Centerline closes up Northern Lights. You keep going, head south to the Carolinas, Florida—"

"And leave you. That's it? You've been lying here doing the math and . . . *that's* the best you can come up with!"

Paul looked away and jaw set, stared up at the curved track holding the draped fabric curtain that muted the glare from the huge bank of windows in his room. From where I was sitting I could see what was promising to be a magnificent sunset out there—the brooding blues and purples of the clouds backlit by the flaming orange sun as it slipped behind the horizon. I had told him from that vantage point he actually could see my motor home, snugged safely on its pad down there, waiting.

"I swore to heaven," he said, "one way or another, I'd never let anyone face something like this on my account, Lib. *Not ever.*"

"Then we've got a problem," I said slowly. "Forget the fact that if there's a pain-free route through life, I haven't found it and neither have you. You were there for Ginny—your choice and hers until the end. I never had the chance to find out whether or not Dan was capable of letting me love him like that. But I know this. I'm a big girl, Paul. I want a relationship where I can give, not just take, where I can nurture, not just feel sheltered, held at arms length in the name of love. And I won't settle for less."

I took a deep breath, then hit him with the rest of it. Capable of even inducing guilt-trips, I was discovering, if that's what it took to shake him out of his funk.

"You've heard all that good stuff about love being a two-way street," I said. "You loved me when I was vulnerable, about as broken as a person can get. Now it's payback time."

The words were barely out of my mouth when I knew my lame attempt at making light of the situation had backfired. A muscle worked along the ridge of his jaw.

"I do . . . *not* need anyone feeling—"

"Sorry for you?" I said it rather than hear it coming from him. "Trust me, I do. For me, for us. I feel . . . terrible, absolutely devastated—for the both of us. Emphasis on 'we'. And if you need a motive, to know beyond a shadow of a doubt what brought me here . . . try *love.* That pretty much covers things!"

I let that sink in, watching the struggle playing itself on his face. He closed his eyes and when he opened them again, I saw only a bottomless well of sadness and pain.

"It's been a great run," his voice was barely audible, "but the season's over, Lib. We'll never know what could have been . . . it's just that simple. When you know your new address, I'll make sure the check is in the mail."

This had to be the morphine and the depression talking, I told myself. Still, I couldn't have felt worse if he had slapped me. The silence between us was beyond tense, ominous.

"Paul, you're . . . you can't just—"

But he was and he could and common sense told me now was not the time to back him into a corner. He was exhausted, so was I. Slowly I got to my feet.

We both needed to get some sleep, I told him, and I had some phone calls to make. I left out the usual part about wanting to avoid saying something we would both regret. There was quite enough of that out there between us already.

I would be back, I said. Paul didn't respond one way or the other.

Alone in the motor home the enormity of what lay ahead hit home with a vengeance. Bad as the accident was, what it triggered was far more life-shattering and the severity of his injuries were the least of the problems. We both knew it.

The irony of the situation was almost more than I could bear. I had come to Northern Lights anticipating this very moment—when I could take off on my own, confident and sure of myself, carving out a future for myself wherever the road might lead. My relationship with Paul Lauden was a detour, not on any map or atlas.

My instincts were right when I told Annie I was afraid to come down here. Go, Paul demanded—exactly what the man had empowered me to do. Whatever he needed right now, it was not me reminding him how vulnerable he was. The only logical choice was to give him space, easier said than done.

There had to be something. Too drained and numb to function, I sat there at loose ends for a long time before I finally picked up the cell phone and redialed that number I had jotted down for Paul's son. After the tenth ring, I gave up. This time Josh apparently had turned off the answering machine.

Around midnight it began to rain, a gentle soaker that slid off the roof of the motor home most of the night. Sometime between then and dawn, through random bouts of sleep and insomnia, it came to me what I needed to do. First light, that audacious plan was still churning away in my skull.

It occurred to me to rent a car. In the end, I just bit the bullet—disconnected the motor home in the dark and headed south. Driving into the sun what seemed like decades later, I found myself in Detroit, crawling from gas station to gas station asking for directions to Dender Communications.

It turns out I needn't have worried about recognizing the place when I saw it. The signage was a gigantic billboard, ostentatious in the extreme, with garish digital graphics of radio and TV towers and their call numbers morphing into trendy programming promos and a larger-than-life portrait of what had to be the empire's founder, Frank Dender.

Inching my way into the parking lot, I threaded my way down aisle after aisle looking for somewhere to stash the motor home. I ran out of options virtually at the base of the sleek glass-and-steel high-rise in a private cul-de-sac populated by an intimidating array of luxury vehicles. All were carefully signed and labeled according to their owner's executive status.

Lauden. A Hummer stood in the spot. Josh was at work.

Paul wasn't exaggerating one bit when he described what he had left behind him. In danger of losing my nerve entirely, I abruptly cut the engine and parked, if you could call it that, in the only place I could—right in the middle of the lane behind that formidable line-up of vehicles.

My watch read 11:58. At least my intended target was not going anywhere for the foreseeable future, including lunch. That motor home wouldn't let a thing pass in either direction. If the policy was to tow interlopers, good luck to anyone trying to get my rig out of there.

Locking the motor home door and pocketing the keys, I squared my shoulders and headed for the nearest entrance. The receptionist in the lobby was multi-tasking, but looked up from her Sudoku and on-hold phone connection long enough to direct me to the fifth floor executive suite.

Palms sweating, I fumbled with the elevator button, felt the pit of my stomach turn over at the swift ascent. There was no going back now.

"Do you have an appointment?" The chic young gatekeeper to the executive suite's eyebrows lifted as she gave me the once-over.

I hadn't even thought of wardrobe in my haste to get on the road. Jeans, scuffed work boots, tank top and flannel overblouse weren't exactly the fashion statement of choice for visitors in this corner of the world, I suspected.

"Family. Josh Lauden and I spoke on the phone several days ago," I told her.

It wasn't exactly a lie, but then I wasn't taking any chances either that the receptionist would call me on it. Brushing past her desk, I headed for the heavy paneled door with its embossed brass nameplate, *Lauden.*

"Ma'am, you can't just go in there . . ."

The door handle was already yielding to my touch. I hesitated long enough to get my bearings, then charged straight ahead until I was within arm's length of a huge wooden desk that took up nearly the entire acreage in front of the floor to ceiling wall of windows.

Behind that gleaming expanse of walnut sat a man in his early thirties, a younger version of Paul—recognizable even down to the same wary look that had greeted me upon my arrival at Northern Lights. Uncanny, but there it was.

As far as the younger Lauden was concerned, I was a nonentity "What the . . . Ms. Frennow, how in the heck did this person get in here?"

By now the receptionist had followed me into the room and had a vice-grip on my arm. "But she said . . . Ma'am, you're going to have to leave—"

"I've come from the hospital, Josh," I said. "Your dad is pretty beat up, out of ICU now though still in a lot of pain. If the leg doesn't begin to heal, they may have to resort to bone grafts. Main thing, he's going to make it. You haven't been returning my calls so I thought I'd drive down and bring you up to speed myself."

Josh Lauden just stared at me—open-mouthed—as if he had been thrust violently into the middle of a home invasion. I could have imagined it, but I thought my terse news-flash at least seemed to loosen the receptionist's death-grip a little.

"I'm going to give you ten seconds to get out of here," I heard someone growl, "and then I'm calling security!"

It was only then I noticed there was someone else in the room—cell phone in hand. That graying hair and fleshy bulldog face had patriarch Frank Dender written all over them. He wasn't waiting for me to respond.

"Security . . . there's a break-in in progress on five," he barked, "Get the hell up here . . . *now* . . .!"

"Frank, right?" I said quickly "Don't worry, I'll be on my way fast enough, if that's what you want. But before you toss me out of here, I suggest you reconsider how all this would play out on the rival networks. I can't name them off-hand, but trust me, I'd find out."

Josh was on his feet now, his palms braced hard on his polished desktop. "You're bluffing."

"Try me."

I had, at one time, been amazing at poker, five-card stud—as long as I was playing for clothes pins, not cold hard cash. Mercifully, young Josh and his chairman-of-the-board of a grandfather didn't know that. The stakes here boggled the imagination.

"Whatever is going on in your head right now," I said, "it all comes down pretty much to two choices, Josh. Keep feeding this vendetta you've let yourself be talked into or grow up and make your own decisions about what constitutes love and loyalty. Your dad loves you, in spite of everything. He needs you. Whatever you think you've won here in this fifth floor executive suite, in the great scheme of things it's just chump change. A time will come when you're sitting all alone behind that desk of yours and you'll appreciate that fact. I just hope your Dad is still around when you finally do."

The clock was ticking. Agitated voices and heavy footfalls down the hall told me the gendarmes were seconds from carting me off to the precinct. Josh obviously heard it too and started to maneuver around the desk in my direction, stopped.

"You all right, Mr. Lauden?" the first of the uniformed personnel demanded.

Eyes narrowed, Josh looked at me and then over at the security guard. "Just a false alarm," he said slowly. "Ms.—"

He left it to me to fill in the blanks. "Aventura. Lib Aventura."

"Ms. Aventura, I believe we're through here."

It wasn't a question. With a sad twist of a smile, I nodded. "I was just going."

Off to one side, arms akimbo, Frank Dender was looking at the both of us with thinly veiled contempt. With a shudder I realized that if

Paul's son hadn't taken charge, the outcome here might have been very, very different. Be thankful for small favors.

"I'll keep you posted," I said, "about your dad."

Josh didn't react one way or the other, except for that muscle twitching along the edge of his jaw. For a split-second I thought I was going to lose it.

Like father, like son—or so I had to hope. That tightening of the jaw was Paul's 'tell' when he was struggling to make sense of what was going on around him. Not much as inroads went, but under the circumstances, something. If I had been expecting anything approaching an equivalent willingness to reconsider on the part of his grandfather, the hard, brutal set to the older man's features disabused me of that quickly enough.

"Delighted to meet you, Josh. I'll tell your dad, you asked about him . . .!"

Turning on heel, I headed back out the door. The cordon of security personnel blinked, but let me pass. All but running the last ten yards to the elevator, I braced myself against the doorframe, dizzy from holding my breath and impatient for escape. I never looked back.

For a change, even backing up the motor home didn't phase me, despite an audience of very annoyed company employees waiting for me to get out of there. I put the thing in gear and hands tight on the wheel, inched out of that cul-de-sac into which I had maneuvered myself. It took a while to navigate the sixty feet and I had to get out a couple of times and reconnoiter. But I did it, aided toward the end by a very twitchy and anxious security guard who had positioned himself between me and all those high-end vehicles I was skirting.

Success must have gone to my head. Retracing my route out of Detroit, I got so thoroughly lost that by the time I spotted an interstate on-ramp, early rush-hour traffic was revving up. Hands glued to the wheel, there was nothing to do but focus on the two or three tail-lights immediately ahead of me in what seemed like way too many lanes on either side of the motor home for comfort. Construction zones and periodic lane squeezes didn't help one bit.

Stuck in that high-stakes bumper-pool ride, I just drove without any real sense of where I was going or to what end. "Just don't hit anything," I muttered periodically to myself.

The little pep talks must have worked—I managed to get out of there unscathed, though by the time traffic began to thin and the urban landscape gave way to wide open green spaces, I had had it. A rest stop cropped up on my right and I took advantage of it. Easing into a pull-through in the truck and trailer lot, I parked the rig, then crawled back to the bed intending to cat-nap enough to take the edge off.

I must have fallen asleep. I woke with a start, groggy and disoriented, sensed through my sleep-drugged haze that the sun had already set. It would be dark soon and I had no idea where I was—only that in this twilight No-man's Land, the mile-markers telling me what to do next were few and far between.

To the north lay Petoskey, where another day of grueling physical therapy would have only strengthened Paul's conviction that he was taking some moral high road, one he was determined to travel alone. The expectation—once mine and my daughter's as well—was that I head south on my own. If I balked and chose west toward Madison and my family instead, all I would do is find myself right back where I started.

One thing was clear. This rest stop was no place I wanted to spend the night. After slipping a can of caffeine-laced soda in the driver-side beverage-holder, I got the motor home back on the highway without incident, though by now the on-coming headlights were making it harder and harder to see. There wasn't much choice but to find someplace to camp and reconnoiter in the morning. I was running on empty.

Mercifully I saw an exit coming up, marked by a string of roadside services signs—among them reassuring symbols for food, gas, lodging and wonder of wonders, even a campground, 3.7 miles off in the opposite direction. On impulse I took the off-ramp, followed the arrows through a stretch of wooded and uninhabited countryside. Finally up ahead on the left I saw a lighted sign for a small private campground.

There wasn't a car in sight, behind or in front of me. I dispensed with the turn signal and eased the motor home into the narrow, tree-lined gravel lane.

The office was dark, closed for the night, but a message on the office door invited me to pick a site, register on the envelope provided and leave the cash in a locked metal box bolted on the campground bulletin board. I took them up on it. The fee was an odd amount and I couldn't make change. Finally I just rounded up and called it good.

In the process I couldn't help but notice the faded calendar of events still stapled alongside the cash box. From the look of it the program season ended at Labor Day, pretty ordinary stuff and a far cry from what Paul and I had set in motion. As is, less than a dozen of the sites were occupied, all by RVs of one kind or another.

I quickly found a grass-and-gravel pull-through, with nary a tree in sight, and parked. Relying on the light from the nearby bathroom-laundry building, I was able to hook up the motor home in record time.

Typical down-state, the night was surprisingly warm compared to what we had been experiencing up north in recent weeks. Alert and edgy after all that running around, I thought about taking a brisk walk around the maze of campground access lanes to clear my head. Instead I cobbled together a supper of fruit slices and cheese, then washed it down with my daily ration of merlot. If that didn't put me out for the night, nothing would.

On the road again. The song seemed stuck on auto-play in my head, like the nagging voice in my skull defying me to articulate what I had intended or hoped to accomplish with my borderline-reckless junket to Detroit. By now that unsettling introduction to Josh Lauden and his grandfather felt like a half-lifetime ago. The results were ambivalent at best. Still, as I drifted off into a troubled sleep I felt a certain peace with what I had done—whatever came of it, I had survived the trip and could never fault myself for trying.

Twenty

Morning dawned uncannily like the one that had set me on this course in the first place so many months ago—gray with a chill edge to the wind that seemed to be threatening rain. Stiff and sore from yesterday's drive, I took my time improvising breakfast and unhooking the motor home, slugged down a couple of ibuprofen with the day-old dregs of that super-caffeinated diet soda as a chaser. It was only as I began to retrace my route from the campground back to the interstate that I realized exactly what I had done.

In all that bumper-to-bumper traffic and confusion after leaving Josh Lauden's office, relying on instinct not maps, I hadn't given a second thought to the sequence of highways to get me out of that morass. I had come down from Petoskey on I-75 along the eastern side of the state. From some strange force of habit, on the return trip I headed due west instead—the first leg of the route up the middle of the Mitten sometimes favored by tourists on their way north to bypass the I-75 industrial corridor.

No wonder that off-ramp seemed so familiar last night. My gut twisted as I put it all together, like a compass swinging suddenly true North.

Right now I was cruising along on the interstate less than twenty miles from the tiny bedroom community outside of East Lansing where

Daniel and I had lived the whole of our life together. Beyond surreal, old Sigmund Freud would have had a field day with this one.

Ignoring the angry sound of a driver behind me leaning on the horn, I slowed down anticipating the exit I knew lay dead ahead. At the end of the off-ramp I brought the rig to a halt, turned left and headed into town.

Homing. Our culture has whole industries devoted to the instinct. Entire TV channels celebrate our obsession with the process—selling homes, buying them, remodeling them. I had lived in that world for most of my life, treasured those memories.

Still, as I cruised slowly past the two-story frame house in which I once had raised my children, I was shocked to find that I barely recognized the place. The current owner had painted the siding the color of a jar of German mustard, which didn't help. Totally out of character, our once happily dandelion-infested front yard was miraculously as thick and flawless as if someone had brought in a truckload of sod. The house next door and another down the block sported large For Sale signs.

Dodging an occasional parked car on the narrow, tree-canopied street, I retraced the route my children had walked every day to elementary school. From the scaffolding and a swarm of workers on the facade, I guessed the building was having its brick re-tuck-pointed. As I worked my way through the downtown grid looking for my old office, inexplicably a whole new forest of one-way street signs stood in my way. The entire mini-mall where Senior Tours had been was now gone, replaced by condos.

Life moves on. With a shock, I realized I was fully capable of doing the same—precisely what Paul Lauden had demanded of me. Like stumbling across that familiar off-ramp last night, I had found myself at this emotional watershed before. Going back wasn't an option. I had ceased to allow myself to be afraid of what lay ahead.

Maybe right now Paul couldn't see beyond one pain-wracked step after another, but I could. Time was passing. For better or worse, I knew exactly what I needed to do.

❖

Traffic was light and the cross-winds minimal. Still, another half-day had passed by the time I checked back into that tiny campground in Petoskey. I took it as a good sign that my old camp spot was still empty. Methodically I hooked up the motor home, showered and changed and walked over to the hospital.

For all my resolve, I was quietly relieved that Paul appeared to be dozing when I stuck my head in the door of his new room in the orthopedic ward. Prepared to wait him out, I settled down in the chair, watching the rise and fall of his breathing, the slow drip of the fluid in his IV.

I could have imagined it, but it seemed like there was not as much tension in his face. It could just have been the light, but the lines bracketing his mouth had relaxed a little—good, if it meant the pain level was becoming more manageable. When he finally stirred and his glance strayed in my direction, I forced what I hoped was a smile.

"You know, for the record," I said quietly, "sometimes you behave just like my daughter, Danielle—dead set on taking the weight of the world on your shoulders and steam-rolling anyone or anything that tries to object. I can't say I'm crazy about that little habit."

The muscle twitching along the ridge of his jaw told me I had caught him off guard. "Last night," he said, blinked as he tried to put my presence in some kind of context, "earlier, when they had me up on my feet, you weren't . . . the motor home was gone."

At least he had cared enough to check, no easy business under the circumstances. I decided to plunge ahead.

"I've been on a little road trip," I told him, "roundabout fashion, wound up in East Lansing—go figure. I lived there most of my adult life. Funny thing was, when I finally got there, all I wanted to do was to get back up here, as fast as I could."

"You were . . . *where*?"

240

"At one point within a stone's throw of the Michigan border. But then I turned around and drove back. A guy can cover a lot of ground in 24 hours, if he puts his mind to it."

The set of Paul's jaw told me that was probably just wishful thinking. "Not in a walker," he said. "Nothing has changed, Lib. I can't guarantee you that I'll . . . ever—"

"Don't bother with a list, we both know what's on it. Walk . . .? Maybe not a lot of fun right now, but you can't have everything. Run? Climb Mt. Kilimanjaro? I'd say, probably not operate any more backhoes. *Caveat emptor.* Love doesn't come with a warranty. I'll admit I wasn't obsessed with reading the fine print on product labels anyway."

"You may think all that now, Lib, but—"

"I could get hit by a bus tomorrow or we could wake up to the Apocalypse," I shrugged. "One thing's for sure, you could have died out there in that mud. And horrible as it was, what happened in that bog reminded me with a vengeance that there are no guarantees in this life. Absolutely none. Trust me, I understand how very depressing this is. But even wallowing in whatever it is you have seized on to wallow in, I am *not* going to let you do this, throw away everything we—!"

"Lib, I can't expect . . . you don't have to—"

"No, I don't. But you do. And that's put your money where your mouth is. You started all this with that little road trip to talk to your son a couple months ago—swore you were serious about us, if I remember correctly, willing to risk everything. Well then, prove it!"

"I love you. All the more reason why—"

"Good. We're making progress here. At least you're still talking present tense!" I told him. "Because heaven help me, if you were smart enough to ask, I've decided that I would . . . *marry* you, even stubborn fool that you are at the moment. Though if I have to, I'll settle for you glaring and growling at me over the top of my computer terminal in that double-wide along Route 2 for the foreseeable future, if that's what it takes until you finally come to your senses."

I didn't give him time to respond. "And before you say another word, if we can weather the next two minutes—while you chew on the fact that you are *dead wrong* here—then we can survive absolutely anything . . ."

For once the man was speechless. As I watched, my heart beating wildly in my chest, the corners of his mouth twitched in what I hoped was a smile.

"Not your everyday, run of the mill proposal, Lib," he said finally, "though certainly . . . creative . . ."

"*And . . . ?*"

"Sorry, getting down on one knee isn't an option—not likely for some time to come, if ever. And with me more or less locked up here, you'd have to be the one to scrounge up a guy with a round collar . . ."

I was having trouble getting my head around what he was saying. "If that's a Yes, at least getting the blood tests shouldn't be an issue, given where we are," I said finally.

"Do they still do that?" His rumble of laughter ended on a stifled groan. "So much for only hurting when I laugh."

"At least we still can—laugh, that is. Though apparently there's something else you haven't been telling me."

"Forgot. I've been having fun while you were gone. Hard to tell in my banged up state, but they also think I have a torn rotator cuff, maybe a cracked rib—"

"Oh, Paul . . ."

One of my former neighbors went through a bout of problems with his rotator cuff, no fun at all. It could mean more surgery, immobilizing that shoulder for weeks, extended physical therapy and up to six months of recovery.

"Still time to back out," he grimaced. "All of this sure as heck is going to slow down our love life for a while—though at least, I seem to have drawn a get-out-of-jail-free card. They're talking about hauling me off to some rehab facility any day now, here or St. Ignace, take your pick. A week and change after that and I'm back at Northern Lights, provided Arvo can rig up a ramp by then."

242

"Paul, that's absolutely—"

"I suggest reserving judgment about how good it is until I actually shuffle across the Northern Lights parking lot," he said. "Point is, you're conveniently avoiding the subject."

"I've seen the dune chapel. That will do nicely."

Paul shook his head. "We're definitely going to have to call out the mountain rescue folks to lower me down those stairs. Not a pretty sight, but then I guess how much worse can it be than getting me out of that . . . damn bog?"

I didn't know whether to laugh or cry. "Much as I love the setting," I said, "sorry, you're right. I am not taking a chance on you winding up in surgery again, any more than I'm prepared to sit around and wait for you to change your mind."

"Suggestions."

"That rehab place in St. Ignace must have a chapel," I shrugged. "Or we tie the knot on the porch in front of the campground office. It's where you met me after all, give or take a few feet."

"And entertain the campers? Too blasted cold this time of year."

"Then we'll make it Annie's. She would be thrilled."

"Better than some rehab chapel, that's for sure," he said. "It wouldn't look so much like—"

"A potential mortuary?"

His laughter ended on a frustrated outrush of breath. For a second his eyes flickered shut and I sensed how exhausted all this had made him. No sense in pushing our luck.

"I should go," I whispered, "and let you—"

"*No.*"

His hand reached out and his eyes dark with longing, he coaxed me into snuggling precariously alongside him on that hard and narrow hospital bed. Trying my best not to jostle him in the process, I complied.

"This can't be . . .they're going to kick me out of here, Paul."

Awkwardly he reached across with his good arm and caught my hand in his. "Let 'em try."

I hesitated to remind him of his earlier instructions, how close we had come to the abyss. "You do have an unfortunate habit of doing that yourself, you know . . .giving me my walking papers."

"Just caught me on a bad day, that's all." With thumb and forefinger, he was thoughtfully tracing the length of my ring finger. "A little makeshift, but if I could snag a washer off one of those . . . *gizmos* they have me tied to, I'd make all this official."

When he reached the faint indentation where up until now my wedding band had always been, he abruptly stopped, tried to shift on the pillow so that he could look up at me. For a blessed moment, it was simply love not the meds or the pain I read in his eyes. I shivered as his hand closed hard around mine.

"It was time to tuck that away," I breathed. "Somewhere safe, so someday Dani can have it."

His voice was hoarse with the same potent brew of emotions I found myself battling on a daily, almost minute-by-minute basis—regret, anger, resolve to get through this. At least we were prepared, finally, to do it together. "So, I gather, you're not concocting some bizarre retribution then," he said softly, "for my outrageous—"

"I've been so desperately worried, Paul. You have no idea."

I felt the tension drain from my body as it cradled his, breathed in the warm and reassuring scent and taste and feel of his presence. We would have our share of bad moments ahead. Right now, this one had ended so much better than anything I had feared or imagined.

"I love you," I told him. "A hard time prying that out of me, I'll admit—"

"Oh, I heard you . . believe me I heard, loud and clear, when they were loading me into that ambulance. Sometimes I think it was the only thing that kept me going that awful dark stretch from the campground to St. Ignace, then Petoskey. As impossible as it sounds, given the way I've been behaving the past couple of days, I love you, too, Lib!"

"I know . . .," my voice cracked, then steadied again. "And believe it or not, I never doubted that for a single minute."

244

❖

Life never ceases to amaze, I was discovering, even this late in the game—starting with my daughter's reaction to the wedding. After thinking things over, I told Paul that we needed to wait a month so my kids could clear their calendars to come, if they chose. He had just gone through a horrendous afternoon in therapy when I suggested it.

"Why do I think your kids are going to go ballistic," he said, "and start to google ways of slipping an air bubble in one of my IV's?"

I laughed. "You've been reading way too many mystery novels in that lending library of yours. Besides, you ought to be off that darn drip by then."

His eyebrow arched. "They'll think of something."

"Your therapists or my kids?"

"Both."

I amended my prognosis. "Danielle might be tempted to read me the riot act, but in the end I think both she and her brother, David, are smart enough to use the road time getting here to decide—how did you put it?—that they know a good thing when they see it."

Low blow, I realized, throwing his own words back at him from all those months ago when he tried to persuade me to start dating. They stuck in my head all this time and then, as now, the point had been made.

"You . . . speaking of Josh, I gather that somewhere in all this chaos and high drama," he said softly, "you called my son."

There was no easy way to put it. "He listened. Not long, unfortunately. But he listened."

I toyed with, then rejected the notion of sharing the rest—that when Josh took to blocking my calls, I set off on that wild expedition to Detroit. There didn't seem to be any point.

"It was wrong to put you in that position, Lib. I'm sorry."

"My daughter has had her moments," I shrugged. "You stuck with me through all of them. We just need to give them a chance."

As it turns out, at least when it came to Danielle, I won the bet. Supportive through the accident from the get-go, this time she didn't even resort to her usual ten-second pause to consider.

"Of course, we'll come," she said. "And since you've got more on your mind right now than shopping or frou-frou. I'll take care of the flowers and get brother David to handle the cake. He's been surprising me for years on my birthday, double-chocolate extravaganzas from bakeries I never heard of. Whatever he comes up with, you'll love it."

"I was hoping maybe the grandkids could participate. Nothing extravagant, just walk Grama down the aisle."

Danielle laughed. "Louisa will probably insist on wearing that May-Day crown you gave her even if it's starting to look more than a little chewed-up around the edges. That aside, it would be adorable. I'll talk to David about his brood. Have you found a dress?"

"Not high on the priority list. There's no way in heck Paul is going to wiggle into a suit, but at least we won't be decked out in open-backed hospital gowns either, mooning the grandkids. Right now he's hell bent on standing through the whole thing and walking me out afterward, all of which could take quite a bit of doing. I'm holding out for a golf-cart myself."

Even over the cell phone, I could picture my daughter's slow intake of breath. "You two . . . you *are* really sure you know what you're doing?"

I smiled. "Do we ever, any of us? It may be hard to teach an old dog new tricks, but at least I've figured out one thing these past weeks and months. Life isn't over until it's over, unless we stop risking and growing. I've been given a remarkable chance to do both, and for better or worse, I'm taking it. We've got that better or worse part of the vows down pat already, by the way. Although Paul says maybe, under the circumstances, we ought to rethink that bit about sickness and health. Not too subtle. . .maybe even downright creepy."

Danielle laughed. "You're . . . incorrigible, you know that?"

"That's what Paul tells me. I guess there are worse things you

246

could come up with for a eulogy."

"Seriously, Mom . . . you'll let me know if we can help? Besides the cake and the flowers, I mean."

"You already did and have," I told her. "Just knowing you understand, that you're going to be there is all the help anyone could want."

My throat tight, I told her I loved her, listened while she haltingly wished me every happiness. When I told Paul about the phone call, the tears that finally came on both sides were of relief and quiet joy.

"I can't say I'm crazy about all that fuss she's proposing, though," I said.

Paul turned the notion over in his head. "Maybe Danielle has a point . . . this isn't just about flowers or cakes, after all. Is it so wild to want to let our friends celebrate, even spoil us a little? You're the one who is always throwing that back at me. I assume somebody could sew me into a tux."

"You're kidding!"

"It's just hanging back in the apartment, moth-bait. I may as well put it to use. In the meantime, when we're in St. Ignace, why don't you prowl around downtown when they're torturing me in PT and come up with something you like. Floor length . . . the whole nine yards . . ."

I had been living in boots and slacks so long, the thought of something more feminine sounded absolutely wonderful. As it turns out, the week Paul was in rehab, the end-of-the-season sales in St. Ignace were in full swing. I prowled the racks and finally came up with an empire-waist chiffon mother-in-law gown, a deep wine that brought out the hints of auburn in my hair. If nothing else, it might work well in future as a get-up at Nordic weekend next season. A couple of phone calls also located a tailor willing to experiment with redoing Paul's tux for the occasion.

When we asked Annie if we could use the diner for the ceremony, she let out a whoo-hee that could have rattled windows in Escanaba. "You can't imagine how wonderful it will be just to close this place and celebrate for a change," she said. "We're handicap accessible . . . so even my John can come and trust me, he will—if I have to hogtie him to do it!"

The event quickly was turning into a crowd scene out of the Exodus. "Ya don't need a limo, Lib-girl," Arvo informed me with a smug little grin. "Earl got a couple of the guys at the diner to pitch in and give that old bus of Arnie's an overhaul. Plan is to pick up the whole darn county before we're through. Pastor Bob is threatening to wear his fire helmet with his priest-outfit, just in case Lauden needs CPR when it's time for his I-do's!"

I laughed hard enough at the thought, the tears weren't far behind. At least, for once, Arvo had the sense not to tease me about it.

"By the by, has Boss said anything about where you're gonna winter," he wondered instead. "It's starting to get a little dicey out here on Route 2."

I didn't have any answers for him. While there was still no sign of snow, it was just a matter of time. Paul and I needed to make a decision before then what we were going to do.

"I'll bring it up with Paul," I promised, *again.*"

Truth was, although Paul's rehab was proceeding on schedule and he even was taking back some of the reins at Northern Lights again, I had honest doubts about whether we could survive in that apartment of his in the double-wide all winter. When I said as much, he was not in the mood for discussing it, much less any solutions I had to offer.

"Seriously, if we stay up here," I told him, "I think at least we should leave the apartment in Arvo's hands, rent a couple of rooms for the season in St. Ignace where we aren't so far from everything. If you're going stir crazy, I could schlep you out to Northern Lights once in a while to make sure everything's okay."

Paul winced. "Glare ice and snow up to our armpits. . . all that with my sense of balance like this? I don't think so."

"So, then we're back to driving down to Florida in the rig."

"With me spread eagle on that bed in the back like some beat-up

248

DaVinci Vitruvian Man . . . *lovely picture!*"

I stifled a smile at the prospect. "Well, at least you could be doing those awful forced marches of yours out of doors surrounded by palm trees," I said. "We can retrofit the motor home with a wheelchair-lift if you can't navigate the stairs or a ramp. I've booked all kinds of crazy tours in my day. Why not a north-south do-it-yourself PT junket that lands us on the Gulf Coast somewhere for the winter? Lord knows with the demographics down there, they must have darn good specialists if we need help."

Paul looked at me as if I had just lost my senses. "You would have to do all the driving. And with that unwieldy walker, a wheelchair . . . and God knows what else in the back of the motor home."

"With luck, you'll be on a cane by then and we'll strap the wheelchair on the back. If the trip's too tiring for either one of us, we'll just stop a lot. I'll drive a hundred or so miles, then we'll hunker down for several days while you put yourself through your paces. Baby steps. Then move on until we decide it's warm enough to winter over in style. Your doctor can give us a list of referrals in case—"

"All right, I give up, surrender—you win," he groaned, "and I'd throw in the proverbial towel, only that darn rotator cuff is *killing* me too much to throw anything!"

"Cheer up, we're almost good to go, you said so yourself. Northern Lights is all but shipshape for the winter. Arvo would be thrilled to death to hunker down in the apartment for the winter. The calendar is more or less in place for next season and we can handle the publicity blitz long distance just as well as staring at some four walls in St. Ignace. True, I'll admit, a motor home isn't exactly your everyday-run-of-the-mill honeymoon suite—"

"Are you *through* yet?"

"Pretty much," I said.

Paul's smile was enough to melt the polar cap. "Good," he said, "because I was thinking the whole idea was starting to sound pretty darn sexy myself."

Twenty-One

After all our jokes about All Saints as a "biggie" on the Northern Lights calendar, the weekend before turned out to be the only date my family could make the trip. After considerable soul-searching we had decided to send Paul's son an invitation though neither one of us expected a response. With precious little help from Paul and me, the Day arrived and with it my kids, David and Danielle, and their families who promptly went to work helping Annie clear the decks at the diner for the ceremony.

There was no point in being a stickler over tradition about brides not seeing grooms on their wedding day. I drove Paul over from Northern Lights, his wheelchair stashed in the back of the SUV. Pastor Bob was waiting for us at the door. One look inside that little diner was enough to tell us that our friends had been giving my family and Annie an awful lot of help.

Somehow between close of business yesterday and mid-morning, they had transformed that functional eating place into what could pass for a chapel, moving the tables out of the way and setting up tight-packed rows of folding chairs. At one end of the room stood a lattice bower—goodness knows how they even got it in through the diner's doors. My daughter had brought along enough silk floral arrangements to decorate a good-sized cathedral, including lush sprays and ropes of brown-eyed Susans, ferns and wine-colored ribbons that wound around not just the lattice arch but even the institutional-looking metal support columns of the diner's pole barn interior.

"No way . . . what on earth are the two of you thinking?" Annie scolded when she saw us coming. "Paul, you've seen the last of your bride until the ceremony . . . !"

She started to whisk me away to her tiny office, then made a detour long enough to introduce me at long last to her John, a ruggedly handsome man with an endearing, almost boyish smile. From his wheelchair near the front of the makeshift chapel, he wished the two of us every good thing.

"That goes for the both of us," Annie breathed.

Moved beyond words I let her hold me, willing myself not to just give in and let the waterworks flow. "At this rate, I'll warn you," I told her finally, "my mascara is going to start running, I'll look like a racoon . . . and darn it, Annie, it's all your fault!"

Half-laughing and half-crying, she let me go. Perfect timing. We could hear Arnie's shuttle bus coming a half-mile away thanks to Earl Forester, who in addition to springing for new tires and painting the crazy thing sea-foam, apparently outfitted the bus with an air horn that played the first couple of bars of "Here Comes the Bride".

Sonja told me about it as she swept into the office for moral support and to check on how I was holding up. "Earl says the old rust bucket really needed a paint job," she shrugged between gales of laughter, "and the price was right,"

The whole thing boggled the imagination. "Sea foam?"

Sonja shrugged. "Why in the world would anyone paint anything on wheels that color if they didn't snag the cans off the bargain rack. Earl wanted to turn the bus into a Norse-mobile, but red and black are too popular to land on any overstock sales . . . lucky for you!"

"Have you seen Paul—is he still okay out there?" I fretted.

"With John and Pastor Bob, solving the problems of the universe."

That little office of Annie's was getting way too crowded. I was convinced the adults were getting nuttier about all this than the kids. My granddaughters were carrying the matching nosegays Danielle had made for them like they were laced with poison ivy. I couldn't even imagine how she had managed to convince the boys to wear sprigs of greenery pinned to their starchy white shirt collars.

"Mom, for crying out loud, what are you . . .*doing*? I've still got your bouquet," Danielle fussed as she shooed the grandchildren in my direction, hell bent on trying to organize what could pass for a bridal procession.

From the general noise level coming from the diner, it was high time. I squared my shoulders and the whole crew of us moved out through the swinging doors that separated the kitchen and office from the large public room.

No one prepared me for what came next. At the point my oldest grandson, David's boy, started toughing out a vaguely recognizable version of the Clarke "Trumpet Voluntary in D" on his trombone, I almost lost it again—except I knew Paul and a roomful of people were waiting.

As he saw me coming, Paul set his jaw and with a subtle assist from Pastor Bob, got up out of that wheelchair and proceeded to stand as we repeated the vows. The familiar greeting, "Dearly Beloved", calmed my anxious heart—that, and the love in Paul's eyes—and somehow we both made it through. Everyone in that room, whether friend or family, knew how much effort it was costing the groom in the process. I could have hugged Pastor Bob for speeding things up toward the end.

"I am proud and delighted," he said, "to introduce to you, Mr. and Mrs. Paul Lauden."

At the whoops and cheers that followed from Arvo and his cronies, I felt myself blushing crimson as my dress. My daughter and I made eye contact. Her face awash with tears, I saw her shape the words, "I love you."

Paul gently began to urge me in her direction. "Go to her, Lib."

I did, but not until he was resettled safely in the wheelchair. Beyond words, I let Danielle hold me until my heartbeat began to steady again. Even her brother, always the quintessential purveyor of calm, hugged me until I thought my ribs would crack—like the little boy he once was, suddenly latching onto a long-outgrown teddy bear.

"I'll never forget this," I told them both. "How you were there for me, when I needed you to be—so very, very badly."

Lord knows how long the universal partying went on because Paul and I cut things short. He had been pushing it, was clearly worn out and we knew only too well what we had ahead of us by way of a honeymoon. The days and nights in Paul's former bachelor pad were spent alternately holding one another and commiserating between grueling bouts of his physical therapy.

"At least we're here, together," I reminded Paul every time he lost heart and was tempted to apologize or complain, "more than we could have banked on a month ago. Trust me, I'll settle for that."

During his daily regimen pacing out the dimensions of the office porch with his walker, the last of the geese were straggling south overhead, reminding us how much still had to be done before we headed that direction with them. Finally a week before we were supposed to be on the road, Earl helped us locate a used wheelchair lift that would work with the motor home. In another day or two, plan was to make the move formally from apartment to the rig—a trial run.

With the campground closed, we weren't getting a lot of calls. Our last night in what was now our home in the campground office apartment, Paul's cell phone rang and I found myself scrambling half-way across the room to get it. I instinctively checked the time by the faint glow from the night-light in the kitchen. Four AM.

"Lauden's," I said.

At first, silence greeted that pronouncement. I was half contemplating hanging up, thinking it was a wrong number.

"It's Josh," the voice on the other end of the line said. "Could I

. . . I need to speak to Dad."

"Hold on, Josh . . . I'll get him." Suddenly wide awake, I clamped my hand over the receiver mouthpiece. "Paul, it's your—"

"Josh. I heard."

Paul had awkwardly propped himself up in bed, hand extended, waiting for me to hand him the cell. After a terse, Hello, he just listened without comment for what seemed like a very long time. Heart thudding, I strained in vain to catch bits and snippets of what was transpiring on the other end of the line.

When Paul finally did respond, his voice was raw with emotion. "You know I'll help any way I can, Josh. All you have to do is call . . ."

I couldn't read much from that reaction and in the dim light, it was impossible to see Paul's face. By now his son was talking again, calmer judging by the level of sound filtering my way.

"I'll tell her," Paul said, "and thank you for that. We're heading for Florida in a couple of days, by the way. If you like, we could stop in Detroit en route for a day or two."

Silence. "I understand," Paul said finally. Then as I listened, he told his son he loved him, clicked shut the cell phone.

My throat felt tight. A huge weight had settled on my chest, making it hard to breathe.

"Frank Dender had another heart attack," Paul said quietly. "He's on a ventilator, was way too stubborn for a health-care proxy, and Josh eventually is going to have to authorize the hospital, maybe even go to court to pull the plug. He wasn't asking me what to do. But I offered to help just the same, if it came to that. The next week should tell."

"Oh, Paul . . ."

"In passing," he said, "my son also told me how much he . . . appreciated that little junket you made to Detroit in the motor home in September."

It felt as if all the air had suddenly escaped from the room. "He told you about that?"

"Apparently it made quite an impression," Paul chuckled softly.

"The security guards are still talking about the way you parked in the entire upper management of Dender Communications with that rig of yours."

"And Josh wants us to . . . he'd like us to visit?"

"He didn't exactly thank us for the wedding invitation, that's going a little far. But he left things open, which couldn't have been easy for him. I'd say it's possible, yes—maybe not now, but on the way back in spring."

"Something," I said. "A start."

"Whatever Josh thought or thinks about you and me, all of this," Paul hesitated, "he definitely admires your guts, as he put it, for administering a rather . . . compelling reality check."

"Paul, I know I should have—"

"Asked me? Told me? Probably. Maybe. But then I certainly have to agree with my son about the bottom line."

In the darkness, I felt his sensitive artist's fingertips gently tracing the curve of my cheek, heard the rise and fall of his breathing subtly escalate. A major production as intimacy had proved to be since the accident, I knew where all this was leading.

"We've come a long way since you showed up on my doorstep," he said softly. "All of us, Lib . . ."

I shivered, thinking about it. Two more days and we would be on our way, headed across the Mackinac Bridge with me at the wheel. How far, indeed.

Travel, it seems, was becoming both our life and our business. The rhythm of the road—the joy, the pain, the heart and soul of the journey—was transforming what we felt and believed, how we lived and loved. I had plotted so many strange itineraries over the years, none more life-changing than my own.

Some things in life are beyond even the power of the GPS to track or compute. I found myself giving silent thanks for every single moment and mile that lay ahead.

Photo: Cara Loriz

ABOUT THE AUTHOR . . .

With her best-selling 2006 novel, *TIME in a Garden,* continuing to enthrall new readers and book clubs from Maine to California and draw rave reviews on-line, Mary Agria has turned her unique gifts as a writer to *IN TRANSIT*—a story based on her long-time love of family camping and the RV lifestyle. As a bit of whimsical hands-on research, she made her first coast-to-coast book signing tour in 2007 for her second novel, *VOX HUMANA: The Human Voice,* in a 25-foot motor home and looks forward to many more opportunities to connect with fans wherever the road takes her in the years ahead. She is in demand as a speaker on issues relating to older readers and their families, gardening and spirituality and the writing process.

Ms. Agria turned to novels after a distinguished career as author of numerous non-fiction works in the field of rural community development and work force issues. Her column "Winning the Rat Race" ran for twenty years in newspapers around the country and led to a college-level text by the same title. She also currently authors a column on gardening and spirituality, based on *TIME in a Garden.*

The proud mother of four daughters, Ms. Agria loves to travel the globe with her husband, retired university president and professional photographer, Dr. John Agria. She weaves, enjoys liturgical music and gardening. "As human beings, our life stories are sacred," she says. "It is a deep privilege to explore the hopes and dreams of older readers and their families in my work."

To experience chapters from her novels, essays, special features and photos of signings and readings, including the coast-to-coast summer 2007 tour, visit on-line at maryagria.com

IN TRANSIT BOOK CLUB QUESTIONS

1. Discuss how the lives of all the characters in the novel, in one way or another, are "in transit". How does "rootedness" or involvement in "community" change these life journeys from fearful to empowering experiences? Discuss how Lib, Paul, Arvo, Annie, Sonja and Earl grow as they reach out to one another.

2. How do the various characters in the story define "home"? Discuss how those definitions change over time for them.

3. How do "traditional" gender roles contribute to Lib's struggle to face the loss of her spouse and begin again? Discuss how she struggles with such stereotypes as the novel progresses.

4. In what ways are generational relationships crucial to the story? Discuss how Lib's family dynamics impact the plot and her own personal growth.

5. Lib's daughter, Danielle, faces demons of her own when her father dies. Discuss how Dani's childhood contributes to how she relates to her mother in time of crisis and as Lib tries to rebuild her life.

6. Discuss Paul Lauden's struggles to deal with his grief, his past life choices and cope with the aftermath of his own wife's death. What factors limit his flexibility as he tries to begin again?

7. Contrast and compare the response of Paul's son to losing a parent and the way Lib and her daughter are facing similar issues. What factors make it difficult to cope with how their surviving parent's lives are changing?

8. How do the marriages of Annie and John, Earl and Sonja, the elderly campers in the Minnie Winnie, even Arvo and his lost love, play a role in Paul and Lib's growth as the novel progresses? How do attitudes toward "work" vs. "retirement" shape those relationships?

9. Some 500,000 households are currently full-time RVers. Why can that full-time RV lifestyle be so appealing? Discuss what couples and singles can do to make that life choice more successful long-term.

10. The Lauden's and the Aventura's in many ways can be considered typical of families struggling with loss and change. Discuss how treating life as a "journey" not a destination can make such turning points survivable. Discuss how imagery and the novel's setting contribute to conveying the spiritual side of that world view.

For more book club materials, author reflections and sample chapters, visit the author on-line at maryagria.com

Other novels from Mary Agria...

TIME in a Garden...

the 2006 best-seller that started it all. Set in northern Michigan's resort country, this unforgettable story of Eve Brennerman and Adam Groft and their little crew of senior citizens trying to beautify their struggling rural community, celebrates perennial gardening, family and the enduring power of human love.

"A compelling read. Adam and Eve in the garden . . . is a delicious tale . . ." Five-Star judge's review, 2007 *Writer's Digest Self-Published Book Awards*, Literary Fiction.

VOX HUMANA:
The Human Voice. . .

The intriguing worlds of pipe organs and weaving come together in this poignant story of love and forgiveness. A career counselor forced by early retirement to take her own advice, Char Howard wasn't looking for the love of her life when she returned to her hometown of Hope in western Pennsylvania. Life had other plans.

"A five-star book in every way. It would be difficult to choose what I like best. The characterization was excellent . . . fascinating details made everything seem real . . . music, organist's secrets, liturgy, the details about weaving. I learned so much by reading this book. Special . . . excellent work." Judge's review, *Writer's Digest Self-Published Book Awards*, 2007.

And coming in 2009...
A Community of Scholars

a thought-provoking novel about the sometimes brutal politics of higher education, and a professor who struggles to rediscover his faith in the world of the humanities and learning to change lives, including—most surprisingly—his own.

A woman in jeans and a blazer, green book bag in hand, had taken up vigil in the corridor outside A. J. Ferinelli's basement office in the Academic Center. It wasn't an everyday occurrence at seven o'clock on a Thursday morning in October. But it certainly was an improvement, he decided, over the night janitor finishing his rounds.

Her back was turned, revealing dark hair in an intriguing twist at the nape of her neck. She didn't hear him coming. They had installed new carpet over the patchy tile flooring of the building several months ago.

"Looking for someone—?"

She swung around in his direction. Her reaction was a trifle too quick, anxious and he could sense the questions close to the surface in those intense blue eyes.

"Professor Ferinelli. . .we talked some time ago," she said, "at a faculty meeting. That schedule on the door says you come in early on Thursdays."

A manila folder full of quizzes tucked under one arm made it hard to maneuver, but A. J. managed to shift his briefcase and keys so he could shake her hand. Her grasp matched her eye contact, straightforward. Still something about her body language, tense and guarded, told him whatever brought her here at the crack of dawn, it was not to discuss class scheduling.

For sample chapters of Mary Agria's novel, calendars of upcoming events, slideshows and reflections on her work and the art of writing, visit maryagria.com